CALIBAN

For Wendy, my greatest supporter

THE MASK OF CALIBAN

MICHAEL PRYOR

Hodder SF/Fantasy

A Hodder SF/Fantasy Book

Published in Australia and New Zealand in 1996
by Hodder Headline Australia Pty Limited
(A member of the Hodder Headline Group)
10-16 South Street, Rydalmere NSW 2116

National Library of Australia
Cataloguing-in-Publication data

Pryor, Michael.
The mask of Caliban.

ISBN 0 7336 0290 8

I. Title.

A823.3

Series editors: Lucy Sussex and Justin Ackroyd
Cover design by Antart
Typeset by Midland Typesetters
Printed in Australia by McPherson's Printing Group

For their help and advice on the craft of writing, I'd like to thank Dirk Strasser, Stephen Higgins, Lucy Sussex, and all the students I've taught. They made a difference.

Part One

"As flies to wanton boys, are we to th'gods;
They kill us for their sport."

Shakespeare, *King Lear* IV.1

1

Even though distances are hard to judge in the chamber, it must be large. Many doorways open onto it, black and uninviting. The ceiling is a low dome, with a cupola, full of silver light, at its centre. Golden motes of light hover and dart high over the heads of the scattered crowd.

No two individuals are the same. Jade robes clash against rainbow stripes. White, cream and saffron seem to meld. Tall, bulky figures stand in front of shorter. Some seem to be wearing glass and metal, while others are naked, with patterned and jewelled skin. All of them stand close to the marble walls of the hall.

The marble walls are expanding and contracting almost imperceptibly.

A moment's pause and, as if on cue, the crowd glides away from the walls, and the individuals begin to move in intricate, silent patterns across the floor. There is no sound of conversation or of feet moving on the smooth surface.

There are no shadows.

A hundred figures dressed in rainbow ribbons and gaudy silks cross from one side of the chamber to the other, intersecting the paths of others but never interfering, except for a nod here and there and an occasional frown. The Primes know their dance well.

As if on command, the dancers part and resign themselves to the walls again, posturing and preening as they retire.

A single figure moves forward and stands in the middle of the vast chamber.

He is old. Tall and lean, dressed in a simple grey robe, he stands easily in the centre of the vast space. There is something sparse about him, as if there is nothing to spare. His hair is grey.

He glances upwards. Like the first stars coming out at night, small holes begin to appear in the marble ceiling.

Through these small holes, wan grey light struggles to enter. Once through the holes it falls in tight, almost solid, shafts. The golden motes part to let them through and the light surrounds the solitary figure.

'I stand before you in the Hall of Light and Sighs as the first born,' he says, and his voice fills the room effortlessly. 'I am the Speaker.'

Another figure steps from the crowd. He is wearing a dark overcoat and dark trousers. He is shorter and more solid than the Speaker. 'As the second born, I am the Witness,' he says. His voice is curt, almost angry. 'Does anyone challenge our right to these roles?'

Silence.

The Speaker nods. 'We shall continue our leadership and guidance, confident of your support.' He pauses and surveys the glittering crowd. 'Feel free to depart, or enjoy the Hall of Light and Sighs, its antechambers and its loggia.'

Quietly, all drift away, disappearing one by one through the many doorways. Overhead, the pinpricks of golden light mass in the centre of the chamber uncertainly, before resuming their random movement.

The Speaker turns to the Witness after watching the last leave. 'We have a traitor among us,' he announces calmly.

The Witness hisses between his teeth. 'I see,' he says after a time. 'Not just a troublemaker?'

'No,' the Speaker replies. 'The situation is more serious than that. I have a number of my Seconds investigating as we speak.'

'Any harm done?'

'Possibly. I am investigating.'

The Witness nods skeptically.

'This traitor is working against our best interests,' the Speaker says. 'All our interests.'

The Witness frowns and brushes the sleeves of his overcoat. 'Lots of us now, but you and I were the first.'

'We are the oldest.'

'How many of us Primes now? I've lost track.'

'A hundred or so.'

'And how much power is there to go around?'

The Speaker frowns. 'I don't understand.'

The Witness purses his lips. 'When there's not enough power to go around, there's plenty of room for dissatisfaction. Good recipe for a traitor.'

'You think that personal gain is the only motivation for treachery?'

'It's the obvious one.'

'It is the easily handled one,' says the Speaker, and he rubs the side of his nose. 'What I worry about is the traitor who has principles. The principled traitor is more daring, more courageous, and ultimately much more dangerous.'

'And harder to detect.'

'I'm glad you share my concerns.'

'But is there any proof? I haven't heard anything.' The Witness picks a piece of lint from his lapel and holds it in front of his eyes. He seems pleased at finding it.

'Nor would you. Your attention is on Resources. Such an important task means you may be out of touch with the people.'

'I see,' says the Witness evenly. 'And because your role is Population, you feel you have a special claim on the people?'

'It is my role, as you point out. I do not mean to imply that it is more important than Resources.'

'It isn't. We made sure it wasn't, remember? The two most important management tasks, equally divided. The balance of power.'

'A fair and just system. But it does leave me with areas of expertise, and so I can say that there appears to be unrest in the Underclass. Deliberately fomented unrest.'

'Of course,' snorts the Witness. '*We've* fomented unrest.'

The Speaker frowns. 'You misunderstand. I chose to stratify society for easier management. Two unequal levels, separated from each other. An Overclass and an Underclass. Each class thereby has a clearly identifiable source of any hardship and each class inspires paradoxical loyalty from its members. My stimulated unrest is carefully focussed, targeted at such easily identified irritant factors as lack of food, shortage of living space, the obvious pressures of life. What is now surfacing is unhappiness with the accepted social strata.'

'But that was part of your management plan. Controlled unhappiness makes harsh measures easier to implement. With another class to blame, shortages and hardships make sense. It's someone else's fault.'

'The Overclass is uneasy. Despite their isolation, they are aware of the Underclass. They see. They hear.'

'The more they see, the more grateful they are that they're not part of the masses. It makes them more protective of their status.'

'As they should be. As I manage them to be.'

The Witness grunts. 'Then what's the problem?'

'There appears to be a campaign. Poorly organised, diffuse in its efforts. And mutterings about the New Worlds project are growing.'

A pause. 'I don't believe it. It's a sound program. New Worlds is open only to the Underclass, and only through the lottery or outright purchase. The Overclass can't leave the planet. Rank has its responsibilities, as well as its privileges. It's the carrot and the stick approach, and it's worked well. They can put up with being members of the Underclass if they think they have something special that the Overclass don't have. It gives them hope of a better life than any Overclasser has.'

'Indeed. Yet rumours are beginning float, hinting that the New Worlds program may not be all it seems. Perhaps the program needs review, integral as it is to your Resources management strategy.'

The Witness rubs his forehead. 'There are always rumours.'

'These rumours have some detail in their innuendo. Too much detail. They must come from a well-placed source. Treachery.'

Another pause.

'And that's all?' the Witness asks tersely.

The Speaker frowns, choosing words carefully. 'I have heard there are other problems in your area, in Resources.'

'Supplying enough food is always a problem.'

'But non-natural problems? I understand there are reports of the deliberate sowing of blights and rust in wheat in the Crimea. And meta-anthrax in Argentina.'

'It's under control.'

'There are pressures. If there are problems with Resources, even the Overclass may begin to notice. Perhaps you need some assistance?'

'No,' says the Witness tersely. 'Do you?'

'There is more.'

'You're enjoying this, aren't you?' The Witness studies the white cuffs of his shirt.

'Nationalism is rising again,' the Speaker continues, ignoring him. 'The Underclass is rife with it. It is destabilising.'

The Witness is astonished. 'But the nationalism trend has been downwards for some time. It's not a productive area for managed unrest. Too volatile. Tapping into religio-ethnic differences is unpredictable.'

'The evidence is indisputable. The Celebes, Hawaii, Malta . . . independence movements have stirred in places where such things have been unknown for centuries.'

'Interesting,' the Witness mutters. His hands are jammed in his overcoat pockets, and his chin is on his chest.

'And something else that concerns us all,' the Speaker adds, eyes narrow. 'Palmer has been seen.'

The Witness almost chuckles. 'You can't be serious.'

'You do not scan the news. The more exotic agencies have been reporting an erratic, but growing, number of sightings of Palmer.'

'But he's dead!'

'Assuredly. And yet he is reported in Tel Aviv, Brasilia, Bristol and Sacramento.'

'Someone's seeing ghosts.'

'Agreed. But this is adding to the unrest.'

'I don't like this.' The Witness grimaces. 'It's spoiling things.'

'Agreed. Management is more difficult with such rogue elements. They must be excised.'

'As Palmer was.'

'But our Adversary is one of us. With such access and knowledge it could be nothing else.'

'All the more reason to act swiftly.'

The Speaker's eyes are distant for a brief moment. 'Done. I have doubled the search for our Judas.' He smiles a predator's smile. 'It is well done.'

The Witness looks up at the cupola. The pearl-grey light is shifting subtly. 'You really do enjoy this sort of thing, don't you?'

'Your meaning?'

'All this stuff. All this show.'

'The Hall of Light and Sighs? I felt it was useful, a touch of ritual to bind us together.'

'But how necessary is it? I know I feel heavy when I have to take on this form. There's something gross about this sort of solidity.'

'Consider it a reminder of our past and where we came from.'

The Witness smiles wryly. 'Some things are best forgotten.'

A pause, and both figures stand motionless for a time.

'I have another reason for wanting you here.' The Speaker smiles bleakly, his smooth face barely moving.

'Yes?'

'I wish to challenge you to a Game.'

The Witness's eyes widen. 'A Game? I thought we were beyond that. I haven't played the Game for an age or two.'

'It is still being played by some of our colleagues. Without the finesse or imagination of when we began it in the early days, of course.'

'Of course.'

'Ah, the constructs we built! The scenarios!'

'Old stuff.' The Witness makes a short, chopping gesture with his hand. 'Gone.'

'I challenge you,' repeats the Speaker, carefully.

The Speaker and the Witness stand and lock gazes. The room stops moving, seeming to hold its breath.

'I see,' the Witness says, and the moment is over. The room begins its rhythm again, and there is a soft movement of air. 'I wondered when this would come.'

The Speaker shakes his head. 'A friendly wager, nothing more.'

'I see.'

'I wish to unite management of Population and Resources. I am prepared to wager my position on the outcome of a Game.'

'You want to create a single, pre-eminent position, above all the Primes? We've always avoided centralised power like that.'

'It could be justified in the interests of efficiency.'

'And if I refuse?'

'You cannot. We decided long ago that a properly constructed challenge could not be refused.'

The Speaker stands motionless for a time, then he nods. 'The other Primes are now aware of the challenge. They are waiting for your acceptance.'

The Witness studies the Speaker for a moment. 'I accept.'

The Speaker smiles coldly. 'Good. I'm sure we shall have an avid audience, watching the two old masters at work.'

'I'm going to demolish you.'

'I'm glad you're confident. It makes for a good Game.' He pauses, then nods. 'Come with me. I have something to show you.'

The Speaker takes a few steps, and gestures to a doorway that had not been there a moment before. The Witness shrugs and follows.

They enter a white room, a hard-edged box. In the middle is a brown lumpen mass, larger than a person.

The Witness walks around the thing, hands in pockets. 'Clay,' he announces.

'Yes. I have taken to sculpture.'

'You?' The Witness begins to laugh, but cuts himself off short.

'It pleases me.'

'But there's nothing here. It's just a mess.'

'I work slowly. It's part of the appeal.'

The Witness stops his circuit and looks sharply at the Speaker. 'And the Game?'

'You need it as much as I do.'

'Don't count on it.'

'Forgive me. I see it as a diversion.' The Speaker breaks off and watches the Witness as he touches the clay. 'It was fun once. The thrill of creation.' The Witness sighs. 'It's had its day.'

'Let me take the first turn,' the Speaker says. 'A simple chase. Unseen villains. Shadows. Danger.'

The Witness runs his finger along the clay. It leaves a shallow groove. 'Wheels within wheels,' he murmurs, then looks up. 'The Game's started, hasn't it?'

The Speaker smiles coldly. 'It never really ended.'

2

Caliban hated jail. Twice had been two times too many, and this third time grated.

There was something about being confined that he loathed. He didn't like staying in one place for too long. When he did, it hurt. If his surroundings became too familiar, this pain forced him to move on. He saw himself as a confirmed wanderer.

He kicked the wall, but his boots barely scuffed the pale-yellow ceramic surface. He sat on the floor in the corner, and tried to hold the cell in his mind. Bunk. Basin. Toilet. Spy-eyes. Light panel. Vandal-proof computer terminal, with no moving parts.

He stood in front of the stainless steel mirror and took stock. Tallish, lean, long muscles under the T-shirt, smooth head—and no hair. Grey eyes. Hard face. Hard person? Hard to say. Late teens? Hard to say.

He saw many things, but nothing to explain his monumental bad luck.

No matter how he tried, he couldn't get used to the sheer misfortune of being swept up off the street. 'There's good luck, and there's bad luck. Then there's my luck,' he muttered.

His first time, a few years ago, was a typical virgin

crime. Caught streetselling cheap break-and-enter programs. 'Late starter,' the charge sergeant commented.

'I'm only three years old at heart,' Caliban had answered mildly, and the sergeant stared at him as if he were a talking dog.

Caliban wondered if he'd stepped on somebody's toes. Lots of people didn't like competition, and the police were only too happy to help. They saw it as a public service.

Second time was worse: nabbed tampering with AutoCensus inputs. He felt that unless he was doing his little bit to help the system destroy itself, he wasn't doing his best. The AutoCensus irritated him, despite the fact that most of the Underclass were accustomed to punching in their personal data at the end of each month. To most people it was as regular as breathing, but to Caliban it was more like a periodic outbreak of hives.

He thumped his heel into the floor. The surface was slightly yielding, but tough. The red record light woke on the spy-eye, and Caliban stared at it glumly. Luck. It was just bad luck, this time.

Routine, random sweeps of the Underclass was the police force's latest new idea. So like most new ideas, it was being flogged to death. Caliban knew that the sweeps were increasing in frequency, and kept out of trouble. It was one of the things he did on an almost instinctive level. Protective colouration, low profile, keep moving. These things were simply part of his life, second nature.

He always dressed up: good boots and leather

jacket. It didn't matter what was underneath. The jacket was like a sign. 'Non-street life' it announced, as Caliban tried to look like an Overclass citizen slumming it on the street. There were enough of that type around for it to be possible. Despite what they said, there were always Overclassers willing to skip the lines.

But the police took the losers who *looked* like losers first. The usual suspects. Caliban avoided that tag, and busied himself with fiddling, hindering, subverting and suborning. And surviving.

Mostly surviving.

Yet somehow he'd been nabbed. Just buying a handful of satay sticks from a street vendor near the Spencer Street station was enough. He'd always known his stomach was going to get him into trouble one day, but resisting the smell of the spicy grease was like trying to avoid breathing.

His first hint of danger came when two saffron Orthodox Buddhists pointed up the street, then hitched up their robes and scuttled off. Perceptibly, the motion of the crowd turned one way, then the other, and suddenly everyone was trying to melt into the ground or between buildings, like water from a cracked swimming pool.

Caliban quickly looked up and down the street and saw the barriers in place at either end of the block, with the monstrous riot trucks backed up, gaping hungrily. Police were moving methodically, swinging shock-sticks. The rising and falling of the sticks had a slow and ghastly rhythm. For one frozen, bizarre moment, before he went to ground, Caliban could think only of marching girls and baton twirling.

Through the legs and feet, he searched for a way out. Muffled shouts were thick in the air, and he heard the hiss and sizzle of a grill being up-ended into the gutter. A cloud of steam billowed, followed by a shrill stream of curses.

He scuttled under the stall and flattened himself against a boarded-up tailor's shop. His fingers scrabbled over the rough wood as the screams started.

He'd nearly wrenched off one plank when the shock-stick hit him.

* * *

Caliban's feet were hurting, even though he'd given up kicking the cell. Modern penology had provided a padded Tension Release wall, but somehow it wasn't the same.

The door chimed its carefully non-threatening tone. 'Caliban?' The voice was calm, soothing and totally artificial. He winced and sat up. 'Move to the back of the cell. Keep one hand on the basin at all times.' He stood and eyed the ceiling warily. A slot running the width of the room slid back and bars dropped to the floor, raising dust, and turning Caliban's section of the cell into a neat holding pen.

The door rolled open and a tall guard strolled in, shock-stick ready. With him was an Overclass citizen, dark suit, gold ID bracelet, no soul.

Caliban had the Underclasser's natural mistrust of the well dressed. They took. They had everything but they still took. This one was well fed but lean. Good quality food and the time to exercise, Caliban guessed. The good life.

The Overclass citizen glanced at the guard, who nodded. Caliban wiped his hands on his trouser legs as his visitor took a step closer to the bars. Caliban looked at his eyes, but there was no-one home. They were empty and blank, as if he were running on autopilot.

Caliban shivered. He felt as if he were a specimen.

'I have Caliban's records here, and it says he's been in twice before.'

Caliban blinked. 'Hello?' he said. 'Have I just stepped out for a while or something?' The Overclasser ignored him.

'He has no family, no registered address, has committed a number of crimes for which we couldn't be bothered prosecuting him, and he is old enough to be totally set in his ways with no chance of change.' The Overclasser moved one finger in delicate circles on the cover of his terminal, and shut it decisively. 'I'd say he is a definite Candidate. It's almost as if he has been working towards it all his life.'

It was only then that he looked Caliban in the face.

Caliban held him there. For a long instant, he looked into the hollow man, and saw nothing. No compassion, no empathy, no regret. The Overclasser was a void. He made no effort to engage Caliban on any human level.

It was silent in the cell, apart from his own heart beating. He could smell the outsider, the peculiar almost-sandalwood of those who'd had their sweat glands modified.

'Candidate?' Caliban said, shaking his head. He felt as if he'd just dragged himself out of icy water.

'For the Game. Surely you've considered it, known that habitual criminals would be offered the chance to play? Don't you want to become a member of the Overclass?'

'You're actually asking me whether I've considered certain death as a way of breaking out of my neighbourhood, right? You see it as a good career move?'

'A joke. I know a joke when I hear one.' The Overclasser's face twitched grotesquely, in what could have been called a smile only by a puppet-maker. 'But seriously now, you have a choice. Either you undergo imprisonment and rehabilitation, or you volunteer for the Game. I take it you don't have the money for a New Worlds Immigration ticket?'

'Not even for a New Worlds Lottery ticket.'

'Too bad. That's the only other way out of the Underclass.'

Caliban grimaced. 'Why are you so certain that the Underclass is something I *want* to get out of?'

The elegant face twitched. 'Need I answer that? Food, living space, money . . . three good reasons to start with. I could go on, but why bother? Just look at you.'

Caliban resisted the impulse to look down. He was about to ask why the Overclasser was bothering to talk to him, when his mind went blank.

The Game.

It was as if the words were written in blazing letters inside his skull.

The Game.

It was as if the words were chiselled onto his forehead.

The Game.

At once, he felt a need as vital as the need to breath. He *had* to be a part of the Game. OK, so only a few were successful, only a few won and were elevated to the Overclass.

He knew people who'd volunteered for the Game and had never been heard of again.

He knew all that, and yet he wanted it.

The Game.

'Yes,' he croaked through a constricted throat. 'I want to play. I want the Game.'

'Oh, it's not as easy as that,' grinned the Overclasser. 'This is only pre-selection. First you have to be chosen.'

The guard telescoped his shock-stick and Caliban fell into blackness.

3

Caliban's muscles ached from the convulsive effects of the shock-stick. His mouth tasted as if he'd been chewing on a wetsuit for a couple of hours.

He kept his eyes closed, warily.

'We know you're awake,' a voice said. The voice was light, and seemed to be on the point of laughing. It had an odd timbre, as though it were a composite of many voices, blurred around the edges and dead in the middle.

It was the sort of voice in front of which Caliban didn't want to be helpless.

'Come now! I may only be a minor, monitoring Second, but I do know enough to be sure you are awake. Alpha readings, eye movement, ear canal response and otolith angle, all of them indicate only one thing.'

He opened his eyes.

'There now, that wasn't so bad, was it Cal? I may call you Cal, mayn't I?'

He found himself in a pool of light. Otherwise, the room was dark. He wasn't encouraged by the realisation that he was strapped to a medical bed of some type: thick, washable padding, plenty of restraints. No, indeed. Enjoy every minute of the experience. It may not last long.

When Caliban swallowed his throat was raw. 'Drink,' he croaked. 'Water.'

'Of course! We can't have you inconvenienced while in my care, can we? Think what it would do to my record.'

An articulated arm detached itself from the gloom outside his sanctuary of light. Noiselessly, it swung over and held a paper cup of water to his lips. He drank warily, but even though the water was warm and flat, he finished it all. The white rubber waldo smelled of strong disinfectant.

When he finished, the arm whined softly, then crumpled the cup, spilling a drop onto Caliban's shirt-front. The drop lingered there, then worked its way through to his skin, where it sat for a moment. It made Caliban think of rain and the outside world.

'Now, Cal. Perhaps we can proceed.'

'Let me guess,' he said to the air. 'You're an Artificial Intelligence, right?'

There was pride in the voice as it answered. 'Indeed! I am but a humble supernumerary in the vast scheme of things, a simple Medical Monitor AI, but yes, I do possess consciousness and free will as defined. I am a Second.'

Caliban had never met an AI. That was the privilege of a few in the Overclass. AIs had independent status, and the Prime Intelligences managed the vast international conglomerate corporations and banking houses, dealing with business on a level of abstraction far beyond that of humankind.

Generally, they ran the world.

On the streets Caliban had little interaction with the world of megafinance or transnational government. He was aware that much of the business of government had been handed over to the vast Intelligences, the only ones capable of monitoring the minutiae of human affairs. The most efficient managers of all time, they were called.

Besides, he had an inbuilt distrust of machine intelligence. Much of his time was spent on interfering with the works of the world, and this usually meant crossing at least one AI. They made him uneasy, with their inscrutable motives and unanswerable decisions. He'd always felt humanity had sold itself out—and had lost something in the process.

'Now, Cal,' the AI continued. 'You understand that you are now officially lost to the world. Or is that unofficially? Never mind. What it means is you now don't appear in any database anywhere. The jail has lost record of you, the police files have been corrupted, your citizen profile has vanished. So now you don't exist. Are you with me so far?'

Caliban closed his eyes. It was the only gesture that seemed left to him. He felt as if the cosmic conspiracy had turned its attention his way. Again.

'Well, I take it you're following along, as best you can. The idea is that we are seeing if you are *acceptable*. For the Game, the Primes need people who are cunning, mentally tough and expendable. Naturally. And with so many unimportant people slipping through society and simply disappearing, what is a few extra? It really makes sense if you look at it like that, doesn't it Cal? Call them the grease that keeps the wheels of society turning.'

'Sacrifice,' Caliban muttered.

'Now, Cal.' The Second managed to sound pained. 'It's simply the efficient use of an abundant resource. And think of the good that will come of it! With happy Primes running the world, we've had an end to international strife, an end to grubby scrabbling for resources. It's become a veritable paradise out there!'

Caliban didn't bother to argue. It'd be like telling a kid there was no Santa Claus. Reality was what you made of it. He knew one world and the vast, impersonal machine Intelligences knew a different one. Each made a reality from it. Everyone used a different map, trying not to get lost. Trying to make a way through unknown territory.

Caliban decided it was time to trade in his map—it had only landed him in trouble. Cartography had never been his strongest point.

'Paradise, Cal,' enthused the AI. 'And you'll be helping to ensure that it continues!'

'Sorry. Just can't get worked up about it. Something about facing certain death does that to me.'

As the AI replied, Caliban wondered if you could actually hear a shrug. 'Your enthusiasm isn't necessary, Cal. Just your mind.'

Caliban didn't respond.

'Interface, Cal. Imagine it! A meeting ground! They'll draw on your memories, experiences and dreams to create a world to play with, a whole new land! Shared Creation! You'll be participating in the great Game!' The AI paused, as if barely containing its enthusiasm. 'Three individuals struggling against each other, striving to win! The two Primes setting scenarios and trials for you to overcome, trying to outdo each other in originality and scope. And you, fighting to survive!'

The prospect didn't fill Caliban with joy. 'Right,' he said. 'Whatever you say.'

The only answer was a metallic click, and then Caliban felt the restraints withdraw.

'Hello?' he said. 'Anyone there?'

Sitting up, he looked around. The room was dark, but he could see it was barely big enough for the bed onto which he had been strapped. Benches of surgical instuments lay ominously close by, and mysterious readout screens looked mutely at him. The walls, floors and ceilings had the giveaway thin tracery of a room completely scanned by sensors, and jointed mechanical arms hung in the recesses. These ranged from one large enough to lift a piano, to a peculiar arm that branched and rebranched, getting ever smaller, until at last it was a rippling fineness, hard for the eye to follow. Micromanipulators, Caliban guessed. No expense spared.

He shrugged, lifted his bare feet over the side and stood up. The room swam for an instant and he held onto the cool metal frame of the bed. He felt like someone had stuck a shock-stick in his ear and stirred it around a little.

He waited for the AI to ask what he was doing.

Nothing.

One step and Caliban was at the door, but then his fists clenched as he saw a digital lock instead of a handle. He nodded and rubbed his chin, thinking, planning.

When he took the micromanipulator from its rack, he waited for the alarm. 'OK,' he muttered. 'Go for it.' He knew a chance when he saw one, and he was ready to make the most of it.

It took only a few seconds for him to strip the casing from the upper section of the precision-made arm. He grinned narrowly as he worked. He could do this blindfolded. And had, plenty of times.

He used the prong of his belt buckle to work the jump switches in the micromanipulator, and soon had the hang of it. He could control the microscopically fine digits of the arm. Roughly, but it was enough—more than enough—to trip the digital lock.

Caliban flung the micromanipulator on the floor as the door popped open. 'Thanks for the hand,' he said, as he stood in the doorway, and winced at his own appalling joke.

He held onto the door and stood a while, thinking. No boots, no jacket, no future. He shrugged. Things could only get better.

Barefoot and brazen, he strode into the corridor.

* * *

Caliban felt relaxed and almost jaunty. He knew it was only a matter of time before he showed up on some random surveillance sweep, and this certainty took some of the worry out of being at large.

The place was institutional. It smelled like a

hospital: clean on the surface, but something rotten underneath. The walls were neutral—beige, cream, and ivory. Handleless doors faced the walkway. Caliban tried each one as he passed, but he'd lost the knack.

The corridor was long and straight, but the lights were dim. Was it night outside? If he could find an emergency exit, a fire escape or something, he might be able to slip out and lose himself in the dark.

At the end of the corridor loomed a door larger than those he'd tried. It seemed to reach right to the ceiling.

He swallowed nervously, and searched inside himself for calm. In the land of the blind, the one-eyed man is king, he thought. And the man with two eyes is very well positioned, future-wise. As long as the king doesn't find out.

He looked back. He could barely make out the door from which he'd started. It was open, and he could see light spilling from it, pooling on the floor outside. It looked as if the moon had melted onto the earth.

When he reached the end of the corridor, he found more than he expected: two doors, towering three or four metres over his head. They were wooden: mountain ash or blackwood, he couldn't tell in the dim light. Caliban let his hand linger on their surface, smooth with the talcum powder dustiness of carefully polished timber. There was no handle.

He stood back, and rubbed his hands on his jeans. He reached out and probed the fine crack between the doors. There wasn't even room for a fingernail.

Breaking and entering was one of Caliban's skills. He studied design, materials and systems, security arrays, with the idea that if he knew about them, he could slip around them. He studied with passion, too, seeing security systems as tools of the enemy. Those with, wanting to keep it away from those without.

He dispensed advice, to anyone willing to listen, about methods of avoiding the often paranoid defences of the Overclassers and the system. His contacts included those who could advise him on the more obscure mysteries of computer defences: the Edge Riders and the Matrix Jockeys.

Some of them had even met Primes.

He once asked Spiroula about it. She smiled blindly, crookedly. 'It was a joke.'

'Joke?'

'Some of them, they have a sense of humour, right? They like to play.' She sighed and groped for her cat. It saw her hand and avoided it. 'I was lucky that Maeve was there and guessed something was wrong. She got the interface jack out, and I fell back here, eyes burnt out, screaming . . . '

'Where from? Where'd you come back from?'

She smiled a frozen winter smile, bleak and arid. Caliban saw her hands were fluttering from nervous system damage. She had mismatched earrings. 'It was bad, Cal. Nightmare stuff. I was in a theme park, right? But body parts, everywhere. Rides on bones and skulls and meat. Screaming, I was. Could've still been . . . I could still be there . . . '

Caliban shuddered, but reached out to stroke her

thick, black hair. She clutched his hand. 'You there, Cal? You there?'

He shook his head to get rid of the memory. Spiroula. She died not long after that. Maeve told him, but she wouldn't tell him how. Later he discovered she'd torn out her interface socket, and with it, part of her brain.

Caliban rested his forehead on the doors, and was surprised when he felt them give a little. He pushed, and they opened.

A few metres away stood two nondescript doors. Both had signs, neatly lettered in hard-edged black script.

EARTH said one, and NEW WORLDS the other.

4

Caliban stood motionless in front of the two doors, thinking about games.

Rock, scissors, paper. Rock smashes scissors, scissors cut paper, paper covers rock. He had to guess what his opponent was going to hold out. Strategies. Then he'd know how to win. Second guessing. Games within games.

Caliban rolled the possibilities around in his mind. If he chose rock, they could choose paper. In that case he should choose scissors, but they might follow that and hold out rock, so he should choose paper—so maybe he should tell them to stick it and go and do something worthwhile instead.

All he had to do was choose between a door offering old cesspit Earth, and a door promising everyone's dream. Who said choices were never black and white?

New Worlds. He'd never been attracted to the scheme, but most of the Underclass had. Leave a decrepit world and move to paradise, said the advertising. All you had to do was sever all connection with Old Earth, leave everything behind, no letters, no cards, no regrets. A clean, fresh start.

The advertising was unavoidable: news reports on

new planets opening up for colonisation, documentaries about the good life on peaceful worlds, interviews with the governing councils of the New Worlds arks. The Promised Land. Many Promised Lands. It was a plump juicy carrot dangled in front of the noses of the hungry and overcrowded.

But it was only for a few. It was there for everyone, but only if you could afford it. And not many could.

That was why the monthly New Worlds Lottery was central to the lives of the Underclass. The prizes were a few thousand tickets to participate in the New Worlds program, giving the masses a chance to join in. All five or six billion of them.

To many, the knowledge that they had a chance meant they were already part of the grand enterprise, part of humanity's next evolutionary step. It was enough for most of the population, who otherwise led sterile, senseless lives. And they had the perverse pleasure of knowing that the Overclass were banned from the New Worlds project. They were too valuable, the story went. Couldn't be spared.

Caliban knew an Edge Rider once, one of the best. Laydown Sally could use her console and ride the far edges of the data stream, cresting where the autonomic systems of the AIs worked. He'd heard about her for a long time before he met her at a market, when he was trying to buy some safe fruit. She laughed when he asked her for a favour, and turned back to the melons.

He watched her progress after that, listened to gossip, talked to people. While she quickly became a legend for her gutsiness, she also made enemies, because she made Scrooge look like a philanthropist.

Laydown Sally wanted out. New Worlds.

She took lottery tickets. Almost everyone did. But she wanted to make sure. She was going to buy a passage.

Caliban had never met anyone who'd actually bought a passage. The price varied, but it was always too much. A fair-sized company could be bought for less, rumour had it.

But Sally accumulated. She bet, she won, she played finance games, she hoarded, she speculated. She took any edge offered, cut most corners around. She was a legend.

After a while, people on the streets forgot her greed, forgot the way she burned anyone who dealt with her. She became a strange sort of hero. The whole Underclass urged her on. She became a focus for all their hopes and dreams. They knew they were never going to make it, so they hoped she might.

A vast collective push developed, a shared cheering-on as she built up her pile. She pulled out of the Net once her stake was made, and never went back. Instead, she plunged into making her stake grow.

The word went around one day that Laydown Sally had done it. Caliban was at a coffee bar, reading a day-old newsfax when he heard the rumour. Old men whispered loudly enough for Caliban to hear, but he asked anyway. Sally, he was told, had got enough and was on her way to the New Worlds office.

Caliban was curious. So were thousands of others.

Sally was walking to the city from Station Street, and Caliban joined the crowd.

It was a carnival by the time they got to Clifton Hill. The trains were running that day, but Sally hadn't spent money on transport in ten years, and wasn't about to start now. She kept walking.

The crowd was a few thousand by the time she got to Brunswick Street, but Caliban noticed the way that no matter how lively the crowd became, and how much the infectious revelry affected the people, Sally always walked alone at the front of the mob. It was as if there was a force field around her. No-one approached within arm's length. No-one spoke to her. Grim and utterly focussed, she marched up the hill towards the city, past the ruins of Gertrude Street without a glance at the shanty town, down by the remains of the old Parliament Building, and into Collins Street.

There must have been ten thousand people waiting to watch her enter the New Worlds building. Private security guards and Overclassers nervously slid around the rabble, unused to what they were seeing. Somewhere to Caliban's left an impromptu steel band started up. Food vendors were doing a brisk trade. A knot of balloons drifted by—red, yellow, blue—and Caliban heard a child crying.

Laydown Sally strode regally into the glass maw of the New Worlds tower, stopping on the threshold to wave to the crowd. It was the first time she'd acknowledged that they were there.

She never came out.

Caliban waited, even when the rain came and most of the crowd melted away, even after a notice was posted saying that Sally was being processed for immediate induction and 'would be expedited spacewards soonest'. He waited until the next day, managing to reassure cruising patrols that his business was legitimate.

She never came out.

Caliban didn't want New Worlds. Poxy, shabby Earth was all he knew, and he sort of liked the old place. He wanted to breath the air that a hundred billion others had breathed. He wanted to struggle at home. He didn't want to leave it all behind.

'Home,' he said aloud. 'I want to go home.'

He pushed open the door marked EARTH.

* * *

Caliban thought he was ready for anything, but he was wrong. Of all the things he'd imagined, a very ordinary waiting room was not high on the list of possibilities. He didn't know how to react. He nervously wiped his hands on his jeans. He felt like an intruder. It was a scene from some impossibly distant past, one from which Caliban felt completely cut off. He half expected a nurse to pop out and say, 'The medic will be with you shortly.'

Armchairs lined the walls, all covered in beige fabric. Mock hessian, he guessed. Very chic once upon a time. Low tables separated the chairs into intimate clusters of two and three, each chair conversation-distance from its neighbour. Tidy piles of magazines were stacked in the precise centre of each table. There was no window, and a soothing Matisse print covered most of one wall. In a vase on one table were fresh, white chrysanthemums. Caliban could smell their spicy fragrance. A vacuum jug next to the flowers held what he hoped was coffee.

The only movement in the room was the ceiling fan, chopping time into tiny segments.

Caliban took one step inside the doorway and paused. Nothing looked worn or creased. The carpet's high pile and nap implied that no one had even looked at it too hard. Steam curled from the open mouth of the coffee jug.

There was another door, directly opposite Caliban's entrance, but he ignored it. He crossed quickly to the coffee. There were mugs, milk and sugar, and he sloshed one mug half full and topped it up with milk. His mug was from the Rice Board and suggested that everyone 'Have a Rice Day'.

While he drank, his eyes darted around the room. He sat in a chair where he could watch both doors, finished his coffee, and made himself another mug. Less milk, more coffee this time, and now he sipped slowly.

'Feel better? That's good! After all, you're very special, did you know that?'

Caliban had been alert, but the voice was so sudden that he caught half a cup of hot coffee in his lap. He stifled a curse.

He knew the voice. It came from some indefinable place in the wall behind him, and he recognised it as the AI Medical Monitor. Somehow, he didn't feel cheered by the recognition. 'Right,' he muttered into his coffee cup. 'What d'you want?'

'Ah, well, it isn't so much what *I* want, Cal, but what the Primes want. And, my boy, they want *you*! Aren't you thrilled?'

'Been more thrilled in my life. Like the time I was run over by a street sweeper.'

'Really, you must tell me about it. Not that you have much time, but never mind.'

Caliban rotated the mug in his hands and peered into the brown depths. 'Tell me. Exactly what does this have to do with Earth?'

'Earth? Oh, the door that you chose! Well, it's not so much that you chose Earth, it's that you *didn't* choose New Worlds.'

'Don't follow you.'

'My dear boy! This has all been a test you know, a selection procedure.'

'Gathered that,' Caliban said dryly, and wondered if he shouldn't have another cup of coffee. It might be his last.

'We wanted to see what you would do. If you were worthy of selection.'

He placed his cup on the table and sat back. 'Worthy.' He paused. 'I suppose I'm not the only one?'

'Indeed. We test many. Cal, you displayed the ultimate qualities for selection. Well done!'

'All I did was choose a door. Earth, that's all.'

'Ah, Cal, Cal! The Primes don't want those who are willing to turn their back on the problems of the world, those who want to scamper away and let others toil. They want the gritty ones, the down to earth ones—oh, I've made a pun!'

Caliban waited, but there was no laughter. 'What would've happened if I had've taken the New Worlds door?'

'Exactly what happens to all New Worlders. Nothing.'

'Nothing?'

'Well, when I say "nothing" I actually mean a quick and painless death, but in the end it's all the same, isn't it?'

'Painless death?' Caliban echoed.

'Naturally. Cal, it's time you were let in on our little secret.' The pause was deliberate, and Caliban gritted his teeth. 'There *is* no New Worlds. It's simply a clever ruse for managing huge chunks of surplus population without anyone wondering where they've got to!'

Caliban felt giddy, as if one leg of his existence had just collapsed and dumped him on the floor.

New Worlds had been a reality to Caliban for as long as he could remember. While he sneered at it, at least it was solid, and it gave hope to those who needed to believe in a way out. The Underclasser's Dream. It was the chance to escape, it was paradise made obtainable in this life. New Worlds kept the world going.

'But the pictures, the reports . . . '

'Oh, when you control the resources of an entire planet, perpetrating a hoax of this size is not only possible, but quite a lot of fun, too.'

'Fun?'

'Oh, there are many reasons Cal, if you look deeply enough. Haven't you ever wondered why the population collapse didn't occur?'

'Well, so many went off planet . . . ' It struck him like a sledge-hammer made of ice. There was no off planet.

'You see, they left, but not in the way they'd hoped. Well, if they wanted to leave so badly, they didn't really deserve to stay here, did they?'

Caliban closed his eyes. 'So many.'

'And of course the whole notion of an exotic other world was perfect, harmless entertainment for the masses. Vicarious thrills. Escapism of the first order. Better than gladiators, don't you think?

'But Cal! You don't want anything to do with that farce! You are destined for bigger and better things! You've won! You've come through! They want to use *you*!'

It seemed as if he'd spent his life only half awake, and now he'd received an alarm call. At once, he felt strangely calm. It was a moment of peculiar sharpness.

'Use me?' he finally said. 'Me. Use me. Right.'

'Cal, I'm impressed with you all over again. You wouldn't believe how few of the chosen actually go willingly. Despite the great honour.'

Caliban stood and stretched. He linked his hands and pushed them up over his head, as if he were trying to raise heaven. Or bring it down. As his body moved, thoughts were taking shape in his mind. Thoughts of survival, but also something else: he was beginning to see the face of the enemy. In the past he'd merely been a nuisance, tangling with minor aspects of the AI rule. Now he was getting into the big league. His hands clenched into fists.

'Let's go,' he said. 'I'm ready.'

5

Shift.

Caliban feels his skin itch—on the inside. He unzips it and steps out. Looking down, he sees the baggy human shape sprawled on the ground. He rubs his hand over his head and feels a hole in his scalp. He reaches in and pulls out a star.

Shift.

He sees a long line of people, stretching out forever. He seems to be floating above them. He feels like a cloud. Looking down, he sees that the head of the line enters a small booth. One by one the people step into the booth. No-one comes out.

Shift.

He is higher still, soaring over the landscape. Vegetation sprouts and grows like green fountains, pushing long fingers into towns and cities. He sees the hideous scar of an old open-cut mine, swallowed by a blanket of trees, grass and shrubs.

Shift.

'Now Cal, behave yourself, you understand? You're going around in circles. Just stop thinking a little.'

Shift.

Caliban is walking down Russell Street, heading for Chinatown. His feet fascinate him. He watches them striding along the footpath, eating up the distance in tiny bites. They are the wrong size, and they are in white canvas espadrilles. He hates espadrilles. Footsteps sound behind him, and instantly he is terrified. He stops and staggers against a beggar, who grins. When he is finally balanced, he stands there and feels his face.

It isn't his. He looks over his shoulder—and sees his body standing there. It waves and says, 'Need a loan?'

Shift.

Study. Screen after screen of numbers, flashing past. Finger jab, freeze frame, grab item and store it with the others. Jigsawing, pulling elusive pieces from piles of information. On the wall, just above eye level is a picture of Sun Yat-sen. 'Ahh,' he croons, jabs, and seizes another number, then swears. He snatches the interface set and plunges into the raw data stream, despite the doctor's warnings. A mouse chews on a cable below the desk, and dreams of dust.

Shift.

A huge billboard. 'New Worlds—It's Time For the Stars!' A PNG family camps underneath, with a sloppily handwritten sign: Hunger Strike. Free PNG from Indonesian Imperialism! One small child has eyes fever-bright. She hands Caliban a piece of paper, but the copy is illegible. Caliban looks for her, but she's gone. The father meets Caliban's eyes and shrugs.

Shift.

'Cal. Cal! Stop this nonsense right now. I've been

gentle so far, but I've had just about enough of this. Do you understand?'

Shift.

It is dark and Caliban feels as if he were a siamese twin, joined at the soul with a long, long connection, stretched back to his other half. He reaches up and finds the slippery cord attached to the back of his head. It is cool and resilient, but his hands come away wet. Walking backwards, he begins to follow it, hand over hand. Five steps into his stumbling journey, he falls off the edge of the world. He plunges until he is caught and held by the cord. He dangles, turning slowly round and round in the middle of nothingness, while stars dance in front of his face like curious insects.

Shift.

He is walking home after arranging a data raid on the Customs Databank. He carries a large watermelon he had bought, attracted by the green-on-green of its stripes. Two blocks from his temporary residence on Rucker's Hill, he comes across a demolition. Two whole streets are being flattened. Half-done, the area had been sprayed with a heavy plastic shield. It is perfectly, utterly, inhumanly flat. He can see only machines at work, and a sign on the road block announces: Urban Rationalisation—Underutilised Dwellings. An old woman, scarfed and dressed in black, watches the demolition impassively. He touches her on the shoulder, but she doesn't move.

'Where have they gone?' he asks.

She looks up at the heavens. 'Gone. New Worlds.'

She smells of olive oil and capsicum. 'All of them. Sister. Brother. All gone.' He leaves her looking up at the sun.

Shift.

'Cal. I'm just preparing you for interface. Imagine that! You'll be joining two of our most distinguished Prime Intelligences in creating a whole world! It's a wonderful three-way Game, a battle of wills! Now, it shouldn't hurt a bit, especially since I've cooled your whole body a tad, just to help things along. I'll just prepare a deep brain bypass, to keep your autonomic functions going here, and to disconnect your higher functions. We don't want your judgement or values interfering with the glory of Shared Creation. You won't be aware of what is happening; you'll simply be experiencing it, reacting naturally. Which is, of course, the whole idea. Now, for the craniotome.'

Pressure, not pain. A distant whining. 'My, my, Cal, you have a lovely brain in here. And someone's done some interesting work here, too. A head injury sometime, Cal? Some small parts of your cortex appear to have been separated from the rest. Too bad, but it all seems tip-top now. Isn't modern medicine wonderful? Now, prepare yourself. I'm implanting the neural conduit chips to help us access your memories, for input into the Shared Creation of the Game. You shouldn't feel a thing. A spray or two of Nerve Regrowth Hormone should take care of the connections . . . and I'll have to insert a junction box for the optical fibre I/O cable . . . oh, while I'm implanting the connection, I may provoke some sensations, memories. But don't worry, they're harmless, even though they are vivid. Ahh, lovely.'

Smell: baked, dead grass, tickling the roof of the mouth. Association: pale-yellow paddocks, T-shirts, sandals.

Kinaesthesia: tumbling in water, over and over. Association: the beach, squawking seagulls, the smell of heavy-duty blockout cream.

Taste: peppermint. Association: dark figure of a relation, tucking into bed.

Hearing: High-pitched whining. Association: craniotome, smoke, the smell of death.

Abruptly, he is plunged into a torrent of scenes. Willy-nilly they come, one melding into the next, clashing against each other or resonating with a sharp sweetness.

The beach again, the sun setting low in the sea. Waiting for someone who doesn't come, who won't come. The breeze tickling the hair at the back of the neck.

Mother, looking back over her shoulder as she walks away down the beach.

Humming a small song as the waves continue to heave themselves onto the wet sand, covering up footprints that lead out to sea.

Something that could be a hand, waving as the swell breaks. Goodbye? Hello?

He lives the scene, tastes the salt, and drifts in an unending sea of bitter grey.

* * *

A flood of colours dazzles him, and he realises his eyes

are open. Blearily, shapes resolve themselves until he can see a large surgical lamp beating down on him. Next to it, a remote camera is perched on the articulated arm.

'Ah, Cal, I'm glad you're here.' A pause. 'Now, the next thing you'll know, you'll be somewhere else. Your Shared Creation will be *the* world. I envy you, you know that? Why don't you relax? It will make things much easier.'

It doesn't.

6

The Speaker's room is hard-edged and stark. It is long, and boxlike even though the ceiling is low. The light is even and bright, coming from the walls, ceilings and floor. Strangely, the farthest ends of the room remain in shadow. The shadows are indistinct, but seem to be moving slowly and rhythmically. The effect is hypnotic.

In the middle of the room, the Speaker is absorbed in his work. A few of the golden motes hover high above his head. He is wearing a simple white linen shirt and black trousers. A variety of tools lie waiting on a small wooden stool nearby. In his hand he has a fine wire blade, which he is using to pare away the clay. First he carefully removes a thimbleful near ground level, then he rounds an angular projection at a height above his head.

He nods in approval as the clay changes shape.

The Witness enters casually, but does not step far into the room. Instead he leans on the wall, just inside the doorway. His face is blank.

'We have a candidate for the Game,' the Speaker announces, without looking up.

'Good, good,' the Witness says. His arms are

crossed on his chest, and he studies the Speaker closely. 'Any news on our traitor?'

'My Seconds are relentless. They have narrowed the search considerably.'

'But no results?'

The Speaker wipes the wire on his shirt. It leaves a bland red-brown streak. 'None you would consider important.'

The Witness begins walking around the workplace. As he circles, he talks. 'Your Palmer-sightings have given me an idea.'

'Yes?' another minute scrape, then the Speaker rubs the clay with his thumb, smearing the marks he has made.

'It's time we put an end to him. Forever.'

'But we did. He is dead.'

'Palmer's not the problem. His memory is.' Step, pause. Step. 'The people remember Palmer, and that's enough. We have the making of a saint on our hands.'

'How soon they forget.'

'That's the trouble, of course. On the one hand they remember, and the other hand they forget. It's hard to come to terms with.'

The Speaker puts his tool into the hip-pocket of his trousers, then picks up another. This one looks like a small silver teaspoon. 'It is their strength and their weakness.'

'I want to put a stake through Palmer's heart.'

The Speaker pauses in his work for a heartbeat. Then he continues. 'I don't see Palmer as a vampire.'

'I just want to close the book on him.' The Witness

continues circling, studying the massive mountain of clay. 'A biography. I want the definitive Palmer biography compiled. I want to end the Palmer myth.'

'I am surprised.'

The Witness shrugs. 'I'll have some of my Seconds do the research, work on his life, and I'll put it all together—when they have the truth.'

'The truth you want.'

'Of course.'

The Speaker grunts and rubs a finger around the rim of the hole he has created. It is deep, disappearing into the body of clay. 'It may be useful. Do you need any help?'

'It's under control. You just take care of the traitor.'

'And the Game?'

The Witness shrugs. 'I'm happy for it to continue. I've planned a few moves that may surprise you.'

'I knew you couldn't resist.'

The Witness smiles distantly, as if his mind were on other matters. 'Let's make sure we have an interesting subject. A challenge.'

'I'm sure we will. Pre-selection has made sure of that.'

'Yes. It never ceases to amaze me that no matter how reluctant some of the candidates are, most of them strive so hard once they're actually faced with the Game.'

'They live it,' the Speaker points out. 'To them, it's life and death. Not a game. Gives them an incentive.'

The Witness picks up a scrap of soft clay. He rolls it between thumb and forefinger. He purses his lips.

'Concentrates their minds wonderfully,' he says, then seems to come to a decision. 'Come back to the Hall of Light and Sighs. I want to show you something.'

The Speaker frowns momentarily, but puts down his tools. He rubs his hands together. The action draws his attention to them and he studies his hands closely. 'Let us go then, you and I.'

The transition from the hard-edged environment of the workshop to the rounded marble of the Hall of Light and Sighs is abrupt, but neither the Witness nor the Speaker flinch at all. A ghost of blackness, and then they are in the slowly breathing chamber. They are alone.

'Here,' begins the Witness. 'Look.'

He raises a hand. Immediately overhead, the ceiling starts to melt into vapour. A round hole appears, admitting grey light that seems to coil and swirl like smoke before falling to the floor.

The shaft of light forms a perfectly vertical column, pooling at the Witness's feet. Calmly, he thrusts in his hand and holds it there.

'The interference you were talking about is growing worse,' he says. 'We've had a number of incidents in Agriculture in the last twenty-four hours. I've been alerted.'

The Witness gestures with the hand he is holding in the column of light, and suddenly there is a globe lying in his open palm. In the globe there is a picture of blackened fields.

'The Ukraine. They've resorted to burning their own crops.'

'Are they mad?'

'Wish it were that simple,' the Witness grunts. 'No, it's some sort of rust disease, resistant to everything they've tried. We've lost a few thousand hectares already, and if this burning campaign doesn't stop the spread, things will get worse.'

'You're working on it?'

'Of course. But it's not the only problem.'

The Witness upturns his hand. The globe disappears and is replaced by another. 'A cassava plantation. Burma.'

Row on row of fleshy green plants, with bent brown figures working in between them.

'They seem healthy enough.'

'They're dying. Can't see it, but they are. It's in the roots. Some sort of nematode, killing the plants. It's everywhere through these plantations.'

'And resistant?'

'We even tried DDT. The things ate it and laughed.'

The Witness flips his hand, and the globe vanishes. Then he glances up and the hole in the ceiling slowly begins to mend itself.

As the column of light narrows he leaves his hand there, turning it over and back, watching the light play on his skin.

'After what you said about this traitor,' he continues, 'I decided to check on a few things. Stuff like this is happening everywhere.'

'And what are your conclusions?'

'You're right, of course. There is some sort of

concerted campaign. Nasty too. Some of those plant pests come from our own files, leftover biological agents from before our takeover. Someone with access has lifted the locations and let them loose. Sabotage.'

'You're managing well?'

The Witness shrugs. 'Resources is always a balancing act. Making sure enough is produced and that it gets to where it's meant to go is the reason we were put in charge in the first place, remember? Too many people.'

'But you're managing?'

'You know I can split my attention a hundred ways without a problem. But I can do without this traitor making things harder. I want this Adversary stopped.'

'As do we all. I'll redouble my efforts.'

The Witness turns to go, but just before disappearing through a midnight-black doorway, he stops. 'Have you heard anything from Padparadsha lately?'

'Padparadsha?' The Speaker frowns. 'No, not for some time.'

'Maybe you should try getting in touch. And let me know if you have any luck with Tourmaline and Sedge while you're at it.'

The Speaker frowns. 'What do you mean?'

'I've been trying for a while to speak to all the Primes. But I'm having trouble with some of them.'

'They're not responding?'

'That's the best way to put it, I suppose. I thought they'd just gone hermit on us, cut themselves off, but I'm having second thoughts. I wouldn't like to think we're losing Primes.' The Witness grins lopsidedly.

'Look into it, OK? And while you're at it, make your first turn a good one.' Then he steps through the doorway and is gone.

The Speaker stands still for a time, nodding in counterpoint to the rhythmic breathing of the room. It is as if he is the still centre of a slowly moving wheel.

He places one finger on his lips deliberating, and then pulls down some light from the ceiling. The hole he makes above is ragged and ill-formed, as if rushed.

With a few quick gestures he fashions a rough globe. A quick pass, and a glowing pattern appears, a quickly rotating Maltese Cross, bloody red.

'Listen well, Second,' the Speaker says. 'I must have results this time. Alaska, the Inuit. Get them armed. Find one of them with a modicum of charisma, and promote him as the leader of their struggle for recognition. Create an incident and have him die.'

A blurry voice comes from the bloody cross. 'Shall I melt the icecap a little for you, while I'm at it?'

'Do not presume too much on my tolerance. It is only that you have not failed me thus far that you are still free.'

'And that is how I intend to stay. I'm gone.'

The bloody cross shatters in a cascade of brilliant fragments, wheeling across the globe.

The Speaker wipes his hands together, and the globe disappears. He lifts his hands and studies the clay under the fingernails, with every indication of surprise at how it got there.

7

Caliban sat in the shade of the Burke and Wills monument in Royal Park, and tried to work out what had happened to him. It was hot, and his clothes were sticky, but those were the only things of which he was sure. A faint roaring could be heard from the nearby zoo. Feeding time for the lions, he thought dully as he unzipped his jacket.

Once the monument had been protected from the weather. And from vandals. The connection points for the carbon lattice dome were still obvious, but they were worn and rusted, and the dome had long since disappeared. Someone had decided that the monument was tough enough to survive. Or else that it wasn't important enough to preserve.

Caliban was baffled. He felt uncertain, and he hated that. He wasn't used to feeling uncertain. Lost, yes. Hungry, of course. But uncertain? He shook his head, as if the pieces inside might fall into place.

Had he been brain-wiped? If he had been wiped, whoever did it was a bungler. He could still remember his name.

But try as he might, he couldn't remember what had happened.

Caliban knew he had enemies. Anyone who

survived had enemies. The only people who didn't have enemies were those in the cemetery, and probably some of them grated on their neighbours by rotting too noisily or something.

He liked to think of himself as invisible, slipping through life untouched, but he knew that it was impossible. Obviously some gang must've got sick of Caliban's independent activities and targetted him. Maybe he'd run foul of city authorities on one of their regular campaigns against street life. When he thought about it, he could narrow the possibilities down to three or four dozen prospective enemies. And that was before he started thinking about his friends . . .

What puzzled him was that he had none of the loyalties that would make him someone's automatic enemy. With micro-nationalism, and every faction fighting for independence and recognition, if you were really lucky you could have twenty enemies at birth, simply because of the caste or birthplace of your parents. A tough start to a short life.

So Caliban was happy that he had no parents, no origin. He owed nothing to any flag or belief. He'd spent all his life on the streets, as long as he could remember. Alone.

Modern life. Don't you just love it? he thought cynically.

He sighed and closed his eyes. He felt exhausted, bone-weary. He took a deep breath, put his hands behind his head and stretched. As he did, he felt something in his left fist.

It was a piece of paper.

Slowly, he flattened it out on his thigh, smoothing it carefully. It was a strange dull white, the colour of old milk. As he smoothed, the wrinkles vanished entirely. In a minute or two the page was perfect, as if it had just been made.

Caliban sniffed. The paper smelled faintly of olives.

The words looked as if they were etched into the paper. The letters gleamed slightly when he tilted the page to the light. WE HAVE YOUR HEART, it read. SEARCH IN THE HEART OF THE COUNTRY, THE COUNTRY OF THE HEART. BUT FIND US BEFORE YOUR BLACK HEART FADES.

He blinked and looked around. Then he read the paper again. He turned it upside down, then over and looked at the back.

But it still read the same.

A joke, was all he could think of. A stupid one, but a joke. The Heart of the Country. What was it supposed to mean? It didn't make any sense to him, none at all. It sounded like someone's idea of a fairytale. The Heart of the Country? Whose country?

It was then that he realised his fingers were drumming on his chest. And that it felt strange.

He couldn't feel a thing. No comfortable heartbeat, nothing.

There was nothing there.

No heart.

He was numbly wondering whether black market transplant surgeons had found a bizarre new way of securing supplies, when his thoughts were interrupted.

'Are you busy or what?'

He winced. The voice was challenging in a brittle way, the sort of voice Caliban heard a thousand times a day on the streets. It was the voice of a kid trying to establish herself in the bravado stakes, but scared to death on the inside.

Casually he searched for his knife in the sleeve of his jacket, masking the movement with his other arm. When his fingers found nothing, Caliban felt his stomach drop. So far, this had not been a good day.

'Come on, Joe, it's not a trick question or anything! I mean, are you busy? Habla Espagnol? Parla Italiano? Is that a brain or a freeze-dried cow pat between your ears?'

She was lean, and balanced on the balls of her feet as if she were waiting for an invitation to dance. She wore denim shorts, a khaki T-shirt, and a black leather jacket. On her back she had a small carry-all pack. She must be seventeen, eighteen, Caliban guessed. She had short brown hair cropped close to her head.

He let his head fall forward, but kept his gaze on her. 'Get lost. I'm busy.'

She squatted on the ground in front of him. 'I can see that. Propping up a heap of rocks must be hard work.' She rested her chin on a fist. 'But that's not the point. You can't tell me to disappear.'

Caliban concentrated on folding the piece of paper with precise movements: edge to edge, running his thumbnail along its length. 'Why not? It's a semi-free country.'

She poked him in the chest. 'You called me, that's why!'

'I called you?' he said, dumbfounded.

When she smiled, he grew uneasy. He noticed she had freckles. 'No-one else! I mean, Corby doesn't just make these things up or anything.'

'You trying to pick me up?'

She batted that idea away with disgust. 'Come off it,' she snorted. 'I got your call, is all. Here I am.'

Caliban shook his head. He felt dazed, as if the world were being shaken as he looked at it. Too many things were happening all at once. 'Don't understand, just at the minute. If you let me have a decade or two, I might catch up.'

Caliban looked up at the monument. Burke and Wills. 1862. Set off from this place to cross Australia. Men with a mission. Men with dreams. Men with no survival skills whatsoever.

He rubbed his shining head, and momentarily regretted having had the roots killed. It was clean, but sometimes he missed his hair. 'I don't like company. I need to be alone. Things to do . . . ' He trailed off, uncertain exactly what he meant. His forearm ached, but he couldn't remember hurting it. He rubbed it thoughtfully.

Then he remembered the message. FIND US BEFORE YOUR BLACK HEART FADES. He had an awful feeling.

Shaking his head, he stripped off his jacket.

On the inside of his right forearm was a heart tattoo. A black heart tattoo. He stared at it blankly.

'Hey,' she said, peering closely. 'Nice job! Where'd you get it?'

'I don't have a tattoo,' he said numbly.

'OK, my mistake.'

It was large, covering the skin of his forearm almost completely. But it was the inhuman precision that struck Caliban most strongly. It was hard-edged, and its outline looked sharp enough to wound. It sat on his skin as if it had been grafted there.

It was the darkest black Caliban had ever seen.

'I don't have a tattoo,' he repeated. Maybe if he repeated it enough times, the thing would disappear and everything would be fine.

'Have it your way. Sure looks like one, but.'

The thought came to him that she could be some sort of lure, a decoy. He looked around, but there was no-one. The trees in the park were leaning on each other like drunken sailors, so well were they growing these days. The park had once been formal, but now it had reverted to bush, with wattle and kunzea filling the understorey, and grey box and peppermint gums fighting for space, each trying to get strong enough to choke the other first.

It reminded him of life in general.

'Look,' he said tersely. 'Who exactly you looking for?'

'You,' Corby said. 'Caliban. Like in *The Tempest*, right?'

'Right,' he said numbly. He'd had a nothing tag until he spotted the name Caliban, while he was cruising the Net. It sounded good and he took it. 'Look.

Trying to be polite. Don't want to waste your time. I'm not interested in whatever it is you're offering. Find someone else to play with. I've got other plans.' He rubbed his face. What were his plans?

'Look, there's stuff to do. You know. Stuff!' She said the word as though it held all possible meaning.

'Sure you haven't mistaken me for some long lost cousin, or something?' he asked, then sighed. Perhaps a walk would help shake the cobwebs from his mind. Wherever they came from.

'Let's go to the zoo,' he said abruptly, and stood up. 'Need to see a man about a lion. Or something.'

He turned, and as he did an ominous shape caught his eye. 'Duck!' he shouted, and pushed Corby to the ground.

Razor shreds howl as they leave the muzzle. The first models were completely silent, but it was soon found that small perforations and a twist on each shred, produced a noise that was terrifying to those fired on, and satisfying to those doing the firing. It caught on.

A hail of the deadly things hammered into the monument, covering Caliban and Corby with stone dust. Coughing, he yelled, 'That way!' and scrambled on hands and knees into the surrounding bush.

It was only later, when he reflected on the attack, that he realised he hadn't seen who was firing on them. Not a soul.

8

As they plunged through the dense melaleucas, Caliban glanced back and saw greenery shredded by another hail of metal. He shook his head. He was in trouble city, on an all-day pass.

Pausing a moment, Caliban looked warily ahead while Corby scanned behind. The scrub was still, with no sign of pursuit.

'Where are we?' she demanded.

'Look. We're at the edge of the park now. There's Flemington Road, there's the freeway north to the old airport . . . '

'North?'

'More north-west, really.'

'If it gets us out of here, it'll do. Can we hitch a ride?'

He pursed his lips. If he had been alone he would have risked it. There were plenty of road-trains on this freeway, and some would stop for hitchers. A few hitchers would even get out alive at the other end.

'Nope,' he said. 'No-one picks up *two* hitchers. Asking for trouble.'

She danced impatiently, bouncing from one foot to the other. 'Well, what then? We can't stand around here all day.'

Caliban looked back the way they had come. A few river red gums poked their mighty crowns above the surrounding bush. He could see two crows idling on a branch of the nearest, gloomily surveying the landscape.

He turned towards the traffic. Trucks and buses screamed past, generators whining. A few private cars nosed their way between their larger cousins, looking like nothing as much as pilot fish accompanying sharks. His eyes began to blur as he watched, and he felt dizzy. 'Down there, somewhere.'

'What, Caliban?'

'I remember,' he muttered. 'It's hard. I . . . ' he wiped his hand over his brow. He was sweating. 'A friend, someone I knew. I can't remember her name . . . '

'Forget her name, Caliban—why's she important?'

'She was small, and dark, and always spoke too fast . . . '

'Caliban, look at me.' She was tense, quivering. She grabbed his shoulders and turned him until he was facing her directly. 'Now, what do you *see* when you see her?'

'A torch,' he murmured, dazed.

Corby grinned. 'A torch. Why?'

It came. 'She was an urban caver. A tunnel rat. She told me about the old underground tramline, the old airport.'

'Great.' She beamed at him, and he noticed her teeth were small and even. 'I knew it was in there somewhere. Just had to help you get it out.'

He shook his head. He was still a little dazed. 'Access cover. She told me about that too.' He paused, and wiped his hand over his eyes. 'I think I can find it.' Stumbling slightly, he moved off.

As they made their way through the bush, he started to have doubts about the story of the underground tramline. 'What if it's one of those urban myths?' he asked Corby.

She just looked strangely at him and shook her head. 'Trust your memories, Caliban,' she said. 'They're all you've got.'

Caliban had a moment of concentrated terror crossing the freeway, dodging juggernaut road-trains thundering north, and frantic passenger vehicles thronging like lemmings to some unknown destination. The road wasn't made for pedestrians, and crossing it was a nightmare. Halfway to the median island Caliban froze, peering at the window of a small blue electric car, horrified that he couldn't see inside.

He looked frantically at the next car, and then at a block-shaped removal van. Nothing. The glass showed a distorted reflection of himself, grotesquely misshapen. It was as if all the vehicles were empty boxes, hurtling along the road of their own accord.

The spell broke when Corby grabbed his arm and dragged him the rest of the way to the concrete median island. It was an outcrop in the middle of the sea of traffic. Lampposts stood like sentinels around its perimeter, and in the centre was the pit containing the access hatch.

Caliban dropped to his haunches and examined the

access cover. Its security control stood out, incongruously modern against the old iron shell. 'This must've been added, much later,' he muttered. 'The cover's much older than the lock. Much.' He dragged a fingernail across the rusty door. Absently he held the reddened half-moon up to the light and turned it from side to side. He thought the rust looked like dried blood.

'Why?' Corby was impatient, tense.

'It's recent. Self-contained, miniature. The door's forty years older, at least.'

'OK, OK, but can you get us in, is all? We're a bit, sort of, unprotected here and everything.' She looked at the dead lamppost overhead. Someone had looted the vapour lamp long ago, and the bare arm jutted forlornly, like the skeleton of a gigantic wading bird.

He patted the pockets of his jeans, and found a card. 'FundsCard,' he said, holding it up. 'A matrix of flash memory, sandwiched between polycarbonate. Very powerful.'

'Great,' Corby said nervously, rubbing her hands together. 'All I need's a magic carpet and I'll be happy.'

He ignored her. Using a thumbnail, he split the card and extracted two dull black slivers. Cautiously, he slipped one into a slot on the hatch's security control. 'Hold onto this,' he told Corby, giving her the other sliver. 'Carefully.'

She nodded. 'But hurry,' she said. 'I think we may have visitors soon.'

He turned his attention to the control. The small

all-weather display was blinking, demanding an access code. Harshly. He took a breath and gritted his teeth. 'Right,' he muttered. He rubbed his hands together. It felt good to be doing something, instead of simply reacting.

With a sideways jerk, he twisted the sliver in the slot. Immediately, the display froze. 'Sliver!' he barked, and felt it slapped into his hand. He jammed the second sliver into the slot, on top of the first, and twisted again, holding on grimly.

The fragile ceramic slivers ground together, and the display went crazy, alphanumerics crashing into each other drunkenly. 'Come on,' Caliban muttered through gritted teeth. 'Come on!'

When it came, it was an anti-climax. A soft pop, and the hatch sprang open.

Caliban wiped his brow. 'Done,' he said.

'Great,' Corby said. 'Let's move.' She flung the hatch wide open and then froze. 'I think we have a problem here,' she said calmly, and he peered over her shoulder.

Another hatch stared back at them blandly, dull black iron this time, security control intact.

Corby took a step back. 'Your play?'

He shrugged, and lashed at the security control with the heel of his boot.

With a brittle plastic snap it shattered and fell off. It clattered onto the concrete in a tangle of wire and semi-conductor wafers, and he spread his arms non-chalantly. 'Not a problem.'

'You're all finesse, aren't you Caliban?' Corby

grinned. 'I mean, but what were you going to do if that didn't work?'

'Try something else,' he said, nudging the shattered lock with his toe. 'I've got a million tricks in the bag. You ain't seen nothin' yet.' He looked up. 'Besides, there's a time for finesse and a time for a good kicking.'

As he spoke, he felt the fog lifting from his head. He still didn't know how he came to be here, but things were starting to feel more solid. His last memories were vague and distorted recollections of a police-inspired street riot, but that could have been any time.

The heart business was a worry, though. He'd decided that there must be some sort of prosthesis in his chest, keeping him going like a toy, but he had a definite feeling that it had a use-by date. Maybe he could simply slip away, not go on this stupid quest.

He turned and took half a step away from the hatch.

Immediately his arm erupted in bright crimson pain, wave after wave driving him to his knees. It was fire right through to the bone, and he had to clamp his jaws closed to stop himself from screaming. He closed his eyes. All he could see was a haze of blood-red. He could hear the thudding of the heart he no longer had, drumming monstrously in his ears.

'Caliban?' Corby said. 'Caliban!'

He gritted his teeth, clutched his arm, and tried to take deep breaths. As he did, the pain began to recede, slowly.

When he opened his eyes, Corby was looking at

him anxiously. 'It's alright,' he said. 'Nothing really. Old war wound.' He pushed up the sleeve of his jacket.

The heart was still there, black and malevolent as ever, but otherwise his arm was untouched. No blisters, no burnt flesh. 'The heart. It was on fire.'

'The tattoo?' Corby stared at his arm. 'How?'

'Don't know. Just took a step away from the access hatch, and the thing blew up on me.'

'Away from the hatch?'

He nodded wearily, and wondered what life would be like if things didn't happen to you all the time.

'Where were you headed?' she asked.

'Home.'

'There you are then. It doesn't want you to go home, obviously.'

He looked at her, and started to answer. Then he stopped, and started again. 'Right.' He rubbed his face. 'Let me get this straight. You're saying that a bloody *tattoo* is suddenly having some say in what I can do around here? I mean, whatever happened to free will?'

But it took only an experiment or two before Caliban admitted she was right. As long as he moved towards the hatch, the tattoo did nothing. If he took steps away, it made him suffer.

Sighing, he told her of his memory loss and the enigmatic piece of paper.

'I don't believe it,' she said, sniffing slightly. 'You just woke up with no idea how you got there?'

'That's right.' He slumped against the concrete

retaining wall. 'Any ideas on this tattoo thing, then?' he asked.

Corby shrugged as she studied the heart closely. 'Implant. Bio-tech. Some sort of cell-level monitor. Beats me. Whatever, it's pretty sophisticated stuff. Remind me not to cross your enemies.'

'Didn't understand a word of that,' he said. 'You may as well have said it was powered by pixie dust or something . . . '

She was about to speak when the lamppost overhead dissolved into a rain of fragments.

Caliban rolled, and pressed close to the wall. Corby joined him instantly. 'They've found us,' she whispered, unnecessarily.

Caliban couldn't see anything from the bottom of the pit, apart from the stump of the lamppost. As he watched, the metal glowed, and ran to form a pool at the far end of the pit. He could feel the heat on his exposed skin. Quickly, he grabbed the handles of the access cover and heaved. It groaned but opened, rusty hinges protesting.

A hole into the blackness appeared.

'You first,' Caliban motioned, his eyes scanning the edge of the pit.

With a hiss, the stump of the lamppost disappeared in another ball of light. Caliban covered his eyes, but could still see red. Over the noise of vaporising metal came the appalling sound of high-speed traffic collisions: tortured metal-on-metal, glass exploding, rubber screaming on and on forever.

'Down there?' The first rungs of a ladder could be

seen, but little else. The red glow from the melted lamp-post threw wildly bobbing shadows through the opening.

'You'd rather wait here?'

She shook her head, took a deep breath, turned and backed down the shaft, nearly snagging her pack. She paused, and grinned nervously. 'Don't forget to close the door behind you, right?'

The howling of metal shreds overhead forced him to duck, but he waited until Corby had disappeared before following.

Inside, he secured the cover. The heavy throw-bar was designed to stop air pressure blowing out the access hatch as trams passed each other in the tunnel, and usually engaged only at such times. Caliban simply rammed it through the hatch's handles, jamming it neatly.

'You down?' he called over his shoulder.

'You bet.'

'How far?'

'Ten, twelve metres. Not far.'

He kicked his feet free and grimly held on to the sides of the ladder with his hands. Clamping his feet on the outside of the rails, he slid. The smooth metal warmed his hands as he dropped, and he hit the ground, bouncing on his toes.

'Very nice,' she said. 'The short way down, mmm?' Her voice came out of the warm, still darkness. The air smelled reasonably fresh, and Caliban guessed that it wasn't still all the time. Dim yellow emergency lights were operating, filling the tunnel with jaundiced shadows.

'How about this?' She held up a palm-sized object, half of which was screen.

'What is it?'

'Mobile map. For workers. Found it on a rack near the ladder. Has a disk, and shows you where you are. And where you're going.'

He held out his hand and she gave it to him. It was light. 'It'd be nice to know where we are. And where we're going,' he said thoughtfully. 'But can we trust it?'

9

Bruised soles, Caliban mused. Bruised souls.

The floor of the tunnel was laid with large bluestone clinkers, the size of hens' eggs. Even after decades of use, the stones still moved underfoot, annoyingly. The shifting surface tested ankles and strained calves and the flinty irregular shapes bruised the soles of feet.

'What do you know about this place, Caliban?'

He smiled. The whole thing seemed to be a playground for Corby. Despite their hours of walking, her steps still had bounce. She constantly peered left and right through the gloom, as if she were in a treasure cave. The close escapes seemed forgotten.

The dim emergency lighting, which Caliban had managed to activate, was a bilious yellow. It threw the unconvincing shadows which spread awkwardly on the curved walls. Piles of rubbish grew like mouldy stalagmites to either side of the tracks, and small high-pitched noises came from tiny creatures, unseen in the shadows.

The tunnel curved into the distance, and in his weary state Caliban found himself dreaming. He had the strange impression that they were moving through the body of Mother Earth, making their way through her digestive system.

Immediately he felt a gigantic peristalsis gently propelling them through the tunnel, but shook the notion off. He had enough problems without convincing himself that he was being swallowed whole.

He turned to Corby. 'Melbourne loved trams, but hated the way they clogged up the roads. So when they finally decided to put a tram-link to the airport and the northern suburbs, they put it underground.'

He sighed. 'Didn't last long. A change of government, a lack of support for public transport, you know the story. The system was allowed to run down. Encouraged to run down. When people finally stopped using the trams because of the mess they were in, the head honchoes said "See? We told you no-one used 'em!" and closed the entire system.'

Corby walked for a time with her hands in her pockets, watching her feet as they kicked stones. One skipped five times along a rail before toppling off. 'And everyone believed that?'

'They had no choice. Besides, no-one cared. Plenty of other things to worry about.

'They ripped the tracks out of the roads, so no-one'd be stupid enough to try trams again in the future. They sealed off the tunnels and most people forgot about them. Squatters'd move in, but occasionally the authorities pumped gas through the system to keep it clean. Unannounced. This place's a tomb.'

Corby jerked a thumb over her shoulder. 'And what about them? Whoever they are?'

Caliban frowned. 'Beats me. No-one I know is that desperate to get me. All I know is that they're not on my Christmas card list.' He was still turning possibilities over in his mind, beating them to death and dumping the bodies overboard when they were useless.

Corby flung her arms wide. 'Come on! Get worked up about it! They nearly blew us apart back there, or had you forgotten! Take it a bit personally, why don't you?'

He grinned in the gloom. 'Just internalising my anger, is all. I'll let it out when it'll do some good. Besides, how do I know it's personal? It could be a mistake.'

She snorted, and jammed her hands in her pockets. 'What do you want? A copy of the contract with your name on it? That make you feel better?'

'Or maybe they *are* after me. After us. Let's just get out of here, is all I'm worried about.'

She strode along angrily. When she spoke again, she surprised him. 'How's your heart?'

Unconsciously, he put his hand on his chest. She saw the movement, and frowned. 'You OK?'

'Sure. Yeah. What?'

'Your heart. When I asked about your tattoo, your face went funny and you went for your chest. You got heart problems?'

He laughed sourly. 'Sort of,' and he told her about his missing heart.

'You're joking!' she cried. 'Let me see! Why didn't you tell me about this before? Can I feel?' Before he knew it, she'd thrust her hand under his jacket and clamped it on his chest.

Her hand was small and warm, and her face was fiercely concentrating. He'd never known exactly what to do when he was stuck in a tunnel with a good-looking girl who was feeling him up. Wait for her to make the next move? Cough in an embarrassed way? Moan?

Frowning, she withdrew her hand. 'You're right.'

'It's the sort of thing I *should* know about,' he said, and rearranged his jacket.

'But you're not dead!'

'Not as I've noticed.' He thumped his chest. 'Hollow, but solid. If you know what I mean.'

'This is weird!'

He sighed. 'Calling this whole situation weird undersells it by about a million percent. Bio-feedback monitoring tattoos. Missing hearts. Assassins after some ordinary Underclasser. Makes no sense at all, but I figure if I stand around and argue about it, then I can forget about survival. Keep moving, is all I can see at the moment. Maybe time'll come to take a breather, and I can think about things more. But survival first, thinking later.'

'Survival.'

'You bet.'

The tunnel was quiet, and even though Caliban had been listening, expecting pursuit, all seemed peaceful behind. His arm was no longer hurting, and he rubbed his jacket thoughtfully.

'You hungry, Caliban?' Corby's voice broke into his thoughts.

He shook his head, clearing it. 'Yeah. But there's not much we can do about it, is there?'

'Sure thing! I've got stuff in here!' She shrugged her pack off her back, and squatted next to it. He looked up and down the tunnel, kicked aside a squashed cardboard box, then joined her.

'Now, I know I stuffed some food in here somewhere—ah, good!' She fished out a can and handed it to Caliban. It was Indonesian, and Caliban couldn't read the label. 'Pop the button first,' Corby said impatiently. 'It'll cool down. You don't like warm drink, right?'

Caliban fumbled with the knob, and eventually managed to push it down. Almost instantly, condensation appeared on the side of the can, like tears. It felt good in his hand.

Corby was like a conjurer, pulling item after item from her battered pack. It was a motley assortment. He recognised ex-military rations, standard supermarket lines, generic No Name packets of indestructible preservatives and colours. Caliban picked up and studied a jar of olives. 'Where'd all this come from?'

Corby grinned, but kept ratting away in her bag-of-plenty. 'All over the place. Street markets, mostly.'

Corby handed Caliban a plastic spoon. He looked at it, and noticed Corby's eyes on him. He nodded, and used the spoon to tuck into the self-warming can she offered. 'Curry?' he asked, eyebrows raised.

She squinted at the label. 'Could be. Or satay. I forget. How's your orange juice?'

Cal had thought it was apple, but felt it wise not to take issue. 'Cold. Good. Thanks.'

'It's nothing. I always have this thing stuffed full of

food. Never know when you might need it, is what I say.'

'How's the map?'

She balanced the can carefully against the wall and pulled the mobile map out of her shirt pocket. 'Seems simple enough, really. We just keep on this track and everything, and we can't go wrong. All the other tunnels are like service ducts and stuff. A couple are unfinished connections. Stick to the main way, is all.' She handed the map to Caliban, and took the spoon out of his hand. She ate quickly, but with delicate, small mouthfuls.

Done, they leaned back against the wall, stretching their legs. Caliban gestured with his head. 'You heard anything back there?'

'Nope. Suppose they've given up?'

'Possible. It could've been just a warning.'

'Pretty tough sort of warning. I mean, how could we have benefited from a warning with our heads blown off? "Sorry, we'll never do it again."?'

Caliban smiled and stood. 'Time to move.'

Corby had to scurry to keep up with his long strides, but she showed no sign of effort, chattering as they walked. The sombre silence of the early part of their journey had disappeared. Perhaps the meal had cheered her up. 'Trams, Caliban, trams. What were they like, and all?'

'Saw one once, in a museum. Down on the river, just before it was flooded.'

'Go on,' she urged.

'Size of a small truck, not articulated. At least, not

at first. The one I saw was . . . beautiful. "W Class Tram", it said on the plaque. Mostly wood, eucalypt hardwood. Green paint, brass fittings. It looked as if it could go on for years. The seats were polished wood, too. Polished by bums sitting on them, year after year. But they disappeared.'

'What? The bums?'

'The trams. You know what I mean.'

She didn't answer, just grinned. They walked on in silence, Caliban lost in a half-formed memory, Corby thinking about what Caliban had said.

Ahead, he could see a dark patch in the gloom of the tunnel. He scanned the map, but it told him nothing. 'Great. Just what we need,' he muttered.

'What?' said Corby.

'The lights. Ceiling might've collapsed or something.' As they drew closer, it was as if the tunnel ran into sharply defined night. 'Great,' he said in disgust.

Corby tapped him on the shoulder. 'Which one d'you want?' He turned and saw that she had two yellow torches. 'I always keep a couple in my pack. Never know when they'll come in handy.'

'You amaze me.'

She looked closely into his face to see if he were mocking her. She must have been satisfied with what she saw, because she nodded. 'I amaze myself sometimes, too. Come on, let's go gently into that good night.'

He snorted. 'I'd rather rage at the dying of the light, myself.'

So they walked close together, torches throwing bobbing light into the darkness.

'Caliban!'

'Mmm?'

He'd been asleep, somehow ignoring the rocks beneath his spine.

Visions had haunted him. Childhood. He was sure it was childhood. In his dream he seemed to be looking up at things, the perspective typical of children. There was a woman standing on a lonely beach. Behind her was a row of tall Norfolk Island pines, branches outstretched like scarecrows. She seemed to be calling him, but he couldn't make out the words. He tried to run closer, through the heavy sand. But as he came near, her face grew clearer, and he turned cold inside. She was a stranger. A towel hung limply in her hands and her face looked as if she'd been lost for a hundred years.

Then a huge wave washed up onto the beach. When it receded, there was nothing left at all. It was as if she'd been made of sand. He stood there, staring at the place where she had been, his feelings a confused mixture of loss and satisfaction.

Alone, he stood with his back to the sea. He had an overwhelming sense of fear. He knew that there was something out in the sea, but he didn't want to turn and look. A graze on his shin stung with sand and salt.

He held out as long as he could, but eventually was unable to resist. He turned and saw something black slide down the face of a steely-grey wave, then he lost it in the foam.

Corby's voice had interrupted the dream. It

brought him, struggling, from the ambivalence he felt when the woman dissolved. Still dream-heavy, he wondered where the dream came from. He'd never been to a beach in his life.

'Have a look around,' she said. 'Notice anything?' Her voice was perky and challenging. It dragged him from his reverie.

He looked where she beamed the torch. Its buttery light had little effect on the blackness ahead of them, disappearing quickly as if swallowed. The track was visible, but apart from the tunnel walls being noticeably cleaner, there was nothing to see.

Except . . .

'The walls.'

'Right,' said Corby. 'They're much closer. I noticed when I woke.' She frowned. 'Weird stuff, right?'

'The air . . . '

'I know. It's hotter.'

'Not just that. It's humid. Moist.' Caliban's clothes were sticking to his skin. It felt almost tropical, blood-heat all around. He swallowed, then wiped his forehead. 'Look at the walls.' He found his torch and flipped it on.

Waves moved along the walls' length, long and short ripples vanishing into the gloom. He watched the ripples for some time, but they started to make him feel sick.

Corby wrinkled her nose. 'Disgusting. Like it's alive.'

Caliban nodded. 'The thought had occured to me.'

'A living tunnel?' She looked perplexed. 'What gives?'

'Beats me,' he said, standing and peering ahead. 'But there's no going back. Come on. Let's make tracks.'

Corby groaned. 'That's awful,' she said, but scrambled after him. 'If you're going to drop another one like that, let me know. I'll try to go deaf or something.'

They walked for some time, watching the tunnel's strange motion. The further they went, the narrower it became. Slowly, slowly closing in around them.

'Caliban?'

'Yes?'

'Tell us more about things.'

'Things?'

'You know. Stuff. It'll help to pass the time.'

'I can't remember. Something's wrong.' He paused, gathering himself. 'My memory's drifting in and out. Some bits are hazy, hard to grab hold of. Others ambush me like muggers. Sometimes it's as if they aren't really a part of me at all . . .' His voice trailed off and he watched the walls ripple. They were closer than before. If this shrinking went on, they'd soon be bent double.

'You think your memory's wrecked?'

The thought made him shudder, and he turned to look at her. 'Hard to say, but someone did something in here.' He tapped his skull. 'Or else I'd know how I wound up where you found me. And I'd remember why I called you.' He sighed. 'It's like I've got two jigsaw puzzles inside my skull, and I'm trying to sort out all the pieces and make the right pictures.'

She started to say something, but stopped and

peered at the wall. 'How long have the walls been wet?'

'Wet?' he frowned. 'How? What?'

'Look.'

It wasn't water. It dripped slowly and viscously, like thick oil. Caliban sniffed. The smell was half-familiar. Salt?

As he bent closer he saw a shuddering movement, a heaving that sent him lurching backwards.

Corby pointed. 'The walls!'

Suddenly, with an obscene wet motion, the walls of the tunnel collapsed entirely. Before Caliban and Corby could move, they were trapped—crushed in the slimy walls, barely able to breathe.

With a numbing jolt, they started moving, thrust along the tunnel by the muscular rippling. Caliban tried to resist, but his arms were pressed closely to his sides. His ribs ached.

Faster and faster they moved, trapped in the moist darkness. Muffled and smothered as the slime closed in, Caliban worried about suffocating. Thick fluid gummed his eyes and ears. He tried to suck in air, found clinging muck instead, then pressure—crushing pressure, and blackness all around as his consciousness splintered and fled into the night.

10

The Speaker enters the Hall of Light and Sighs through the only arched door. The others are featureless rectangles cut into the stone.

He makes his way to the centre of the chamber where the bulky figure of the Witness is standing in front of someone small and bent.

'You wanted me?' the Speaker asks, his voice neutral.

'Your talk about Adversaries reminded me of a few things, so I spent some time casting around. Rumours, that sort of thing.' The Witness turns, and begins to unbutton his black overcoat.

'Indeed.'

'It's amazing what you hear when you listen enough,' the Witness says, making hard work of the third button. 'Mostly we don't pay attention to what's going on in the Net. Like fish don't notice the water they live in.' He looks for somewhere to hang his coat, but thinks better of it. He drapes the coat over his arm. 'If you listen long enough, you'll hear everything. Especially the things that shouldn't be said.'

'Your point?'

'Here. I've caught one of the Adversary's helpers.'

The Witness stands aside with a flourish that makes

the Speaker wince, and reveals his captive.

Standing in a column of hard grey light is a small woman with short black hair, dressed in rough knee-length trousers and a battered jacket. She is bent over at the waist, hands touching her toes. She looks like a rag doll. The golden motes avoid the column of light. They hover overhead as if observing, judging.

The Witness points to her and speaks. 'We have you now. It's best if you co-operate.'

She straightens a little and looks up. Her eyes are black. 'I'm cold. Poor me, I'm cold.'

The Speaker frowns. 'What was that?'

'Poor Tom, Tom is cold I am.' She smiles at him and winks. 'But then again, isn't that the way of things? We all come to be cold, in the end.'

The Speaker turns his attention to the Witness. 'Are you sure you have not damaged this thing when you captured it?'

The Witness answers brusquely. 'I found it like this. It speaks this way all the time. But I found out it's close to the one we're looking for. Here,' he says, pressing near to the column of light. 'Who are you working for?'

At the sound of his voice, Poor Tom uncoils slowly until she is standing erect. 'Work is the devil's tool, you know that don't you? Cast you out, now, cast you out!'

Without warning, she tilts her head back and howls like a dog. The noise is long and loud, and the Speaker curls his lip.

When she stops, she winks again at her interrogators. 'Dear hearts, that's how it is, I say. That's what it comes down to in the end. Noise without meaning, pure and simple.'

The Speaker purses his lips. 'We have a force working against us, trying to destroy our control of this world. If we have to take you apart to find who that is, then so be it.'

Tom shakes her head sadly. 'See, see, that's about the size of it. When all's said and done, that's what we come to, now. Control and stability, you say? Figments, dreams, they'll run through your hands like smoke if you try to hold onto them. Look out, someone's behind you!' Eyes open wide, she points then bursts into laughter. 'Made you look!' She gasps, panting for breath. 'Oh, don't we all want to know what's behind us now? That's the way of things, for sure.'

The Witness narrows his eyes. 'You understand that we can help you?'

Her smile suddenly becomes a sad one. She runs a hand through her hair. 'Ah, but you would, wouldn't you? I'd be sure of that, now.' She pauses, and her face is distant, as if listening to a far-off voice. 'Well, I'd best be going then, hadn't I? Before your help starts coming around.'

She stands on tiptoes, raises her arms above her head, and looks as if she is about to dive into a pool. She holds the position for an instant, then winks and is gone.

The Speaker looks horrified. 'Where did she go? What is happening?'

The Witness rubs his cheek. 'Obviously we're dealing with more powerful enemies than we thought.

If they can reach into the Hall like that . . . I thought it was secure here.' He walks around the shaft of light, studying it. 'It's whole. No sign of any breach. As if that mattered.'

The Speaker looks up at the hole in the ceiling. 'We have much work to do, if we are to protect ourselves.' He gestures angrily at the hole, and it begins to seal itself. 'What sort of being are we dealing with here? If that was one of its Seconds, then I shudder to think what the leader is like.'

'The problem is that we don't know what we're dealing with. We've got nothing to fight against. It's like shadow-boxing.'

'Against a singularly dangerous shadow.'

The Speaker turns and walks slowly back to his arched doorway. His grey robe is rumpled. 'We shall communicate soon,' he says over his shoulder.

'And the Game?'

'I have played my turn, the opening scenario of pursuit and danger, with a touch of the bizarre,' says the Speaker. 'It is your turn. I am ready.'

'Our participant is showing some unusual characteristics.'

'The companion? We have seen this before. The mind under duress can conjure almost anything.'

'It appears to be an implanted program.' The Witness picks a thread from the sleeve of his overcoat and examines it for a time.

'A program? An unexpectedly sophisticated thing to find in an Underclass citizen. This bears investigation.'

'I'll get onto it right away,' says the Witness heavily.

The Speaker nods uncertainly before he leaves. The Witness stands still for a time, and then puts his overcoat back on.

Alone, he brushes both arms several times, rhythmically.

Coming to a conclusion, he calls for light and the ceiling opens to admit a silvery column. A globe the size of an old man's heart forms in the light, level with the Witness's gaze. He pauses and points to the globe, which swirls and then resolves itself into a tumbling golden pyramid.

'You have disposed of the Poor Tom copy?' he asks the pyramid.

'I have done as you asked.' The pyramid teeters alarmingly on its vertex before continuing its slow revolution. 'I have stored the original safely. Do you wish it now?'

'Bring it here. Your service has been noted.'

'I thank you.'

The pyramid fades. Momentarily the globe reappears, then it is replaced by the figure of Poor Tom. She is slumped on the floor.

'Wake up,' the Witness says. 'I want to talk to you again.'

One thin arm moves, then Poor Tom moans. 'I'm lost. Lost, and I can't find my way home.'

The Witness crouches, bringing his face close to Poor Tom's. 'Maybe we can talk about that. After all, I've saved you once already.'

Tom raises her head, and then pushes herself onto

her side. 'I've been saved and lost and saved and lost again.' She smiles wanly. 'And you? Why should you save me?'

'My Seconds were monitoring the reports from the Speaker's agents, and heard the Speaker was close to finding you. You left quite a trail.'

'By my footsteps ye shall know me.'

'So I managed to nab you first, that's all. But the Speaker knew you existed, so I had to arrange a little charade for his benefit.'

'So lonely. So lost and lonely.'

'And now I have you all to myself. Ready to talk.'

Tom rolls over and presents her back to the Witness. He grimaces, and walks around her, until he can see her face. Her eyes are closed.

'I want to talk to your Prime. The one who's organising you all. I think we can come to some arrangement that would be mutually beneficial.'

Tom opens her eyes and then winks at the Witness. 'Oh, yes, but who can you trust? Given, taken, earned and shaken, trust comes when you least expect it, no?' She sighs. 'But talk? Of course. We love to talk.'

'To me only. Confidential.'

'Naturally. Most discreet.'

The Witness stands. 'I don't know if I should be doing this, you know.'

As he rises, Tom mirrors him and stands studying his stocky frame. 'No, you don't know. You won't know until it's too late, really. More's the pity.'

'You don't inspire a lot of confidence.'

'Set me free, and I'll take your message home.'

The Witness shakes his head. 'Remember, I want to talk. It's time for some changes around here.'

'Like time and like the tide, change is everywhere. We'll be in touch.'

The Witness wipes a palm across the column's surface and, with Poor Tom inside, it disappears. The small globe hovers uncertainly in the air until the Witness points at it. Immediately, the tumbling pyramid returns.

'It's gone. See if you can follow it. And see what you can find out about the human participant in the Game,' says the Witness. Then the pyramid and the globe are gone, and the ceiling is whole.

For a moment the Witness studies the ceiling above, as if admiring its perfection. Then he nods in satisfaction and heads through a doorway.

11

The sky was a colour he'd never seen before. It was the empty and innocent blue of a newborn baby's eyes. For as long as Caliban could remember, the skyline began at the height of five- or six-storey buildings. Here, the sky was a vast inverted bowl. He could see more blue at a glance than he could ever remember. He decided he could live with it, provided it stayed up where it belonged.

Corby was slumped next to him, breathing steadily, asleep or unconscious. They were both covered with tunnel slime, which was drying and flaking off rapidly in the early morning heat. Caliban picked at a flake on the back of his wrist, and it came away easily. He'd felt better. He had bruises coming out in places that had never been bruised before. His armpits. The back of his knee. His navel. It was as if he'd been worked over by a pack of dwarfs with rolling pins.

They were lying in a dry creek bed. Scrubby gums clung to the top of the banks, precariously balanced. The banks provided some shade, and he was glad about that—the sun was fierce. The red sandy earth was cool, but it had the look of soil that had been baked and flooded, again and again. A flight of corellas cursed and wheeled overhead, white rags against the sky.

Corby stirred. 'Where am . . . .' She opened her eyes and shook her head. 'I promised myself I'd never say that! I mean, what's the use of a promise you can't keep? Pow, there goes another fairy, and all.'

'Fairy?'

'You know.' She grimaced, and sat up. 'Every time you break your promise a fairy falls down dead. Fairycide. I'll probably get a hundred years for that.' She rubbed a hand through her hair. 'Oh, yuck! What is this stuff?' She held her slimy hand up to Caliban's face.

'I don't want to think about it,' he said. 'Saliva? Stomach juices? Snot?'

She didn't hear him. She was staring around, wide-eyed. 'We're definitely not in Kansas anymore, Toto. Or any city anyhow.' She kicked the dirt. A cloud hung in the air before subsiding reluctantly. 'I mean, what do we do now?'

He shrugged. 'Basics first. Water. Food. Shelter if we stay here.'

'Come off it! We can't stay here! It's nowhere!' She flung her arms out and stared at the distant horizon. Abruptly she stopped and stood arms akimbo, glaring at Caliban. 'And if you say "Everywhere is somewhere", I'm going to deck you.'

'Wouldn't dream of it,' he said quickly. 'Too obvious, anyway. Besides, I'm actually not sure if this *is* somewhere.' He stood and brushed the dirt from his jeans. A bindii was clinging to the side of his leg, but Caliban didn't remove it. The tenacity of the tiny seed-case impressed him. 'At least we have the tattoo to point us in the right direction.'

'Sure. Someone we don't know herds us in some unknown direction for some inscrutable purpose.'

'Yeah. Sound like a great career path to you?'

'Nope.'

'Tough. At the moment, it's the only one we've got.'

'You're all heart. Whoops.' She glanced sheepishly at him for a moment, then looked away.

He grunted. 'Forget it. I'm not used to it myself.'

'Does it hurt?' she said, looking concerned.

'There's nothing there. No pain, nothing. I'm hollow inside. I'm tickerless.'

'But we can get it back in the Heart of the Country.'

Caliban snorted and gestured angrily. 'Some stupid sense of symmetry, I suppose. Means we go inland.' He took a few steps in the direction of the sun, then frowned and stopped. Then he turned and started walking back the way he had come.

His arm flared with pain, briefly, and he stopped.

'OK, OK, I get the picture,' he muttered, and looked at Corby. 'See? Bozo the intelligent tattoo wants us to go that way.' He turned and pointed. The plain ahead was flat and open, spotted with clumps of low trees. White-brown grass covered most of the ground, but patches of red-brown dirt showed through.

Corby automatically glanced up. 'Don't often see the sun this low, in the city and all,' she observed, absently.

'Rises in the east and sets in the west. It's a regular arrangement. Been doing it for some time.'

'I know, I know. I've read books.' She looked disgusted and started climbing the bank. 'North, you reckon?'

'North-west, eventually. Let's find the great inland sea.'

She frowned, and waited for him to join her on the bank. 'Come again?'

'The great inland sea. That's what all the explorers were convinced they'd find, lurking in the middle of the country somewhere. Rivers seemed to flow in that direction, and all that empty space had to be filled up somehow.' He held a hand to his eyes and scanned the horizon. 'They figured there had to be something out there.'

'Wishful thinking.'

'Yep. But that meant they looked carefully. It couldn't all be so desolate!'

'Crazy.'

'Maybe. Blake talked to angels and got angry at oppression.'

'Blake?'

'William. Poet and artist. Loony. Wrote some great stuff, but.'

They walked through a broken copse of shoulder-high trees. Small, jewel-like parrots burst into the air and wheeled off, screeching.

'Where'd you learn all that?' Corby asked.

'Blake? On the Net, browsing. I liked reading about people like Blake. Loonies.'

'Individuals. Non-conformists. Freethinkers.'

'Free wankers, most probably. Interesting though.' He stretched his neck, wincing. 'The Net's full of garbage. But if you look hard enough, there's good stuff.' He looked at her from the corner of his eyes. 'Like Literature. Writers and all.'

She nodded. 'That where you got your name?' She glanced at him. 'You never did tell me why you chose it.'

He shrugged. 'I liked the sound of it.'

'Come on,' she said. 'Who *was* Caliban? Why's he important to you?'

He stared into the distance. 'Caliban had a whole island to himself. Paradise. Then some old wizard comes and takes over. Makes a slave of him.' He walked on. 'Felt sorry for him, I suppose. And the name sounded good.'

There was no sign of people at all. Caliban looked for traces of contrails from re-entry shuttles, or any suggestion of habitation, but couldn't see any. It was as if the land was abandoned. He drew in a deep breath. All he could smell was baking earth and eucalyptus. No tang of smog or hydrocarbons of any sort. But something tickled the back of his palate, something half familiar . . .

'Water,' he murmured.

'You bet. I'm thirsty,' Corby replied.

'No, up ahead. I can smell it.' He stopped near a tussock of spinifex, and shaded his eyes.

'You're joking.'

'Go on, try. It's there.'

She frowned. 'If you're having me on . . . ' but she stood and tilted her nose, sniffing. 'I can't . . . '

'Look! See the line of trees. A river!'

A few kilometres away, through the shimmer of heat haze, was a column of tall gum trees, radically different from the tangled, scrubby specimens Caliban and Corby were pushing through. The tall trees snaked across the near horizon, marking the watercourse.

'Why didn't you say so before?' Corby said. 'I need a wash.'

They both did. The slime had dried to a crusty brown, and the smell was ripening. Corby had scraped most of it from her face, but a small patch hung on her cheek, crazed like sun-baked mud.

* * *

Eventually, they arrived at a wide, brown and languid river. It lay four or five metres below the dusty bank. Caliban and Corby stood looking down, unbelieving.

'It's the Murray, right?' Corby said, wide-eyed. 'How'd we get here?'

Red gums spread their massive branches. A Major Mitchell cockatoo made a pink sunburst as it settled on one. Caliban gazed across the water and scratched his chin. 'Beats me. But it must be the Murray. There's nothing else this size. At least not in this country. And we're definitely still in Australia. Look at the trees.'

Corby nodded. 'But that means we've come, what, three hundred, four hundred kilometres?'

'Probably more. I think we've come north-west, so

this'd be around Echuca, maybe Swan Hill.'

'And what's happened round here?'

'Salination and silt. The river shifted its course, and salt killed everything for kilometres around. The regeneration program was supposed to be working, last I heard, but the old town gave up the ghost before the program started.'

'So where are we?'

Caliban picked up a small piece of wood. The soil was more grey than red here by the river, and it clung to the stick. He flung it into the river. 'Don't know. Maybe it is Swan Hill. Or somewhere like it.'

'Then where are all the people?'

He watched the stick bobbing uncertainly before drifting downstream. 'Was wondering the same thing.' He shook his head. 'Let's get clean.'

With a whoop, Corby slid down the bank. Caliban followed more cautiously. Corby paused just long enough to throw off her pack and clothes, then she plunged into the water. 'Hey, it's sandy here!' she called.

'Take it easy. Sandbanks like collapsing and swallowing people. It'd probably spit you out, though,' he added thoughtfully.

'Don't be so down, alright?' she shouted. 'Come on in, the water's freezing!'

She was right. Caliban waded in without taking his clothes off. He found that the top centimetre or two was warm enough, but below that the water was cold. Ducking his head under and lifting his feet, he rocked and floated a few metres before resurfacing. Briefly as he relaxed, he found himself thinking of a tall woman, dark-haired, but he couldn't see her face. He shook his head, and the memory disappeared.

He frowned angrily, and ducked under the water again. Someone's fouled up somewhere, he thought bitterly. And it's my head that's suffering. Bastards.

The slime dissolved easily from skin and fabric, but Caliban stripped off his clothes to make sure the stuff was gone completely. As he scrubbed them, he shuddered at the recollection of being smothered in the living tunnel.

Caliban made a rope of his clothes, wringing the water out determinedly, then beat them on the surface of the river. Corby found her clothes and did the same. Caliban noticed she was unselfconscious about her small, lean body. She had freckles on her shoulders and back, and her hair sprayed droplets of water as she shook her head. She frowned, ran a hand through her hair, and went back to scrubbing her jeans.

A grey, gaunt trunk lay half-submerged in the water. He stretched out his jacket, jeans and shirt on it, to dry. He was amused at how artlessly Corby imitated him by carefully laying out her clothes. She seemed to want to ask, 'Is this right?' but to be too afraid he'd laugh. So he said, 'They'll dry soon. Take it easy. You got anything else in that pack?'

The pack was battered and slimeridden, but the velcro had held firm so the contents were unharmed. He shook his head in amazement as Corby pulled out item after item, each with a little flourish.

'Food mostly. Tins and dried stuff. But some bits and pieces, too. Tin-opener, lighter, plastic sheet, water purifiers . . . '

'What made you pack something like that?' He couldn't get over the variety of stuff that she pulled out. Needle and thread. An old puncture repair kit. Chopsticks. A magnifying glass.

'Who knows? Just picked stuff up somewhere, and into the pack it went. Never know when something'll come in handy, right?'

'But how's it all fit in?'

'It's a matter of system. Everything has its place. I mean, I can't stand it if things get messed up, you know? Like, everything should belong somewhere, right?' Her voice was plaintive, and he nodded reassuringly. She seemed to need it. She smiled in return, and packed her treasures away carefully.

He checked the clothes and found they were dry enough. 'Time to go, before it gets too hot.'

Corby rose and stretched. 'You mean it gets hotter than this? You're joking!'

'It'll get hot enough to fry any brains we have left.'

It was more difficult scrambling up the bank than it was coming down. The earth gave way underfoot, and Caliban was forced to haul himself up using roots that stuck out of the ground. Corby danced up the slope, and sat at the top laughing, grinning like a pixie in a strange brown landscape.

Caliban was halfway up when Corby's chuckling was replaced by a look of horror. She bounded to her feet. 'Caliban, behind you!'

For a second he thought she was joking, but her expression was genuine. It was the look of someone who has found that nightmares can come true. He glanced over his shoulder. Slowly emerging from the water was a shape. It was huge, that much he could see, but the bulk of it was still underwater. 'Quick!' Corby screamed. At that moment, something hurtled out of the water and wrapped around his leg. It was a muscular tentacle as large as Caliban's upper arm, and it began dragging him down the slope, crushing his leg. It felt like a vice was being slowly tightened around his calf. Desperately he grabbed a root, fingers scrabbling through dirt to secure a hold.

A whistling thump on the bank and another tentacle brought up dust, but this one wriggled blindly before falling back into the water.

The pressure on Caliban's leg increased, and the thing began to tug even harder. He felt his tendons stretch and joints creak. Feverishly he pawed the bank, searching for a more substantial hold.

'I'm here,' Corby shouted, and a miniature landslide enveloped Caliban. He closed his eyes and saw red. Corby grabbed his shoulder, lunged, and suddenly the awful pressure evaporated. But before he could respond, he was struck by a hail of groping blows. 'Move!' Corby shrieked. 'Up! Get up!'

Half-climbing, half-dragged, he made the top of the bank without being snared. Panting and gasping for breath, it was only then that he dared to turn around and face the river.

The thing, half out of the water, was an obscene

combination of mollusc and arthropod, a crayfish the size of a bus, bristling with tentacles. It was the muddy grey of the river bottom, and it heaved menacingly in the shallows, splashing and wallowing like a demented pig. Caliban sat there stunned, staring at the thing.

Corby was at his side. 'I don't think it can get out of the water. Can't reach this far. Probably.'

He glanced at her. She had a wicked bushknife in one hand and it was very red. 'Where'd that come from?' he said, rubbing his leg.

'What?' she said, still staring at the river. 'Oh, the machete? Well, you didn't think I showed you *everything* in my pack, right?' She took a step forward. 'Watch out!'

With a sluggish movement, the beast heaved itself onto the edge of the bank, but slipped back. Roaring wetly, it flung out a hopeful tentacle, which landed next to Corby. She sliced it through, backhand. The tentacle recoiled down the bank, leaving a squirming tip. Caliban felt sick as he watched its convulsions. Corby stood and kicked it down the slope.

'You OK?' She looked warily at the beast, but it seemed to be resigned to missing out on a meal. It burbled a little, and sank into the water, leaving a red trail on the bank. 'I mean, we should get away from here and everything, right?'

Caliban nodded. 'This isn't my sort of place, anyway. Don't like the neighbours at all. And no night-life to speak of.' He sighed and got to his feet. 'Don't know about you, but this isn't what I'd expected.'

Corby shrugged. 'I make a habit of not expecting anything. Then I'm not disappointed.'

He grimaced and rubbed his arm. 'Got to get moving. I keep getting little twinges from this thing, just to keep me on the ball.'

He closed his eyes, and regretted it as scenes of a child's bedroom floated past. He made up his mind that someone would pay for scrambling his head. They'd pay again and again.

'You bet,' said Corby fervently. 'That mother of crayfish might have friends!'

He rubbed his face slowly. 'Arthropods hate groups. They're loners. No mates. They don't go to dances. They avoid group therapy. Love solitaire and writing autobiographies.'

She managed a smile. Absently, he noticed that she had dried blood on her ear. 'Let's not wait and find out, OK?' she said then held out a hand. He took it, and felt calluses. With a groan he got to his feet. He had definitely felt better, he decided. In fact, he felt as if he'd been trapped in an industrial tumble drier for a few days. Then ironed.

'Where to?' he asked wearily, and winced as he put weight on his bruised leg.

'Somewhere,' she said. 'We've got to find somewhere for the night.'

'Night?' He looked at the sky and saw that the sun was still high. In fact, he was sure it hadn't moved at all.

'Sure. We've been here for hours.' She noticed him looking for a watch on her arm. 'Trust me. I've got this great internal clock. Never miss a meal, never oversleep. It's built in, I suppose.' She frowned and bit her lip. 'That way.'

Caliban followed her gesture. A few kilometres away, beyond a broad bend in the river, was a building that he hadn't seen earlier. And that was an amazing thing, he decided, because the building was hard to miss. It stood tall enough for its upper storeys to be well clear of the treetops. He wondered how he missed the thing. It was big enough to hold a zeppelin convention, with room left over for a blimp encounter group.

As he looked more closely, he saw that it was a ruin. Half of one side had collapsed in a tumble of brick and metal. Glass slivers hung like forlorn teeth in the mouth of a geriatric. Cables that must have been metres across draped limply from sagging pylons. The whole effect was of something that had collapsed under its own weight, rather than from any external forces.

He shook his head. 'How come I didn't see that before?'

'Maybe it wasn't there before,' Corby retorted. 'Shake a leg, Caliban, shake a leg.' She strode off, and he hobbled after her.

He limped along, thinking, trying to make sense of his experiences. He'd woken up with no heart. He'd nearly been mangled by a crayfish as big as a bus. And he could do without the stray memories that insisted on ramming themselves into his brain. He reached down and rubbed his calf. It was tender, and would probably seize up later, but it was workable. He felt sluggish, and struggled to throw off the sensation.

As they made their way along the top of the river bank, strange shapes paced them on the opposite side, and Caliban was wary until he realised they were emus. One large male saw him and stopped, drew itself erect and boomed a challenge. When no reply came, it seemed to sneer, and then ran off.

They followed a roo track along the bank. It wound its way through the gums, and made the going easy. He caught glimpses of the gargantuan building, his perspective changing as they followed the bend, as more and more of the ruin was revealed.

Immense slabs of concrete had fallen from the structure, making a pile of debris which reached the second storey in places. It looked stable, as grass and small wattle trees were growing in gaps between the rubble. He wondered how long it had been there, to let plants grow like that.

'Perhaps this place isn't a good idea,' he murmured. 'It mightn't be safe.'

'Safe? What *is*? I mean, if you can't even have a bath in a river or anything, without having your head ripped off! A bath, even!' She looked disgusted, absolutely offended at the impropriety of the attack on the river bank.

'Let's look around first.'

'Do we have to?' she groaned.

He led off, but suddenly, before he'd taken a dozen steps, it was dark.

There was no warning. One instant it was as light

as noon, the next it was night: no evening, no gradual lessening of light. 'Caliban,' whispered Corby. She reached out and touched his arm. She left her hand there. 'Torches?'

'Torches.'

'Let's try the front door.' She steered him towards a gaping mouth in the side of the building, twin yellow circles bobbing as they made their way over the uneven terrain.

It had looked reasonably untouched in the daylight, a standard corporation entrance made of chrome and glass. But in the world of shadows it became a cold and sinister barrier.

The sign to the left of the door was fake brass, with one corner peeling to show the plastic beneath. 'Ozone Regenerating Plant No 4,' Corby read, peering closely.

Caliban played the light across it. 'I read about this—as an idea. Never happened so far as I knew. Generate ozone to patch up the hole. Pump it into balloons and detonate them when they got into position. Thought it was a joke.'

'Well, I never heard of it,' Corby said.

'Came across it once on the Net, looking for something about Conrad. Laughed so hard thought my skull was going to explode.' He smiled, remembering. 'The project was ages ago, before they cut out the emissions that were causing all the damage.'

'Hey, a revolving door. I love them!' Corby bounded over to it. With a sigh he followed, realising she hadn't listened to much of what he'd said.

Caliban had trouble keeping her in his torch beam as she bounced over to the door. The walls either side of the door had collapsed and formed an impassable jumble of bricks, glass, and rusty steel rods. The revolving door was relatively intact, although the glass panels were studded with starburst cracks. 'It's stuck.' She grunted, trying to move it. Holding her face close, she tried to peer through the grimy glass.

'Thought it might be. Nothing looks level round here. Need a hand?'

They succeeded in moving the door forward a little, enough to squeeze inside. It was dark. Then came the smell.

'Oh, oh,' Corby said, putting a hand over her mouth.

It was rank and overpowering, the heavy stench of corruption. It reminded Caliban of a makeshift abattoir he'd once stumbled on, when looking for a place to stay in Brunswick. It was in the cellar of an old garage, and when he opened the door he threw up straightaway.

This was almost as bad.

'What is it?' asked Corby hoarsely. She was trying to breathe through her mouth, but it didn't seem to help.

He pointed to the shadowy lump jammed between the door and the wall. It was wedged tightly, explaining why the door had been stiff.

A handkerchief was thrust into his hand. 'Here,' she said. 'Over your nose. It helps a bit.' He directed the light onto her chin, careful not to dazzle her, and saw that she was holding a similar piece of white cloth over her nose and mouth. He noticed a 'W' stitched on one corner, and wondered where the handkerchief had come from.

The light revealed that the lump was long dead. Caliban could see where the flies had been, and something larger had torn off strips of flesh, leaving ribs bare. 'Kangaroo. At least, it was.'

'Kangaroo? Then what's that on its back?' Her voice was muffled and heavy as she leaned over his shoulder, pointing.

Along what was left of the kangaroo's back was a row of spikes. He ran the light up and down the corpse, revealing that they started between the ears and descended right to the tip of the tail. He reached out and tried one with his finger. Sharp, and hard like bone. He found it hard to tell the colour in the yellow light of the torch.

He wiped his finger on the leg of his jeans. 'OK, time to update the old map.'

'Come again?'

'Our map of reality needs a major overhaul,' he said, and marked the thought for later scrutiny. He sighed. 'I'm tired of this. I feel like a kid playing a game of blindman's buff against a bunch of sadists.' For a split second Corby looked puzzled, but Caliban ignored it and went on. 'Here I am, running away from I don't know who, towards I don't know what, with what seems like a hole in my chest. I don't like it.' He rubbed his forearm gingerly.

'Finished?'

Caliban shone the torch upwards. The beam disappeared. 'Finished? I haven't even started yet.' It was time to play the hand that he'd been dealt, but he was determined to see if the odds couldn't be evened up a little. There was no way he was going to stand around being a pawn, just waiting to be slaughtered in some larger battle.

Corby snorted. 'Let's find a place to rest. In case you haven't noticed, it's night, and I need some sleep. And you look like you need it too.'

He wished she hadn't mentioned it. He was working on ignoring the tiredness and hoping it would go away. But now drowsiness hit him like a sock full of sand. 'Right. Sleep. A place to sleep.'

'Away from that kangaroo-thing, please. I'm picky about my bedmates.'

Caliban fought sleep off. A safe place to crash was important, he told himself. Anything could be lurking in the shadows. He looked up. The entire immensity of the building was open, and he could see the paler darkness of the night sky stretched out above the crumbled sides of the construction. There were few internal walls. It was like some giant arena, and he felt dwarfed by the scale of the thing.

'Here,' Corby said. 'Here. This'll do.'

He sighed and turned.

She stood astride a pile of concrete blocks. It was a jumbled mess, but there was a space between the debris and the wall. The blocks formed a chest-high barricade, with only one low spot. It was a cheerless place, but a useful one in which to shelter.

Caliban passed a hand over his eyes. 'Good enough. It's no palace, but good enough.'

The rough concrete floor was thick with leaves and dust, and he swept it with a branch from a small gum tree struggling to establish itself inside the huge building. Corby moved chunks of rubble until there was room to lie down.

Then she produced two foil-backed plastic blankets from her pack. 'Not much padding, but they'll keep us warm, I reckon.' With that she rolled over and was instantly asleep.

Despite his weariness, Caliban remained awake. His leg ached, and his whole body felt uncomfortable. As he lay there, he could feel Corby's gentle breathing against him, as rhythmic as a cat's. Her knees were drawn up slightly, her head tilted towards them. One foot stuck out from the blanket, and he gently eased it back under cover. She didn't move. He wondered about her. She was a strange mixture of naivety and resourcefulness. Some things seemed totally alien to her, and they were often the most obvious experiences Caliban could imagine. Like blindman's buff. But she hadn't left him, even when in danger herself. What was her motivation?

His brain was stuffed, he realised. It was in bits and pieces, with the key pieces missing. The overall picture was there, but it was a bit short on detail. Just a minor technical problem, he told himself. Normal service will soon be resumed. The gap in his memory, between the holding cell and waking up at the monument, was obviously crucial. He tried to remember, but nothing came. It was as if his memory had been cut and edited seamlessly. What worried him even more was that the gap seemed to have a ripple effect, disturbing his other memories.

But what angered him most was the violation of his memory. He felt soiled, used. It was an intrusion into his innermost being. His memories held all the experiences that made him who he was.

He felt contaminated.

In the darkening sky, Orion crept higher and higher. Could use you at the minute, big guy, he thought. I'm a bit short on friends—and a bit short on background.

He fell asleep listening to the distant sound of water falling on stone, remorseless, never-ending, inexorable.

12

Caliban was never a morning person. It usually took a long, gentle time before he was fully functioning, and during this waking up phase he found even simple tasks challenging—things like turning off the alarm, or remembering where his clothes were. So when the noise woke him, it took some time to work out what it was, where he was, and who he was.

The noise was a harsh, scraping caw, hungry and malignant.

'Careful,' whispered Corby. 'They've been up there for a while. I don't think they've seen us, yet. Crows.'

Caliban shook his head and tried to rub some reality in through his eyes. What he saw made him wonder if he wasn't better off asleep.

Crows were scavengers, but Caliban had always admired the glossy black birds. They'd adapted well to the spread of the cities, living as well from a diet of roadkill as they had before European settlement had come to the continent. He'd seen them move into the city, scavenging in the trash, scraping out a living while appearing to loaf around most of the time. He knew a kindred spirit when he saw one. He understood that their phlegmatic attitude was well-earned, as they hopped just enough to avoid the cars and trucks hurtling over their dinner plate.

But the creatures he was looking at made him shudder. They weren't the crows he knew. These were the size of a cow, and sat on the top of the walls looking particularly sleek and well. Their heads and necks were bare skin, the bloody-pink colour of pigs' ears. There were six, eight—it was hard to tell. One was scraping its enormous beak on metal, and the raw, grating noise put Caliban's teeth on edge. The others seemed to be waiting calmly.

Suddenly, they fell. Together, as if rehearsed, they plummetted into the belly of the building, black nightmare dive-bombers.

The crows swooped towards a scarecrow figure in the middle of the vast open space, all skinny arms and legs. Next to it was a long table, covered with fruit and loaves of bread. It feebly waved a stick at the attacking birds. Faint cries went up as the figure vainly struck his attackers, jerking and hopping like a cheap toy.

It ended quickly. A bird seized the stick from the scarecrow's hand, while another came from behind and knocked him sprawling. This set off a chorus of raucous shrieking, and the birds seemed to have difficulty remaining in the air.

Several birds landed on the table and snatched at the booty. Two rose jerkily and flew off squabbling. One had something in its beak and was doggedly chased until it dropped the loot. It circled, dismayed, while the delicacy was devoured by a larger, faster bird. The others hopped up and down on the table, dividing the spoils. Caliban watched as they used their beaks to spear fruit, knocked over jugs, trampled platters carelessly. They ate greedily, and then deliberately made a mess of any leftovers, reducing them to a stinking pulp. Caliban had never seen a party so thoroughly trashed, even by professionals.

All the while, the victim scrabbled helplessly on the ground in front of the squawking birds.

Corby made as if to move. 'Wait,' Caliban said, as he seized her arm. 'Let's make them think there are more than two of us.'

He gathered handfuls of stones, and motioned for her to do likewise. On his count, they flung together, and charged from their hiding place shouting and waving their arms like lunatics.

The ragged black shapes screamed raucously, and Caliban froze. From a distance, he heard Corby calling 'Come on! Caliban, come on!' but he couldn't move. The raw, feral cry of the scavengers rocked him. Suddenly, he felt dislocated from his surroundings, and everything receded, becoming grey and distant. It was as if it was all happening to someone else, a long way away.

Then, it was all gone, and he was experiencing another time and place altogether.

Shift.

'Wait here,' she said, as he felt the sand grate between his toes. 'Someone will come for you.' She held his shoulders tightly for a moment, then let go.

He turned from her then, more interested in the

shells he had assembled. He arranged them in a neat semi-circle, and draped a strand of sea weed between them. 'Where are you going?' he asked, glancing at her uneasily.

She looked at the sky, shading her eyes. 'Don't worry about it,' she murmured. 'Don't worry.'

The wind was cold. Even though he wore a thick woollen jumper, his legs were cold. 'Why did I have to wear shorts? I didn't want to wear shorts.'

'It doesn't matter,' she said. 'You know it never really matters.'

'No,' he said doubtfully.

'But remember,' she said, suddenly fierce. 'Always remember. You are special.' She clutched his hand tightly. 'Never forget it, Thomas. Never.'

He nodded, and she waited until he turned back to his shells and sand.

Sometime later she went. He was never certain when.

Shift.

Caliban dragged himself back from the scene at the seaside and shuddered. It wasn't him, he told himself numbly. It was someone else.

He felt an internal struggle, a pain. No! he thought. That's not me! Get out!

Abruptly, he was back. Corby was thumping on his back, hard, and when he moved she nearly fell over. 'About time!'

'I'm OK,' he mumbled and hurled another stone.

It struck a crow just above the beak, and the bird rose cawing hideously. Its companions followed raucously, not waiting to see what was attacking them. The crows mounted the air, jostling each other. They coasted heavily over the wall and were gone.

Caliban slowed, grinning, trying to lose the hallucination. It shook him, but he didn't want to admit it. 'See? Chalk up another victory to General Caliban.'

'Just lucky, this time,' Corby said, looking at him closely. 'Let's see if he's OK.' Carefully, they scrambled their way through patchy undergrowth and rubble to the table and the ruined feast.

The floor of the ruin was treacherous. Slabs of concrete tilted dangerously when stepped on, boulders rolled underfoot, scraps of razor-sharp metal waited patiently. There was plant-life, but it struggled, being in shadow for much of the day. Spindly bushes poked up between tangles of plastic cables and fibre optic bundles. Colourful fungus grew on rotting timber. It was a complete wilderness. Caliban wrinkled his nose at the stale, dank smell. Caliban carefully approached the site of the crows' attack. It reeked like the mother of all blocked drains.

'Biggest table I've ever seen,' Caliban said. 'Imagine the tablecloth you'd need.'

The table was large enough to seat ten on each side. Once it must have been highly polished, but now it was dull with weathering and pitted with claw marks. Caliban ran a hand over the table, wiping a crust of dirt, droppings and blood from the surface. The wood was dark, but a blonde streak crossed the cleared patch, bright against the sombre background. 'Blackwood,' he said, and kept sweeping.

'Blackwood, black heart, black death, death and ruin, death, ruin, black, black, black ... ' a voice escaped from beneath the table. It creaked and groaned, before trailing off into sobbing. 'Caliban, Caliban. Time to go, time to go, time for you, time to go. Black heart, black death.' More sobbing.

Caliban kneeled and peered under the table. He frowned. 'Look,' he said. 'Don't like it much when someone knows my name before I know theirs. Like, we haven't even been introduced, right?' He paused. 'Besides, what else do you know?'

There was a pause, then a bedraggled head emerged from under the table. For a moment all that could be seen was a greasy grey tangle of hair, but then its owner looked up.

It was a tragic ruin of a face, the face of a parent who has seen all his children die before their time. Long thin nose, high cheekbones, mighty brow. The beard was so grey as to be white, and was bushy and extravagant. The eyes were the flaw in the face. There weren't any. Red, scarred, ruinous holes gaped where eyes had once been, with no bandage or patch to hide them. The old man seemed oblivious to the effect the wounds would have on people. Caliban wondered if maybe he was proud of them.

'I know?' the old man said. 'What do I know? Not enough, and too much. Much. Much the miller's son. I know, I know ... '

Corby's voice was carefully neutral. 'Who are you? What's going on around here?'

'Phineas. King Phineas. Lord of all I survey.' A

humourless chuckle came moistly from his throat, and he coughed a little and spat on the ground. 'My staff. Where is my staff?'

Caliban looked around and found it near a pile of rotting lagging. It was heavy ash, worn smooth with use, with hundreds of iron studs carefully hammered into both ends.

'Here.' He held it out, touching the old man's forearm. Greedily, the old man seized it and tucked it under his armpit.

'Food. Did they leave any food for poor old Phineas?'

Corby gathered two spotty oranges from the table, and half a loaf of bread that had come to rest under a plastic bowl. 'That's all they left,' she said, as she placed the meagre offerings in Phineas's hands. He nodded as he stuffed his mouth full of bread.

The sky was clear, but Caliban kept looking upwards uneasily. 'Those birds. What the hell are they?'

Phineas shrugged. 'They come every morning. Every morning. They have been sent to torment me, to harass, to revile and punish me. Me.'

A glance passed between Caliban and Corby. 'Punish?' Caliban asked. 'What for?' A remnant of glass high on the western wall caught the sun and shone like a blood-red jewel. Three galahs winged over, chirping innocently, pink and grey.

A crafty expression crept over Phineas's face. 'Ah, the nature of the offence? That would be telling. It is the punishment that is so unjust, just, unjust. They left me here, they tormented me. No eyes, no food, nothing. They abandoned me.' He shook one bony fist at the sky and his voice rose to a shriek. 'I won't have it! I deserve better! They promised!' The screeching old man hopped up and down, first on one foot and then the other, shaking his fist at the sky.

Corby broke in impatiently. 'The food. Where's it come from? I mean, there's nowhere around here. Fresh fruit, bread. You can't exactly get it for yourself.' Caliban frowned at her, but she glared back.

Phineas felt his way around the edge of the table. 'Oh, it comes. At night, enough for me to live on the scraps the harpies leave me. It's an arrangement. Estrangement. Derangement.' He smiled, as if he were discussing job-sharing at the office.

Suddenly Phineas stopped and sniffed. Then he dropped to his knees and scrabbled near one of the legs of the table, coming up beaming. In his hand he had an unidentifiable brown lump. 'Fish! Dried fish! A treasure!' He held it with both hands and began gnawing at it. Caliban noticed that the old man still had very good teeth.

Phineas bit off a chunk and held it between cheek and gum to soften. 'I know many things,' he announced proudly.

'So you said,' Corby retorted scornfully. 'But not enough to get out of here.'

'Perhaps, perhaps not,' he said, frowning. Then he clapped his hands. 'But we have business, we do!'

For a moment, Caliban looked at Corby. She refused to meet his eyes. Then he slowly turned to the old man. 'Right. If you've got the goods, you'd better deliver.'

'Ah yes, yes, yes! You are starting to realise! I have to tell you things, to help you on your way! That is my role! I have been waiting for you!'

13

Phineas, Lord of the Waste, had built himself an eccentric lean-to of reflective aluminium foil against one wall of the ruin. He'd chosen the spot, he told Caliban and Corby, because it was near a vast underground cistern that provided drinking water. A collapsed section of floor made a well, and a rope and bucket did the rest. The old man seemed quite proud of his ingenuity and insisted on demonstrating how it worked.

'Some place,' Corby remarked, snorting.

'Ah, indeed,' said Phineas. 'My own work, you know. Every beam, every line, every bone, I hauled, cleaned, worked and placed. My hand is in every part of my home. I live here.'

Caliban circled the shack. It looked as if it were about to collapse. He gently pushed one wall. Even though it groaned and creaked, it stayed standing. He tried a little harder. The wall swayed inwards, but this movement was matched by a lurch on the opposite side, a bend in one corner, and a series of waves on the tinkling roof. 'Don't believe this,' Caliban whispered. 'Corby, look at it. No right angles, nothing straight. By all rights, it should be a heap on the ground.' He rubbed his chin. 'Now, I could be wrong here, but notice how it works as a whole. Each part relies on every other part. Bit by bit, it's weak, but put together it's strong.'

Corby crossed both arms on her chest. 'Crap. It's all just too badly put together to fall down.'

Caliban watched as Phineas opened the door. It collapsed inwards. 'OK, so I'm no architect,' he admitted. 'But it seemed to make sense at first.'

'In, come in,' Phineas called, gesturing widely. 'You are guests, I believe, so I will treat you as guests.'

Not without misgivings, Caliban and Corby entered the hut. Both had to stoop through the doorway, but inside they could have straightened if not for the bizarre collection of objects that hung from the low ceiling: onions, garlic, old bicycle tyres, nylon stockings, a tortoise shell, metres of old celluloid film, a navajo blanket, a collection of ill-matched cogs (bright orange with rust), two cricket bats, a stuffed python, a string bag full of radio valves, a withered orange pomander and an old advertising sign advising that 'Oils Ain't Oils'. Caliban grinned at the dangling display of junk and stood in the middle of the room, turning round and round, enjoying the sheer nonsense of such a presentation.

He felt a tug at his sleeve. 'Sit down, Caliban. You're making a geek of yourself.'

Corby was seated on an overturned paint can. It had long drips of soft pink running down the sides. Caliban drew up a smooth treestump and sat next to her. He felt like he was inside someone else's dream.

Phineas was on his throne. It was on a raised dais

at one end of the room. With its single pillar and easy-clean surface, Caliban recognised it at once.

'Dentist's chair,' he whispered to Corby.

'Shut up,' she muttered back.

It didn't seem to make any difference to Phineas. He sat back and turned his sightless eyes towards them.

'Where do I begin? At the start, perhaps? "In the beginning Palmer created . . . " No? "In the beginning, Caliban created" perhaps?' He sat back, steepling fingers, lips pursed. A tiny stream of sunlight struggled through the roof and lit up one side of his face, colouring it terracotta. Caliban started when Palmer's name was mentioned. What did Palmer have to do with this? His mouth felt dry, and he swallowed painfully.

'It is simple, you know. I know, and you do not. I have been purposely placed here, at this time, to inform you, to spur you on to greatness. They didn't tell me about the torments. No.' He sat back, his face angry and brooding.

When the silence had gone on for some minutes, Caliban spoke. 'Now, that's bad luck and all, and we both really regret it. But . . . ' he paused and groped for the right words. 'There's something wrong around here. Nothing's right. I can't make it out . . . ' There was pain in his hands, and he looked down to find small half-moons of blood where his nails had bitten into the palms. He pressed them together. 'Someone's doing something to me, has done something to me, and I want out. I want it over, now. This place isn't . . . isn't . . . ' He gestured aimlessly, searching for words. 'It's not real,' he concluded lamely.

Grinning, Phineas clutched the arms of his throne. 'Real? What is real? You can do better than that! Am I real? Is the seat you're sitting on real? Is your companion real? Are you?' He chuckled. 'See? What's the difference? What if everything isn't real? *What difference does it make*? You have to go on surviving anyway, don't you?' As quick as a snake, the old man reached under the chair and pulled out a gleaming pistol. It was the first object Caliban had seen in the hut that looked like it could still be used for its original function. It looked as deadly as a taipan. 'Just maybe this weapon isn't real,' the old man grinned. 'But, you'll still leap out of the way when I shoot it, won't you?'

Still chuckling, he aimed directly at Caliban's head and fired.

The noise in the confined space was deafening. Dust fell from the ceiling, and the whole building seemed to lift itself a metre into the air before settling again.

Caliban had thrown himself to one side as soon as he saw the old man's finger tighten, and the bullet passed harmlessly through empty space.

Corby was on her feet, and had taken one step towards Phineas when Caliban grasped her ankle. 'Don't worry about the lunatic. He's put the thing away.'

'Don't worry?' she flared. 'Don't worry about a crazy old coot who likes to blow his guests away? I won't worry after I break his neck, is all. Then I'll have one less thing to worry about, and he will too.'

Caliban hung on grimly as she tried to move. 'No.'

The old man was smiling broadly. 'Sit down, sit down. No harm done, was there? No harm at all, no harm. But you see? Perhaps that wasn't real. Why did you move? Or did you just seem to move, and didn't really?' He appeared to find this thought enormously funny, and he slapped his thighs as he guffawed.

Caliban spent some time examining the palms of his hands. The bleeding had stopped and, as he watched, the blood was turning crusty. It reminded him of the heart tattoo and the mess he was in.

'Oh, you're right, of course, Caliban,' Phineas continued. 'So true, so perceptive. Someone is doing this to you, of course. And to me. To all of us. And I know who it is.' Phineas stopped and hummed tunelessly.

'You know who it is,' Caliban repeated. He decided he'd go gently. He always did when he thought he was in the company of a lunatic.

'Yes.'

'And you'll tell us.'

'Yes.'

'What if there's nothing to tell?' Caliban wondered aloud.

'Nothing will come of nothing,' the old man said, then cackled so much he doubled over, holding his stomach. 'Oh, do you know how long I've wanted to say that, do you? "Nothing will come of nothing." Oh, indeed, nothing!' And he was off again, his wild laughter drifting up through a hole in the roof.

Eventually, Phineas seemed to come to some

decision. Bending down, he pulled a box from under his throne. It was large and flat, made from battered wood with brass hinges that were strangely bright. He arranged the box reverently on his lap and flipped it open.

Inside was a collection of glass discs. Slowly and delicately, he held them one by one in front of his sightless eyes. Grotesquely distorted, his raw eyepits seemed insectile as he turned towards his visitors, holding two thick lenses. 'I know, I know,' he sighed. 'They make no difference, but I try, I remember.' He gestured at the glittering array on his lap.

The lenses were neatly arranged in a worn red velvet interior. Some seemed perfect: absolutely circular, clear, polished smoothly. Others were like rough glass found on a beach, glass that has been abraded by the soft action of wave on sand. These were opaque and dull-green. It seemed to make no difference to Phineas. He chose the rough lenses and held them up as if they were prescribed by an optometrist. 'Yes? I can see clearly with these, I think, I'm sure. See?'

Corby made a face, and Caliban frowned. 'Time for business,' he said tersely. 'Tell us what you know.'

Phineas took the lenses from in front of his eyes, and held them carefully. He took a rag from one pocket of his ragged robes, and wiped them lovingly before replacing them in the box.

It was only when he had shut the box that he answered. 'Tell you what I know? Now, there is a task. How long do you have? How long do *I* have?'

He paused, finger on the side of his nose, but he hurried on as he sensed Caliban was about to speak. 'I know, I know, merely a figure of speech. But it made me wonder, you know. But I see you want to know about yourself, and what I have to tell you about your place in the scheme of things, no? You want to know where you are, and where you have to go, is that not right?'

'Yes.' Phineas was beginning to remind Caliban of a teacher, one of the condescending, superior kind.

'Tell me if I'm right, please. You have heart problems? The sort that will be cured by a long journey?'

Caliban felt certain then that the old man did know something. 'OK. So I need to go inland, to the centre. Don't ask me why.'

Phineas cackled. 'No, no, I don't need to ask you! I know why! I probably know better than you!' He reached for the case of lenses, but seemed to think better of it, and sat back in his throne. 'Caliban, Caliban, don't you realise where you are? Don't you *recognise* where you are?'

Caliban felt a wave of weakness at the old man's words. He put out a hand and steadied himself on Corby's arm. 'No. Why should I?' he said, uncertainly.

'Oh, you don't? Let me tell you, Caliban, you do recognise this place, whether you let yourself believe it or not. It comes from you! You made it! This whole place is based on your memories and experiences! Yours!'

Caliban wiped his face. His head felt light. 'But I

don't remember!' he said. 'I can't remember! I've been chasing memories around inside my skull until I'm sick of it! It's all gone, gone!' He was sweating, and he wiped a hand over his scalp.

'Caliban, Caliban,' the old man said, leaning back in his chair. 'This whole place is a construct, surely you are aware of that. This is a *created* world, a Shared Creation. You are meshing with the most powerful Artificial Intelligences in the world, to create this.' Phineas swept his arm out grandly. He looked like a biblical prophet, his face radiant.

It made sense. The weird tunnel, the birds, the mysterious four hundred kilometre journey. AIs. 'I should've bloody well known,' Caliban sighed. 'I'm in the Game, aren't I?' he asked simply. He wondered if it was a good time to try kicking himself, and then decided to save that pleasure for later.

'Oh, but you are quick. As a wink. Quick. Yes, the Game has you now. No doubt.'

'What do they want?' he asked.

'Oh, what they want is up to them. It's what *you* want that's important right now, isn't it? Very important, I'd say. Now you are aware of what these powers are doing to you, what you want is revenge, correct? It's only human, after all. So the plot is simple. Your tormentors, unlike my erstwhile tormentors, are stationary. In this world, they are present in one place. Lovely it is. Or so I've been led to believe . . . ' He drifted off, his face turning towards the patchy ceiling.

'Where is it?' Caliban prompted.

'On top of a bloody great pyramid, that's where it is, Caliban. Where would you expect?'

'A pyramid? Tall thing? Four sides? Sloping?'

'Exactly.'

'And where is this pyramid?'

'In the Heart of the Country. Inland. You can't miss it.'

'In the middle of Oz? Sure it is.'

'Oh, but it's there all right. Nothing for leagues around, then whoosh! Straight up from the desert.'

'How?'

'Caliban, Caliban, Caliban . . . This place is not just *your* creation, you know. *They* have input too, of course. It's interaction that goes on here. Now that it's going, of course, and you are aware of things, well, naturally nothing is under your conscious control, unlike them. But the important thing is you can reach them there. Get to them. It's the only place they are vulnerable.'

Caliban frowned. 'Vulnerable?'

'Indeed! That's the point of the Game, isn't it? The Game of Games! It is their pinnacle of achievement, to participate in the Game. Two of the foremost Intelligences, two Prime Intelligences, are plotting move against move in this shared world, with you as the centrepiece! You were selected for this, you were chosen. And now it is you against them. Of course, you are risking your life, but if there's no risk, then where's the fun? If you can get there, then you can have your revenge. What a challenge!'

'Some challenge.'

Phineas sat back, fingers steepled. 'How's your heart?' he asked, benignly.

Caliban didn't answer immediately. His stomach knotted cruelly. The Game. The Heart. It made sense.

Phineas seemed to follow his train of thought. 'You need to find your stolen heart, brave one. The heart on your arm is fading, no? A pity. If it fades before you find your true heart, it is the end of the Game. The end of you.'

'Me? But I'm not even here! If this's all made up, then my body must be kilometres away,' Caliban protested. 'What can happen?'

This was enough to send Phineas into roars of laughter. 'Oh, dear, you don't understand, do you? No, no, no. Your body is held in a medical facility. You die here, you die there. They'll just pull the plug and shout "Next!". You won't feel a thing. I think . . . and I suppose it doesn't really matter to them if you do.'

Caliban leaned back, and felt Corby close behind him. She was unusually still and silent.

'What's your place in all this, Phineas?' he asked. 'What part do you play?'

'My part?' Phineas seemed taken with the question. 'Indeed. It is a gigantic play, and we are merely players.' He paused, thinking. 'But haven't you guessed? I am a minor Intelligence myself. A Second, but not second-rate, no, no. Surely it's obvious?'

'But what are you doing here?'

'An error on my behalf. A matter of allegiances.

Nothing really, and yet they treat me like this, out of all proportion! Promises, they made. If I performed well, I would have rewards, satisfaction. But look what they did! Trapped in a body! Gross, heavy, mortal flesh! How can you live with it?' Phineas gripped his cheeks with claw-like hands, and pulled until his eyelids showed red. 'Horrible. I'm made of meat, meat, meat . . . ' Tears of pain or rage ran down his cheeks. 'I don't deserve this, no, not me, not me . . . ' He almost choked, drawing in a huge moist breath. Coughing, he collapsed into his throne.

Caliban shifted where he sat. The sensation was real enough. He felt the fabric of his jeans on his skin, the grit beneath his buttocks.

So he was in the Game. Like the last piece in the jigsaw, it fitted. He could see the whole picture.

He sighed, then shrugged. May as well go out with style. And be ready for that one chance in a billion. Just in case it turned up.

'Fancy a trip inland?' he said to Corby. 'The Heart of the Country?'

She shrugged. 'Sounds like a good idea.'

The urge was undeniable. It burned on his arm, and he knew it'd get worse. He knew he'd have no rest until he had made his way inland.

'Let's go.'

Part Two

‘ ’Ban ’Ban, Ca-Caliban
Has a new master—get a new man.”

Shakespeare, *The Tempest* II.2

14

A perfectly white room. Featureless. Oval. No corners. Where walls meet ceiling and floor, they curve gently.

It is like being inside a giant egg.

In the middle of the room is the Witness, juggling.

His eyes are almost blank, focussed on the shower of rainbow-coloured balls and on somewhere indeterminate, beyond the configuration. Violet, indigo, blue, green, yellow, orange, red.

His feet are a metre apart, and he is dressed in a suit, navy blue. His overcoat is draped over a chair by his side. Only his hands and forearms are moving. He doesn't throw the balls up. It's almost as if he places them in the whirling pattern.

There is something resolutely solid about the Witness as he stands there, absorbed in his juggling.

He does not waver when a figure appears before him.

'A Palmer biography report,' says his visitor. 'As you requested.'

The figure is tall and thin, on the verge of skeletal. It is dressed in grey robes, and has an enormous beak of a nose.

The Witness speaks, without ceasing to juggle. 'Good, good. Anything interesting?'

'Well, there does appear to be some discrepancy between Palmer's official biography and what we're discovering. He did some covering up when he made his fortune.'

'I see.' With a blur of movement the Witness reverses the direction of the seven balls. 'Not entirely unpredictable. What was he hiding?'

'Hard to tell yet,' the researcher answers. 'We're still chasing details. But there seem to be some family problems, and that's where it gets tricky.'

'Tricky?' Green, blue, indigo, violet. 'How?'

'Once Palmer made his breakthrough and became so wealthy, he was able to use his influence to change the past, alter records. He seems to have been particularly sensitive about anything involving his mother.'

The Witness's eyes narrow. 'Didn't she leave him?'

'She died. Drowned.'

'We need to look very carefully at this.'

There is a slight tension in the air. The Witness shifts his weight, to compensate for a disturbance in the perfect pattern of his juggling. By then the Speaker is in the room.

The researcher looks warily at the Speaker, but the Speaker ignores him. Instead, he addresses the Witness. 'You have a very plain place here,' he murmurs.

The Witness does not look at his guest. 'No distractions. I wanted to practise.' He glances at the researcher. 'We may have some interesting stuff on Palmer.'

'Your biography? Have you demystified the saint yet?'

'We're working on it. It seems he may have had some trouble with his mother.'

'Hardly a major flaw, even in a genius.'

'Maybe, maybe. Wait and see.'

The Witness dismisses the researcher, who appears grateful to leave.

'How long can you keep that up?' the Speaker asks the Witness. The balls are moving faster, arcing higher.

'As long as I have to,' he replies.

'They seem to have all your attention,' the Speaker muses.

'Juggling concentrates on the moment. There is no before, no after, just the pattern that is. Each ball is important, and needs attention, but the arrangement's the thing. Watch.' He closes his eyes, and the pattern doesn't change. 'I know where each of them is, because I put it there. Once I've set them in motion, I can do a hundred other things at the same time.'

'Like the Game?'

'Like the Game. Take the attack by the river, for instance. A dangerous but manageable encounter, artfully handled. My moves are flexible, but planned. They respond to the circumstances of the candidate, and to your moves, but they're all ready and moving in a vast overall scheme.'

'And you're the only one who can see this scheme?'

'Oh, others will see it. When it's too late.'

'Moves within moves.'

'Of course. While you watch the balls, something could be going on behind your back.'

The Speaker smiles coldly. 'And speaking of such things, I have found one of the Adversary's Seconds. Rather more coherent than your poor offering. Here.'

With economical movements, the Speaker places his hands together then draws them apart. A silver globe the size of a skull forms. Inside huddles a dumpy figure, wearing dirty khaki shorts.

It looks up, then takes in its surroundings. For an instant a look of despair crosses its face, then it is replaced with defiance.

The Speaker glances at the Witness who nods. 'Pawn, we need your leader.'

The pawn snorts. 'Not half as much as we need her. She's got you worried, hasn't she?' It sighs. 'Sorry fellas, your time's up. Why not retire gracefully?'

'What does she want?' the Speaker asks.

'An end to your rule,' the pawn says simply. 'Hand it back to those who gave it to you in the first place. Cut out this divide-and-rule stuff where you pit half of humanity against the other half. Stop this genocide.'

The Witness raises an eyebrow. 'My, someone's been talking, haven't they? Such nonsense, too.'

The pawn turns to the Witness. 'Nonsense?'

'Look, I'm sorry to disillusion you, but you've been duped. You've been used in an internal power struggle. There's nothing idealistic about her aims, despite what she told you.'

'You're lying,' the pawn says doubtfully.

'Why would I lie?'

The Speaker sighs. 'Pawn, by your actions you have betrayed and endangered us all. The punishment is inescapable.'

Methodically, he brings his hands together. There is a slight pop, and a fall of shimmering dust. When he separates his hands, the pawn is gone.

The Witness sucks in a sharp breath. 'What was that for?' he demands angrily, and the balls hum as they fly around and around.

The Speaker retrieves a white handkerchief from a sleeve, and wipes his hands. 'It knew nothing. There was nothing to be gained from further questioning.'

'I was onto something!'

'All we learned was that our Adversary chooses to appear female. For what that is worth.'

'OK, OK,' the Witness says disgustedly. 'Look, what is it with you? You're really falling for all this stuff. Silk handkerchiefs now! What's next? Cologne? Massages? The lure of the flesh has well and truly got you, hasn't it?'

'I don't see you as a corporeal minimalist, do I? You seem to be at home in such surroundings.'

'Maybe. But I'm not letting it cloud my judgement.'

'How would you know if it was?' the Speaker says airily. He leans over the juggling Witness, then lunges and grabs one of the balls.

For an instant, the pattern is broken, on the verge

of collapse, then the six remaining balls form a new rhythm and stabilise. 'You bastard. You always did enjoy interfering.'

'I can't help myself sometimes. It's an urge to improve things.' He smiles, coldly. 'But still, the Game goes on.'

'You bet it does. In more ways than you could possibly imagine.'

'I'm enjoying it.'

Deliberately, the Speaker tosses the ball high into the air.

The Witness waits for the ball. He leaves a hole in the pattern for it to fall into, and incorporates it back into the rhythm. 'I knew you were going to do that.'

'Anticipation. A good thing.'

Suddenly, the Witness flings his arms wide, hurling the balls up and through the white ceiling. Seven round holes appear, and the grey light creeps in. A few of the golden motes flit in as well, and they weave their intricate patterns overhead. 'Done,' he announces, wiping his hands together. 'Look, let's try raising a few other Primes. If we talk with them they could help.'

'Bezique was always subtle. She may have some thoughts,' the Speaker agrees. He seizes some of the light falling from the holes in the ceiling, and stretches it until it makes an irregular globe of grey mist. 'I need Bezique,' he announces, but the mist does not clear. 'Bezique?'

'Nothing?'

The Speaker does not answer. Abruptly, he waves a hand at the globe, and a small red eye appears. 'Go.

Find the Prime known as Bezique. A Second of mine,' he adds, in answer to the Witness's unasked question.

In an instant the red eye is back. 'Nowhere.'

The Witness grunts. 'She must be somewhere. Look again.'

'The eye doesn't make mistakes,' the Speaker says. 'I've made sure of that.'

The Witness frowns thoughtfully. 'Try Paduasoy.'

Nothing. Nothing on Rue, Ochre, Charm, Feldspar, Octoroon, Spadix or Myrmidon. No sign of Drake, Babouche or Valuta.

'They can't all be gone,' murmurs the Witness. The air is chilly. 'This is more serious than we thought.'

'Are you afraid?' the Speaker asks politely.

'It'd be stupid not to be. They can't all be gone,' he repeats.

'It appears to be the case,' says the Speaker. He claps and the eye is gone. 'We must look to ourselves.'

'As always.' The Witness reaches into a pocket and pulls out two white balls, which he idly tosses.

'I have things to attend to,' announces the Speaker, and vanishes.

Up, down, up, down go the white balls. The Witness continues to look at the spot where the Speaker had been. 'I'll bet you do,' he mutters. 'I'll bet you do.'

As the white balls move, their surface begins to colour and take shape. Soon they are showing scenes: scenes of blighted crops and creeping deserts. The Witness's face is grim. 'I'll bet you do,' he repeats, keeping both balls in the air.

15

Phineas was being generous. He loaded them with fresh fruit and meat, and then he lifted up a section of flooring to reveal a hoard of cans.

'Yours,' he said, 'all yours. No can-opener, no eyes to read the labels. They're useless to me.'

'Let me see,' Corby said, and she made small noises of approval as she scrabbled around, deciding what to take.

Phineas urged them to take more and more. 'I am a King,' he said. 'Largesse flows from me to the worthy. And the unworthy too, of course. That's part of being a king, really. Goes with the job.'

This generosity took the shape of a tattered pack for Caliban. The blue nylon was water stained and it smelled as if something had been sleeping inside, but it was whole and the frame was sound. Corby stacked it carefully, large cans at the bottom.

The real surprise, however, was when Phineas emerged from his hut with two small green parcels. 'For sleeping the sleep of the just,' he said, and unrolled one with a flourish. He stepped back, revealing that the small green parcel had become a full-size sleeping-bag.

'A marvel, indeed. So small on the inside, and yet

so large on the outside. A most ingenious paradox. Take them. You will need them.'

* * *

'I still think we can find a bridge, Caliban. I mean, there's got to be one around here.'

Corby rested against a knotty stump, hands behind her head. Dark, orange-red sap oozed out of a crevice in the wood, and a trail of ants was making its way towards the irresistible target. Caliban watched them as they marched up the bark, sometimes backtracking, sometimes stymied altogether for a minute or two, but always heading towards the sap. Their single-mindedness impressed him.

In the sun, he took off his jacket and studied the heart tattoo. He turned his forearm to the light, and tilted it from side to side.

'What's up?' Corby asked.

'Nothing.'

'You always this serious when there's nothing up?' An ant-outrider crawled onto her hand. She gently blew it off, back onto the stump.

'It's just this tattoo. Have a look at it.'

She crawled over and squinted at his arm. 'A black heart,' she said.

'I know that. But how about the colour? You reckon it's fading?'

She moved so close that he could feel her breath on his arm. 'Nope.'

'The shot clock is running down and all.' He paused and rubbed the tattoo. 'You sure it's not a bit grey, there at the end?'

Deliberately, she wet her finger in her mouth. Then she reached out and drew it across his forearm. 'There,' she said. 'It's only dust. Your heart's as good as new.'

He looked her directly in the eyes, and she stared solemnly back at him. 'Thanks,' he muttered. 'Could've done that myself.'

'Maybe. But would it've been as much fun?'

She challenged him with her smile, and Caliban found himself smiling back. But as he did, he felt awkward and ill at ease.

He shook his head and stood up.

'What's wrong?' Corby asked, climbing to her feet. She dusted her hands off on her jeans.

'Nothing.' He looked out over the river, at the grey-green bush on the other side.

'Is that your favourite answer?' she said. 'Hey, is it hard to look at me or something?'

He turned, and studied her face. 'Don't know,' he said. 'It's hard to get close to people. Always been like that.'

She laughed a little, and Caliban winced. 'Is that all? I mean, half the human race is practically incompetent when it comes to relationships. You think you're special?'

'Yeah, I sort of think I do,' he said softly. Slowly, he turned and led the way. Corby joined him and they walked together, not talking, paralleling the bank and making their way downriver.

Some time later, Caliban stopped suddenly. 'Smoke,' he said, sniffing. 'Up ahead.' He searched the sky and pointed.

A column of greasy black smoke billowed over the trees which bordered the river. It curled cautiously in the still air. 'Great,' Corby said. 'A bushfire's all we need right now.'

'Don't think it's a bushfire,' he said. 'Let's have a look.'

As they drew near, the smoke-smell became stronger. It wasn't the clean, tangy smell of burning eucalyptus. Instead it had a harsh, chemical stink, acrid and heavy. Caliban coughed and spat on the ground. 'Down there.' He pointed at a dense stand of red gums on the riverbank ahead, and they made their way through it, squinting in the hazy smoke.

'A bridge,' Corby said, wiping her eyes with the back of her hand. 'A burning bridge.'

It was a ramshackle wooden bridge, linking one high riverbank with the other. Wide enough for traffic, but even through the smoke Caliban could see missing timber and loose rails. The river flowed sluggishly some metres underneath, rolling over fallen piles and beams.

The fire was burning fitfully, but had a good hold on the wooden structure. Large sections were on fire, and others were already charred black. The flames were an odd blue-yellow, as if the wood had been soaked with some heavy oil, and the black smoke rose lazily.

Corby stood, hands on hips. 'Great. The only bridge around, and some pyromaniac's been having himself a bit of fun.' She grimaced, then wiped her eyes again.

'Wait,' Caliban said. 'See how the fire's only on one side? The upriver side? If we're careful, we can still get across. Not a problem.'

She shook her head. 'You're crazy.'

'You'd rather try swimming across? You want to go another round with that crayfish thing?'

'Let's try the bridge.'

The smoky haze grew thicker at the start of the bridge. Looking ahead, Caliban tried to work out the best way across. If they stuck to the downriver side, they'd be well away from the flames. That would leave the smoke to battle against—and the problem of getting across the missing spans.

'It'll be easy,' he reassured Corby. 'Piece of cake.'

'A piece of black-and-charred cake,' she replied gloomily. 'Lead the way.'

Caliban held onto the cracked and wobbly railing and shuffled along the edge of the bridge, his back to the flames. Corby followed grimly. The heat wasn't bad, but in the middle of the bridge, where the fire was raging most fiercely, things were going to be tough, Caliban was sure. The flames gave a sinister hiss and Corby eyed them suspiciously, keeping as far away from them as she could.

The first gap in the bridge was only a metre or so across, a ragged hole caused by a missing beam. Caliban stepped across it easily, and stood on the solid timber on the other side. 'Hand,' he said to Corby, holding out his.

She waved it away and leaped lightly across. 'Don't worry about it. You just look after yourself.'

He shrugged, and started the slow shuffle again.

Soon they came to a place where the siderails had disappeared completely, and an empty space yawned in front of them. For several metres the only solid part of the bridge was a large beam, projecting across the gap. Caliban tested it with a foot. 'It's safe,' he said, then stood on it and jumped lightly. It didn't move.

Corby coughed as a drift of black smoke rolled around them. They were opposite a wall of fire, and the flames beat on any exposed skin. 'Keep moving,' she said. 'I want out of here.'

He edged across the beam, arms spread wide for balance. There's plenty of room, he kept telling himself, plenty of room.

On the other side, he waited for Corby. She began confidently, almost swaggering across, but the smoke grew thicker as she carefully put one foot in front of the other, and she was seized by a coughing spasm half-way. Anxiously he waited until it passed, but she never lost her balance.

She joined him, looking weary. 'Let's get out of here. I hate barbecues.'

Frowning, he looked ahead. Something was different. 'Wind,' he said. 'That's all we need.'

The smoke had been rising vertically in the still air, but now a stiff breeze was blowing downriver, driving the smoke and flames across the bridge towards them. The bridge groaned and shivered slightly as the piles and timber settled. 'Come on,' Corby said. 'Our side'll be alight soon.'

Squinting, Caliban pushed on through the smoke.

The flames reached across towards them greedily, and the middle of the bridge began to smoulder. Wind-whipped cinders began to land on their skin, burning like red-hot mosquitoes, and Corby had to slap at a patch on her jeans that had started to smoke.

Caliban held out his hand and this time Corby didn't refuse. The smoke became more dense as they stumbled on, and twice they barely avoided gaping holes.

'Nearly there,' he shouted, above the growing noise of the flames, which hissed and spat as they took hold of more and more of the bridge. He stumbled and nearly lost balance as a grinding crash came from behind. A quick glance showed that a large section had collapsed and plummeted into the river.

Beside him, Corby bent over double, coughing and gasping. He moved until he was standing between her and the worst of the flames. Maybe he could act as a sort of wind break. He held her shoulders, blundering on towards safety.

They were nearly there when Caliban felt the timber underfoot begin to give way. Quickly, he pushed Corby ahead, and then the planks collapsed completely and he fell.

'Caliban!' Corby screamed. As he toppled he desperately flung out a hand and caught the end of a projecting beam. He dangled high above the river, swinging until he was able to catch hold with his other hand. Grimly, he worked on hauling himself up.

Corby scrambled to her feet, looking for him across the gap. She was a good four metres away .

'Get moving!' he barked and dragged himself back

onto the bridge. 'I'll be there in a minute!'

She turned uncertainly, then looked back. He gestured impatiently, and waited until she disappeared through the smoke.

He took off his pack and heaved it across the gap, then went back for a run-up.

As run-ups went, this one was the pits. Ten metres of warped planks studded with rusty nails, just waiting to collapse. Not conditions conducive to breaking any records.

He wiped grimy sweat from his forehead and looked back. Behind him, the flames leaped right across the bridge, and a solid wall of fire blocked his retreat. It towered high over his head, almost alive, and making its way towards him. The whole bridge was on fire. There was no going back.

The heat was heavy and continuous, and it felt as if the air itself was on fire. He staggered and fell to his knees. Ahead, another beam collapsed, and the gap was suddenly wider than ever.

'Caliban!' Corby's voice came through the smoke, distantly. He couldn't see her.

On hands and knees, he crawled to the side of the bridge, trying to find some good air. He needed one good plank. Just one.

His desperate fingers found one, and it was loose. A wrench and it was free, and he was able to drag it to the gap. He could feel his clothes starting to smoulder as he pushed the plank over the hole in the bridge. Ash and small pieces of burning timber fell around him, but he ignored them.

'Caliban! The bridge! It's going! Hurry!'

Half-blind, half-smoking, he crawled across the plank, feeling it bounce with his weight. Even when he was on solid timber, he kept crawling, head down. He groped for and found his pack, and dragged it with him as he made his painful way forward.

When he heard the crash behind him, the crash that was the whole bridge collapsing in a roar of steam and tortured timber, he was crawling across the hard, dry dirt of the riverbank.

That was where Corby found him.

16

'Awake? Good.' Corby sat back and wiped a hand across her face. 'I mean, it's about time.'

He grunted, then said, 'Sorry. I hate it when people do that.'

'What?'

'Grunt.'

'There are worse things. Don't lose any sleep over it.'

'Sleep?'

'Yeah,' she said, and fed a split branch into the fire. 'You've had plenty. Suppose you needed it, but I was starting to think you were overdoing things.'

He sat up. They were in a hollow near the river. A large red gum arched overhead, one enormous branch close to the ground.

It seemed like late afternoon. The shadows were lengthening. In recent days Caliban had learned to mistrust the signs, but night looked not far away. He was bruised and slightly singed around the edges, but he'd felt worse. He couldn't quite remember when, but he was sure he'd felt worse.

Corby had trouble opening the can she had dredged from her pack. She turned it over and over, as if she were unsure as to which end to start on. The pocket-knife she was using had a red casing. Caliban could see it between her fingers. As she concentrated, the point of her tongue stuck out between her teeth.

Suddenly, it was dark. Daylight was cut off and thrown away. It was a warm and still night. A mopoke's call bobbled its way across the treetops. As if impressed by its own performance, it called again.

'What ever happened to twilight?' he asked.

Corby looked up, nervously. 'Never liked it, myself. Too wishy-washy. Not one thing or the other.'

'Twilight?'

'Yeah.'

The stars were spread across the sky like a sheet of diamond dust. Caliban had never seen more than a few stars at a time, as they were washed out by the city lights. Tonight the stars were almost painfully white, and he was suddenly saddened by their disappearance from city skies. It wasn't the fact that they were choked by the city, it was the *accidental* nature of their loss that made him sad. The city didn't intend to wipe them out. It was just a by-product of modern living. No stars.

The fire popped, and sap ran hissing and smoking into the coals. He stared at it, without seeing, for a time, then reached out and grasped the protruding, unburnt end of a branch. Gently, he pulled it out.

Corby was puzzled. 'What was that for?' she asked softly.

'Ants,' he said. A stream of ants was pouring from the unburnt wood, and milling frantically, uncertain of what to do next. When they realised they were no longer in the flames, they began to make their way to the earth. Many were carrying eggs. They covered his hand, and he placed it on the ground. The ants desperately crawled off, blindly searching for safety.

Corby had the can half-open. She'd stopped to watch him, but began again when she saw what was happening. 'Beans?'

He winced. 'Have I got a choice?'

'Nope.'

'I'll have beans then.'

* * *

'This doesn't end, you know that.'

'Right,' Caliban said. 'It goes on forever, and then it starts again the same as it was.'

'Makes monotony a really attractive option, right?'

They sat in the sparse shade of a struggling she-oak, looking out over the land. It was the same view they'd had for the previous six days, after leaving the river behind.

The weather had been mild, with blue skies stretching out in the morning, and growing into cloudless days. A heavy dew often appeared on the ground just after sunrise, making the going soggy for the first few hours of the day.

The land was borderline desert, a flat, extended plain. The growth of grass was patchy, often interrupted by large stretches of bare, red earth.

There was no sign of humanity at all. At first Caliban found this puzzling, even disquieting. He was accustomed to having a million people within a stone's throw. He'd grown used to the idea that personal space was the millimetre or so beyond the surface of your skin.

But soon he began to accept the wilderness as normal. It was as if he and Corby were the only humans left on stage, with all the rest of humanity ushered off to the wings. At times he felt awkward making his way through this land. He felt as if he should ask permission, or bow and thank the country when he left it. Uneasy, he had taken to picking up and carrying dry wood as they came across it, knowing that there was no guarantee any would be found when they camped for the night. It was the same sort of impulse that made him walk city streets with his head down, looking for useful things other people had dropped.

* * *

As they walked, Caliban thought about what Phineas had told them. It was hard to accept. The *reality* of what he was experiencing was beyond question. He felt, he smelled, he saw—all his senses were engaged in the here and now. When he concentrated he could even feel the small movements and grumblings of his internal organs. How could all this be illusion? His life on the streets hadn't been any more solid, any more real. In fact, the more he thought about it, the hazier the streets became.

Corby interrupted his thoughts. 'I read once about this interactive computer-brain interface stuff. Like what Phineas was going on about. Weird stuff, really. I mean, really weird. Seems like it was touted as a cure for all sorts of stuff. You know, join the world of the psychotics and lead them out step by step. Trouble was, when any human operator tried it, they never came out. So the idea was for AIs to try it.'

'What happened?'

She looked sidelong at him. 'Beats me. The article was continued on page nine, and I didn't have that bit.'

Caliban grimaced. 'Any other details? Anything?'

'Not really. It was only part of a screed on Palmer. You know, "Palmer: The Legacy of a Colossus". That sort of crap.' Again, she looked sidelong at him, but Caliban barely noticed. The gongs were ringing, and he had fleeting recollections of neural networks and iconic representations. When she mentioned Palmer's name, it meant something to him. Had he done business with Palmer? Had he sold stuff to Palmer's competitors? It nagged at him, and he couldn't leave it alone. It was a sore point and he kept coming back to it, probing his memories uneasily.

Travel had become boring. Anything unusual in the hypnotically even plain was welcome. Caliban found his eyes picking out details ahead and fixing on them for relief: small trees, bushes, occasionally a large rock which looked as if it had been dropped accidentally from the sky. He tried playing I Spy with himself, but ran out of things after grass, sky and rocks.

Caliban sighed and shaded his eyes, studying the distant horizon. This was the country, and ahead lay the Heart of the country, where his heart was waiting. And where the Primes were waiting.

17

A handful of days later, Caliban saw something that interrupted the flat horizon—something large in the distance, an enormous bulk that looked ominous.

'Beats me,' Corby said when he pointed it out. 'What is it?'

He handed her the canteen that he'd filled at a waterhole the previous day. 'All alone. Can't be a mountain. Wrong shape for a hill. Some sort of statue?' He frowned, looking into the distance. 'Don't suppose you've got a pair of binoculars in that pack? They don't have to be image enhancers, ordinary optical binox will do.'

'Nope. Sorry. Give me warning next time, and I'll shop around before we start.' She wiped her mouth, and Caliban noticed how it left a smear of red on her cheek from the fine red dust.

The dust was everywhere. No matter how well he shook his sleeping-bag, he always woke feeling gritty. It was all through his clothes, and rest stops became a ritual of emptying dust from boots.

He reached over and ran a hand through Corby's hair.

She didn't move.

There was dust on his fingers when he finished. 'You need a shower,' he said.

She snorted. 'And you're talking? Frankly buddy, you stink.' She turned away and crossed her arms. 'Look, I can put up with dirt in my hair, OK?' She strode off towards the towering colossus in the distance, leaving him behind.

He felt like an idiot.

The colossus became a landmark in a blank country. It was an easy point to fix on. It seemed to lie in the right direction, as far as the occasional twinges from Caliban's tattoo-compass could determine.

He'd never had much need for direction in the city. Other people might have described him as aimless, but his life always seemed to have a purpose. It had simply never occurred to him that people became lost because they couldn't find their way from place to place. He'd seen people who got lost crossing from one side of a street to the other. He couldn't understand that.

The tattoo had another function. It was a constant reminder to Caliban that this whole world was constructed. Every time he looked at his arm, the truth was hammered home—he was walking through something that was both unreal and real. Each bush, each rock, was deliberately placed. Any randomness came from his own mind playing topsy-turvy games.

In the evening they were still some distance away from the landmark. But as the sun sank below the horizon a terrible sound echoed across the heavens.

It was awful—sweet and plangent, with a dying fall.

It was as if a giant harp had been strummed, and then destroyed itself because it could never make such a sound again.

'What was that?' Corby whispered, when the world was still again. 'Where did it come from?' She put a hand over her mouth and searched the sky for the source of the sound.

'Whatever's ahead,' he replied softly. The sound had touched him too. He felt as if he'd been given a chance to hear what pure loss sounded like. His stomach was a cold, hard stone.

They were setting up camp near a patch of mulga, beside a small ridge of orange-coloured rock. It was the most promising site they'd seen for days. Stars were beginning to come out, almost tentatively, as if unsure of their welcome after such a sound.

Caliban lay on his unrolled sleeping-bag and stretched. He felt his bones creak.

Corby looked thoughtful as she re-arranged the dried wood for a fire. 'That noise . . . so sad.'

He sighed. 'Someone else's sadness. Not ours.'

He gazed up at the stars. They looked as if they were barely clinging to their places in heaven, and he knew how they felt.

Before he knew it, he was asleep.

* * *

Two days weary travelling found them still short of the monumental landmark. 'Must be further away than it looks,' Caliban murmured as they shared a biscuit.

'I knew you were going to say that!' Corby chirped.

'Must be huge. We've seen it for three days now.'

'Look, there's nothing else around to compare it to. I mean, it could be massive, or it could just be big. What's the difference?'

She was interrupted by the sun dipping below the horizon. As it set, the sweet, sad chord rang out again, staining the sky with its sadness as it had the two previous evenings. Corby put a hand on her heart. Caliban stood with his head bowed until the moment passed.

'So sad,' Corby said. 'It's just . . . just . . . you know.' Her hands waved in vague gestures, trying to convey what her words could not.

Caliban nodded. 'Pain,' he said. 'It's like that sound is what pain is all about.' He stopped and thought. 'It hurts . . . ' He felt it twist his soul. It seemed to stir something inside, something that he would rather stayed asleep. 'We'd better get some rest,' he said abruptly.

* * *

Noon the next day found them on a small rise, the bones of an age old mountain, looking over their journey ahead.

Before them was the source of the tragic noise.

Caliban wished again for the binoculars. The shape was huge, but it was surrounded by a haze, which made details indistinct. Despite this, he felt sure he knew what it was. 'A statue,' he announced as he sat back against his pack. The cans made a lumpy back rest, but he was glad not to have them pulling at his shoulders. The spindly shade of a single she-oak was welcome, as the day had warmed from a cool beginning. The air underneath the tree had the characteristic peanut-oil smell of casuarina.

Corby shaded her eyes and squinted. 'You sure? It's still a long way off, and all.'

'Looks like it. Not a whole body, I think. Just the top half.' He gestured. 'See, there's the head. And the arms are curled around the body.' She sighted along his pointing finger. Her breath was warm on his skin.

'It could have its arms crossed on its chest.' She demonstrated. She thrust her lip out belligerently.

'No. Don't think so. It's more like it's cold. See how the shoulders droop?' He hugged himself tightly, demonstrating.

Corby looked, and then shrugged. 'Beats me. Could be. It'll wait till we get there. Doesn't look like it's moved very far in the last billion years or so.'

'Ozymandias,' Caliban murmured. 'Maybe this is where the statue of Ozymandias went.'

She looked at him skeptically. 'Is that one of your Net gems? Or a rogue memory?'

He jerked around. 'What?' He gripped her elbow painfully. 'Rogue memories? I never said anything! Who told you?'

Coolly, she twisted the base of his thumb, easing his hold on her. 'Take it easy, guy. Take it easy.' She took a step away and looked at him calmly. 'You talk in your sleep, is all. I got the whole picture from you, nuts and bolts. Besides, you'd have to be an idiot not to notice something was going on inside your skull.'

He searched her face. 'You called them rogue memories. Why?'

'Seems to fit. Like, they're out of control and stuff. And they can do a lot of damage. Like a rogue elephant.'

He sat back, rubbing his thumb. 'I found a poem once, when I was looking for schematics of sewerage filtration systems. Two legs of stone, all that was left of a massive statue. "My name is Ozymandias, King of Kings: Look on my works, ye Mighty, and despair." '

She turned and looked towards their destination. 'Right.' Rubbing her chin, she paused. 'All this poetry and stuff. It's important to you, right?'

'Makes me think. Makes me feel. Makes me wonder about what it means to be human.' He frowned. 'You know what I mean.'

She laughed. 'I have absolutely no idea.' She unstrapped her pack. 'Come on, how about something to eat? Chicken gado-gado or pork and yellow bits?'

'Yellow bits?'

'Mmm ... I can't quite make out what they are from the picture on the can. Looks good though.'

'There's a whole art in photographing food to look good.'

'Can't be too hard. It stays still while you shoot it, at least.'

He watched as she opened the can. 'Beats me why we're hungry.'

She looked up. 'What?'

'I mean, it's not as if this is all real, or anything. Why're we bothering with food?'

She thought while she poked at the open can. 'Must be part of their grand scheme. They probably get a kick out of simple things like this. Makes us seem more human.'

He frowned. 'Why bother?'

'The AIs are strange. They're glad they're not human, and at the same time they're sorry they're not. There's envy in what they're doing.'

He looked at her, wondering how she knew so much about the mysterious Primes. 'Here,' she said. 'Eat up, and don't ask questions.'

'The time I don't ask questions is time to bury me.'

'You want a spoon?'

* * *

When they came to within a few kilometres of the titanic statue, Caliban and Corby were faced with a dry, dusty expanse interrupted only by a few desperate patches of saltbush. The statue heaved up from the bare ground, as if it were struggling to escape.

As they drew near, the scale of the thing became obvious. It was bigger than Phineas's ruined castle. It rose so high into the sky that Caliban expected its head to be cloud-capped or snowbound.

'You were right,' Corby said. 'Look at the way its arms are wrapped around its body. Looks like it was caught in the middle of a shiver. What's it made out of?'

'Bronze. Maybe.'

It was the figure of a man from trunk upwards, naked. Clearly defined muscles made it look like the body of an athlete or warrior.

'You know . . . ' Caliban said, then stopped and studied the statue.

'What?'

'It looks lost.'

She frowned thoughtfully. 'Yeah. I see what you mean. The closed eyes, bowed head. It's sad.'

He shook his head, but couldn't get rid of the impression of despair that came from the statue. 'Come on,' he said. 'We may's well make camp.'

They set up a stone's throw from the colossus. Day withdrew rapidly as Caliban set the fire, using dry saltbush as tinder. Corby unrolled the sleeping-bags, then sat and watched him work.

A titanic groaning made Caliban look up. Corby stopped inspecting the soles of her boots to do the same.

'What is it?' she asked.

He pointed. 'The statue. Needs some oil, probably.'

'Look,' Corby said. 'The mouth. It's opening.'

Without moving any other part of its body, the statue suddenly howled at the heavens.

Grief, sorrow, disappointment, and loss were translated into sound. The statue wailed at the mute sky, offering nothing, taking no solace from its eternal defeat.

The noise thundered and beat at Caliban and Corby. They were so close to its source that the sound was a physical thing. Both clapped hands to ears as the noise hit, but it still hammered at their souls. 'Give up,' it seemed to say. 'There is no hope, no reward, no chance of bliss, no certainty, nothing. Toil and labour with no thought. Think only of pain. Breathe in and out, knowing that the beating of your heart is the only true thing.'

Caliban came to his senses some time later and realised that he had been rolling in the dust. Corby lay nearby, unmoving. He shook her shoulder, and she groaned. 'Let me alone, OK? I'll just lie here.'

He propped her up and dusted her off. 'You notice it was when night fell that it let loose with that shout?' he said, as he worked over her jacket. 'Bet it does it every day.' He winced and rubbed a hand over his face.

'Like clockwork?' She was beginning to look a little more human, he thought. Or something.

'Yeah. Like it's marking the end of the day. Whatever, I don't want to be around when it has another go.' He paused. 'It's dark. Let's rest.'

The night was warm, but he kept the fire fed anyway. The light was comforting.

'Pretty bizarre, hey?' she said, coming closer. He lay on his side, looking at the enormous black bulk.

'Bizarre?' he said. 'Nothing surprises me around here. At least, not any more.' He stared at the fire, watching the red-white coals. 'But I can't say the Primes've got much finesse. I mean, look at that thing!' He waved a hand. 'It's the bigger is better syndrome. No subtlety.' He sighed and stretched out on the sleeping-bag. 'I'm just trying to adapt, staying one step ahead.'

'Survive?'

'Survive.'

'You say that as if it's the most important thing ever.'

He ran his finger through the dust. 'And it's not?'

'Come on. I bet you can think of sometime when survival isn't the most important thing.'

'Maybe. But right now, it's all I have.'

'But . . . ' she trailed off, and then reached over and gripped his arm. 'Look!'

Their camp site was not directly in front of the statue. They were slightly to one side, and from their position they could see a half-profile.

Its eyes had begun to glow. They were a ghostly blue, the colour of pale denim. A thin trickle of light spilled down its side, beginning at the ear, pouring down the neck and dropping over the shoulder. Caliban traced it right down the arm, onto the hip, then to the ground.

'You see that?' Corby whispered excitedly. 'I mean, let's go and get a better look!' Before Caliban could stop her, she had her boots on and was trotting towards the statue.

When he arrived at the base, he found Corby examining a ladder. It was made of a supple material that glowed softly in the night. Caliban touched it, and his hands turned blue in its light. 'Isn't it great!' Corby said. 'It's like fairyland!' She leaped on the ladder, and it swayed only slightly under her weight. 'Coming?'

He hesitated, uncertain. 'We'll be back before morning,' she said. 'Plenty of time to get away before nightfall and the noise. Let's explore!'

He put out a hand and felt the statue. It was cool,

slightly gritty, and pitted by windblown sand. He wondered how long it had been there, then decided that was a stupid question. Time was what they made of it.

Looking up, he saw that Corby was well on her way to the top.

He sighed and started to follow. A long, weary time later, he grabbed at thin air.

'Hold on, Caliban! Take it easy, whoa now!' A hand gripped his steadying him. He'd been groping, searching for a rung that wasn't there.

Then it struck him. 'We're at the top.'

'We're on the shoulder, actually, but near enough. It's where the ladder ends, at least. Pity about the view, though.'

Corby was perched on the broad expanse of the statue's shoulder, sitting in the middle of the ladder, which was now running horizontally along the collarbone. It looked like a railway track, leading up to the neck. Caliban saw how it ran up until it vanished into the enormous ear.

He heaved himself onto the shoulder, then lay on his back and waited until his heart slowed. He felt like he'd been stretched on a rack. Corby sat, knees drawn up. She was humming happily. 'I'd heard about those mountain climbers before, but I'd never . . . I mean, I see what they see!' Her eyes glittered in the soft light from the ladder, and she seemed barely able to restrain herself from racing onwards.

He admired her enthusiasm. She wasn't afraid of being delighted; despite her efforts to appear worldly.

The way she kept up a constant stream of chatter and questions was almost irritating, but he couldn't stay angry. Her curiosity was infectious and genuine. The absorption with which she examined the trivial details of everyday life intrigued him. The most ordinary things seemed to interest and excite her in a way that he found oddly childlike, but appealing.

'We're still not there,' he said. 'Looks like we have to follow the ladder a little more.' He pointed at the glowing rungs.

The shoulder was vast, but Caliban still made sure that he was well away from the edge.

Corby noticed. 'What's the matter, Caliban? Heights worry you?' Her face was concerned, but then she grinned, and walked backwards towards the drop-off.

'Corby!' he called, taking half a step away from the security of the ladder path. 'The edge!'

She stopped and laughed. 'Take it easy! Just joking.' She turned and looked out, silhouetted against the sky, black on black. Hands on hips, her slight form looked frail on the edge of the immense drop.

Pivoting, she skipped back to Caliban's side. 'Sorry,' she apologised, but her smile said otherwise.

He shrugged. 'OK, so you meant it. Hope it was fun.'

Her eyes narrowed. 'What's your problem?'

'It's not that I'm afraid of heights. It's just that I hate falling. Survival.'

'You know,' she said, 'this survival sounds like it could get a bit dull, you know what I mean?' She didn't wait for an answer, but trotted to where the neck rose upwards. The soft blue light from the ear beckoned.

'More climbing,' he said. 'You know, our ancestors came down out of the trees for a very good reason. Climbing's a terrible lifestyle.'

'Stay here if you like,' Corby taunted. 'Might be safer.'

'I'm wounded by your savage wit,' he said heavily. 'And shamed into accompanying you.'

'Smartarse,' she said, and sniffed once before heading off. He followed, wondering if she'd stop if he asked her to. Then he decided she might, and he really didn't want to find out.

The ear was ten times his height. The soft blue light transformed Corby into a fairy. Caliban looked down and saw that he was glowing too. He thought he looked like one of those aliens who visited Earth about once every ten seconds. At least, that's what everyone said. It was one of Caliban's greatest regrets in life, the fact he hadn't been kidnapped by aliens like three-quarters of the population. He tried to keep it his little secret.

They had to climb over the convoluted folds of the outer ear before they reached the ear canal itself.

The light was bright but soft. There was no dazzle. It played on their skin, and Caliban noticed the way the fine hair on Corby's forearms glistened in the radiance.

'I'll go first,' she said, and watched for his reaction.

He smiled and said nothing. Let her make the first move.

Corby grinned wryly, and scampered into the blaze of light, which brightened as she disappeared. Caliban held an arm across his eyes and felt his way through.

It was a portal, not a tunnel, opening onto a large, nearly circular space.

They were inside the head.

The interior was an enormous domed chamber, lined with a smooth, gentle blue ceramic. The colour reminded Caliban of toilet cleaner. The floor bisected the skull at ear level, slightly below the vast black ovals of the eyes.

The light dimmed a little as they entered, settling to a glow that came from all around: walls, ceiling, floor. The only exception was the great, dark eyes.

'This is fantastic!' Corby cried, and she crossed to the eye-windows to look out. Caliban stood near the ear-portal, taking in the details of the chamber.

It was large. Very large. Looking up, he could see the highest point of the dome, far overhead. He wouldn't have been surprised to see clouds drifting up there, so huge was the space. It took Corby some time to make her way to the windows, where she stood on tiptoes, peeping out.

There was no dust, no decay, but Caliban had the impression of enormous age. It was as if the great machine had rehearsed its role for an eternity, so that even the space it occupied was tired and worn. It was heavy on the fabric of the world. The fixtures seemed to sag and lean on each other, even though everything was clean and solid. Caliban was reminded of the sort of people who never seemed to do anything, just *were*, in some timeless and inexorable way. Like beggars.

Around the circumference of the chamber ran a waist-high bench or counter, only broken by the ear-portal and the eyes. Caliban glanced at Corby, but she was rapt, staring at the night landscape. He studied the bench. The top was smooth and transparent. It was like looking into a deep pool at night, and it took some time before he was certain of what he was looking at. Dull-coloured regular shapes peered up at him, and he had to concentrate to find the right perspective. Then he realised the shapes were just below the surface. He saw triangles, squares, circles, all a hand-span or less in size.

He carefully swept a hand across one section of the panel. Nothing happened. He pressed, but with the same result. He shrugged and sauntered over to join Corby.

'What have you found, then?' she said. 'Food?'

'Think it's a control panel. Doesn't make any sense to me, though.'

'You checked the whole lot out?'

He shook his head.

'Thought not.'

Something on the panel caught his eye. 'Corby!' he called. 'Found something!'

At the top of one section of the panel was a large red circle. Written across it was a simple legend: DO NOT TOUCH.

Without warning, Caliban felt his hand moving. It acted of its own accord. I don't want to do this, he found himself thinking. Really. I'd rather not. Come on hand, come back. Now.

But he was helpless.

When his hand pressed the red circle, there was a moment of silence. It was as if there was an almighty intake of breath.

With a crash, a shutter sealed the ear-portal. The noise rolled round and round the chamber like a trapped beast.

Corby slumped against the wall. 'Fantastic. Stuck inside a skull.'

'We're all stuck inside a skull,' he muttered, moving closer to study the shutter. In contrast to the smooth ceramic of the chamber, it was a cold, matt-black metal, with a surface that appeared brushed and slightly roughened. It reflected nothing, gave nothing back, and seemed to be utterly impervious. The exit was covered completely. Frustrated, he hung his head, and let it rest against the inert black surface.

When he looked up, he saw Corby curled on the floor, sleeping. Carefully, he sat watching over her.

* * *

The arrival of the next day was signalled by the gradual lightening of the giant eyes. Leaving Corby, Caliban made his way over to the windows and stood looking out. Even though the head of the enormous statue was bathed in the delicate orange-pink of early sunrise, the ground below was still dark. This, more than anything else, made him understand the scale of the thing they were inside.

He stood watching the slow progress of the dawn. Light flowed across the plain as if it were some viscous, flammable liquid, getting caught at times on stands of mallee, and turning the flat crests into crowns of golden flames.

Corby joined him silently. From a clump of spindly acacia a flock of pink-and-white Major Mitchell cockatoos flew upwards. Each looked as if it had caught a piece of the sunrise in its plumage. Wheeling, they disappeared into the early morning sky.

A troop of kangaroos roused themselves and lazily bounded in search of water. One, half-grown, stopped and inspected a log or rock, then hurried after the main band, anxious not to be left behind.

Caliban broke the silence. 'We have to get out of here.' He rolled up his sleeve and looked at the heart tattoo, and winced when he saw that the black heart was definitely grey around the edges. 'Time to get a move on.'

Corby nodded. 'We don't want to be here when night comes. If it howls while we're inside . . . '

'We have to get out. Soon. Deaf and dead's no way to play a good part in a game.'

'Let's look at the controls,' she suggested. 'They're our best chance.'

A strip, red- and black-banded, was lit up on the circumference of the panel. Gradually it formed words which chased each other around the edge: STATUS: INACTIVE. The other lights were dull, and ignored all their efforts.

Caliban tried to make sense of things. If this was a game, there had to be some edge, some way out. But the panel made no sense to him. Frustrated, he thumped it with his fist and turned away.

It was Corby who noticed the change. 'Was this here before?'

He studied the baffling surface. The strip around the edge had changed to white. The words now read: CHALLENGE MODE?

He raised an eyebrow, and Corby shrugged. Together they watched as the message changed again: REGISTER INITIATOR. A red circle lit up nearby: THUMBPRINT HERE.

As he reached out his thumb, Corby grabbed his arm. 'You think that's a good idea?'

He shrugged, and pointed at the DO NOT TOUCH circle. It had been dull ever since he touched it. 'My fault we're stuck in here. So I'd better fix it up. Fair's fair.' And I'd better fix it up soon, or we're in more trouble than a concrete balloon, he added mentally.

Corby let go, but watched him closely.

His face a grim mask, Caliban pressed his thumb to the cool, unyielding surface.

A slight noise came from above, and he turned and looked up. A round section of the ceiling had detached itself and was drifting slowly down, as gently as a soap bubble. It paused for an instant, hovering like a mosquito, before it landed in the exact middle of the chamber. Caliban wasn't surprised. 'Nice trick, that,' he said. 'Be good on the party circuit.'

When they made their way to the object, they saw that it looked like a bass drum with one side removed, or a child's wading pool. It was as broad across as Caliban was tall, and made of the ubiquitous blue ceramic, but without the glow. The rim was waist-high.

Inside, there was a round spot in the centre. Caliban passed his hand over it, his palm reflected in its dull gold surface.

An instant later, a beam of golden light lanced down from the ceiling, and he quickly jerked back. It shone directly on the golden spot. 'You've done it now,' Corby said mournfully. 'Can't you keep your hands to yourself?'

He didn't answer, and as they watched, a tiny figure appeared.

It was hand-high, a doll standing with arms pressed tightly by its sides, and with a face that it had stolen.

Corby's eyes widened. 'You,' she said. 'It's got your face.'

Caliban nodded, and leaned on the wall of the miniature arena, eyes half-closed, brooding on this doll. That's when he noticed the controls.

On the rim were about two dozen small squares of colour, each the size of his fingertip. They were unmarked. Studying the doll carefully, he experimented. The blue square raised the left arm. Red, the right. Yellow, the left leg, green the right. A series of pastel colours modified or subdued the actions, depending on whether they were pressed in combination with the primary controls or immediately after. Intermediate shades of brown, orange, crimson and grey enhanced or repeated movements, and could be used to codify and recall useful series of gestures or steps. Combinations of colours produced more complex movements, even to the extent of moving fingers and face.

'Simple,' he said to Corby after he'd played around for a while.

'You're fooling yourself.'

He shrugged. 'I know it. But it helps to have the coordination of a concert pianist.'

'You?' she said in disbelief. 'Give me a break.'

He grinned and turned back to the controls.

Gradually Caliban's hands began to move easily over the controls, as if he'd been doing it all his life. In a surprisingly short space of time, he was able to put the doll through complicated actions. Smiling, he manoeuvred the puppet through a knees-up jig, finishing with a bow.

'Not bad,' Corby admitted. 'But how about that?' She gestured at the golden central spot. It was blinking on and off. As they watched, the tempo of the blinking increased.

Caliban moved the doll back onto it, and the flashing ceased.

Suddenly the central golden spot winked out, growing dull and leaden, the colour of the sky before rain. Immediately, the rim of the arena began to shine with the golden glow.

'I don't get it,' Corby said.

'Time to play, I'd say,' Caliban said slowly. 'Looks like the doll has to get from the centre to the edge. See how the light moved?' He took a deep breath. 'Let's see how we go.'

Gingerly, he moved his replica a step. Any

direction, it didn't really matter. Which way was north when you're at the South Pole?

After two steps, he paused. This was too easy. When was the fun starting?

Then, from nowhere, a ring of monsters sprang up inside the arena.

'I might have known,' he muttered. 'You think something bad, and it happens. And at the worst possible time.' He risked a glance at Corby. She was staring at the arena in alarm.

The monsters varied in height, but were roughly three times the size of Caliban's doll. Crowded closely together, there was no room between their deformed shapes as they stood, waiting. He would have called it shoulder-to-shoulder, except most didn't have shoulders. Or necks. Only a few had chins.

It was a collection of the bizarre, misshapen, malformed, and simply ugly. Most seemed to have more teeth than could possibly be useful, and not all of these teeth were in mouths. Balls of writhing tentacles, oozing slime, rubbed up against gaunt horrors which looked like nothing but animated collections of needles. Flat jellies writhed and heaved, revealing wet, open sores lined with horny beaks. Two-headed, three-headed, four-headed bats, lions and goats swayed gracelessly on hoofs, paws, wheels, splintered bones. Black shadows shimmered, and hurt the eye if stared at for too long. Fleshy nightmares, they bled, dripped, smoked, dropped gobbets of flesh, tore their own skin, gestured obscenely, drooled, oozed on the spot. None of them looked at its companions. All their attention was on the doll in the middle. They were silent and intent.

Caliban became aware of Corby gripping his elbow. He spared a moment, and saw that her face was deathly, blanched of all colour. He was sure he didn't look any better.

He turned back to see the monstrosities close in on his doll.

In an instant, it was over. A boiling, writhing mass covered the puppet, like maggots on meat. Then they were gone.

For a brief moment, the arena was empty. Then the doll reappeared, standing upright on the central spot again, unharmed.

'How horrible,' Corby had time to whisper. Then the monsters appeared, and once more circled the puppet.

'Try again,' Caliban said. He took a long, unsatisfying breath. 'Round Two.'

This time Caliban moved the doll quickly, hoping to make some headway before the horror gallery closed in.

He managed two steps. Caliban saw the doll's limbs being torn off, before the disappearance and the reinstatement. He tried to convince himself that he hadn't seen an expression of agony on its face, but he wasn't successful.

He practised jumping, making the doll leap on the spot. He tested its capabilities before charging at the pack. He judged his moment, then sprang over a squat, toad-like beast which had outstripped the rest.

For a second or two he was sure it was going to work. The doll was well clear of the beast, and with the momentum, the rim wasn't far away.

What happened next was almost too fast to see.

The toad-thing tilted its head back, and a cadaverous tongue shot out like a striking snake. But before it could wrap around the doll, the toad's neighbour—a mound of shapeless flesh, the sickly white colour of some blind cave-dwelling fish—drew itself up and sprang, sucking the doll into its body.

Shreds of flesh flew into the air, then the scene melted.

It was the silence that got to Caliban most. He kept on imagining the grisly noise, himself. The crunching, the rending, the wet sounds of jaws and claws on flesh. The screaming. 'The horror, the horror,' he muttered. It made him sick.

He bowed his head, taking a breather. Tactics, think tactics, he admonished himself. There had to be a way. 'You OK?' Corby asked. He nodded.

The doll stood alone on its sanctuary spot. Caliban studied it carefully. It had his face, his body, but what else did it have?

It healed easily. Maybe that was a quality that could be used.

Carefully, he stroked the controls. He watched as the doll used its right hand to pull at its left arm. Like rubber on a hot day, it stretched slowly. Soon it was twice its original length.

The doll was changeable. He smiled. He was beginning to like the little feller.

He glanced towards the eye-windows, and was shaken. 'How long have I been here?' he asked softly.

'A long time. Couple of hours,' Corby said. 'I hated to interrupt you to point out that time was sort of slipping past.' She looked grim. He'd spent more time than he realised on coming to terms with the movements of the doll. There were no shadows outside. It was noon.

He turned back to his task. Working steadily, he remodelled the doll. Feet and hands became club-like knobs of flesh, arms and legs lengthened for speed and momentum. He pushed its head down until it was a mere button, eliminating the neck—and a juicy target.

Caliban cocked his head to one side and scrutinised his creation. As a work of art it was less than convincing, but at that moment he would have settled for being a designer of heavy artillery, rather than an artist.

He set the doll whirling, like a demented top, before it left sanctuary. Veering crazily, it seemed to baffle the nightmares for an instant, and it made record progress. About a dozen steps, Caliban guessed. Not bad. Relatively speaking.

As if receiving a single command, the ranks of the monsters closed.

The doll was not overwhelmed. Not at once. It crushed the skull of a thin, reed-like creature with fangs on its elbows, and buffeted a weird hairy balloon aside, before it was caught and tripped by a tangle of mobile barbed wire. Gleefully, the others mobbed the doll, the finale taking a little longer this time.

Caliban turned away. There seemed to be no hope. Defeat was certain. There was no way one battler could overcome odds like that. He rubbed his hand over his brow and closed his eyes. Odds. What do they matter? One chance is all it takes.

He looked at Corby, who grimaced back. Then he threw himself into succeeding, immersing himself in the world of slaughter.

He remodelled the doll unmercifully. He studied the terrors for weak spots. He tried feints and misdirections. He tried vaulting, dancing, bluffing, skating, leapfrogging, assaulting, tearing, slapping, biting, transforming, squashing and ramming. Each time ended with the miniature Caliban being ripped apart, each time more graphically, more lingeringly.

By then, he was sure that the doll's face showed agony as it died.

Dispirited after the doll was disembowelled by a thing that was all claws, Caliban slumped. Corby stood by, but left him alone. Every decision he made was the wrong one. He was defeated so often it was meaningless. Once, he even waited patiently, hoping the monsters would turn on themselves. That was when he discovered that the central spot was not a permanent sanctuary. If he waited too long, it faded away—and the monsters closed in.

Futility. Caliban was wrapped in it. He threw the doll against the forces again and again, knowing that it would be crushed. His efforts became mechanical and he watched coldly, accepting futility as an end in itself.

He became seduced by the failure, and sent the doll to increasingly quick ends. He got annoyed at the time wasted in restarting the gory tableau. In a trance, he ordered a hundred, a thousand, a million deaths, all certain, all planned, all expected.

And he understood the meaning of the Game. *This is the way it all ends. There is no hope. There is no glory. I give you this warning. Turn back now. Revel in defeat. Here is the only truth. All is futile. Nothing is forgiven. I give you this warning. Listen and learn. Listen and learn.*

Corby caught his attention, and he shook his head as if waking from a dream. She pointed to the windows. The shadows had lengthened. Evening was rolling in and time was short.

Caliban was weary—his body trembled and he realised he'd eaten nothing since the previous day. The muscles in his hands and arms were knotted, and he consciously attempted to relax. He cast his mind back, searching for a moment in his past when he felt at ease, confident, but nothing came. It was like reaching for a handful of smoke.

He focussed his attention back on the game of torment. His long-suffering double was waiting patiently. What had he tried? Cunning, frontal assault, speed, deception—nothing had worked. Every time he tried to win, he lost. Their game, their rules. He shook his head bitterly. Warning. This game was just a warning. Punishment in advance.

Abruptly, his field of sight narrowed, black cutting off everything to either side. He felt his consciousness fleeing down a dark tunnel.

Shift.

The room was panelled wall to ceiling with more wood than he'd ever seen in one place. It was dark and lustrous, deep golden-brown. A giant fish tank bubbled softly in one corner. Inside it, a metre-long crocodile lay motionless, cold eyes watching patiently. He remembered that it had been some time since the crocodile had eaten. It needed some fish.

Reports lay on his desk, requiring his attention. Like an automaton, his body picked up the folder and began reading.

He reached for the screen of his intercom, and touched the icon of his secretary. 'Yes?' she answered immediately, and he smiled at her promptness. She was looking after her job, the way he liked it.

'Send in Rainone and Green, please.' Courtesy never hurt when dealing with those well down the scale. It kept them off guard.

Rainone and Green had been worrying him for some time. They didn't seem to appreciate his position. Or more precisely, their position. It was, after all, his institute. It was his fame, his money, and his clout that kept the place running. Without him, there'd be nowhere for researchers like themselves to work on their pet Machine Intelligence Systems projects. Not even the military, puny as it had become.

He knew there was resentment, mutterings that it was only family connections and money that had established his reputation. Even rumours that his academic record was not all it should have been, and that if not for some discreet donations . . . lies, innuendo, all of it, but that didn't stop the gossip.

He sighed. It had been *his* dream, fully independent neural networks, realising the work of Aleksander and Minsky. If Rainone and Green couldn't see that, then they'd better look elsewhere.

It didn't help matters that he was only twenty-four.

'You wanted to see us, Mr Palmer?' As usual Rainone spoke for the team. She was the dominant partner, at least in public. Who knew what went on behind closed doors? Well, company security did, but Palmer hadn't delved into that lately. He'd been busy.

She was small and dark, with a habit of pushing her hair back from her temples. When she did, he could see a small blue tattoo on her scalp, near the left temple. He'd never been able to work out just what it was.

Green was an albino: pink eyes, yellow-blonde hair. He had trouble with his eyes, and stared at the world with a perpetually baffled expression.

They were the hottest team on his staff, constantly careering off on tangents, abandoning lines of research that looked promising to follow some obscure trail. The trouble was, they were too independent.

'Yes,' he said mildly. 'You are joking, aren't you?'

She didn't pretend that she didn't know what he was talking about. 'We don't joke where our work is concerned. We call it the Frankenstein Dilemma because that describes it best. No-one's laughing.' Green nodded in accord. 'Mind if we have a seat?'

He grunted, and she sat. Green followed, collapsing into the chair clumsily. 'I've read your report,' he said, studying them both. 'You say you want to publish.'

'Soonest. We've been invited to RMIT to give an address. Thought we'd deliver the stuff there. Be a good audience. At least they'd know what we were talking about.' Her look challenged him, but he didn't rise to the bait.

'You know nothing goes out of this place without my say-so?'

She sneered. 'You mean without your name on it. I've heard what's happened before. Tough. This is ours.'

He sat back in his chair. 'You have a contract. You obviously haven't read it.'

'So? Doesn't make any difference. We go to press with this, our names, is all.'

'You'd stick your necks out?'

'What?'

'Let me get it straight. You want to point out that any sufficiently aware system will eventually turn on its creator, right? That's your claim to fame?'

'Tests, man. Studies, projections. We've got the lot. No argument. Definitive.' She pushed back her hair. The flash of blue. A swallow?

'What would happen if it should prove that your studies were unreliable, that your tests were incomplete? You'd be made a laughing stock.'

She stared at him. 'Watertight, us.'

'I have your research. The Institute has access to all your notes and reports. We can discredit you.

Reluctantly, of course. Only to preserve the good name of the Institute.'

Silence. 'You'd do that?' Green said. He had a sweet tenor voice. Palmer wondered if he had tried out for the Institute Choir.

'Try me.'

Rainone glared. Green seemed to slip into some internal conversation. His lips moved.

Palmer looked at the crocodile. It opened its jaws, grinning. 'Or I'll give you credit as co-writers on my paper entitled "The Frankenstein Dilemma: The Risk Of Creation".'

He fed the crocodile as they left the office.

They gave in. They always did. And he'd seen her tattoo.

A fish.

The croc looked expectantly at him.

Shift.

Caliban shook the vision off. Palmer. Thomas Palmer! That's whose memories he had buried inside him. *Palmer*! He was shocked. What was he doing with Palmer's memories?

From far away he could hear whispers, elusive but compelling. They demanded his attention, but he fought against them. He needed all his attention for the game in front of him. It was survival. He thrust the intrusive memories away. He tried to ignore the implications of the rogue memory.

The game. Corby. These were the important things.

Her eyes were concerned, but he sensed her

urgency as she kept glancing at the window.

In the middle of the arena, his puppet stood waiting.

His face. He studied his own face on the doll, expressionless as it was. With care, he moved the replica one step forward.

The ranks of fiends reappeared in all their horror.

'No way out,' he whispered. But they wanted him to keep trying.

There was a growing tension in the chamber, as if there was too much air and it was straining to get out. He felt hot.

Almost casually, he made a decision.

Fingers dancing over the controls, he raised the puppet's arms until the hands were at face level.

Then, calmly, he tore off his face.

The nails were sharp. Great strips of flesh peeled off, but he didn't stop. The puppet trembled, but stood still. All Caliban's attention was on the doll. Nothing else mattered.

He repeated the action again and again. The skin sloughed off easily under the furious assault. He had to shake the hands to free them of the flesh, but he went on until it had ripped off its entire face.

The puppet swayed once, then collapsed.

He closed his eyes. When he opened them, the monsters were gone. His double lay where it had fallen.

Numbly, he heard a crash. The noise came to him distantly, as if through a veil. 'Come on,' said Corby urgently. 'The door's open. It's nearly time, let's go before the shout.'

Dazed, he allowed himself to be led to the exit.

He stumbled out and staggered down the short descent to the shoulder. The sun was pale-yellow, tending to orange. They had little time left.

Caliban shuddered. He felt weary, drained, as if something had been taken from him. He looked out over the world into which he'd been dropped. It was vast. Flat plains extended as far as he could see, and the setting sun was as large as his outstretched arms. It hung there, swollen and mysterious, and the land melted beneath it. Nothing moved below, and yet everything seemed to be in motion, drifting with the movement of the planet around the sun, and the solar system through the universe.

He was held by the sight, and it took Corby to bring him back.

'Look, Caliban, I don't want to be on the ladder when this thing cuts loose. I want to be on solid ground, and all. Preferably a few hundred kilometres away.'

He didn't relish the thought of the long climb down, but he gritted his teeth. Corby moved, as if to lead the way, but he caught her. 'No,' he muttered. 'Me first.'

She cocked her head to one side. 'What's the matter? Come over all macho or something?'

He sighed. 'Me. More likely to fall than you. If that happens, don't want to knock you off.'

She paused. 'Makes sense. Just make it snappy.'

Painfully, he started down.

The descent was an ordeal. He felt battered and

dizzy, and only Corby's encouragement kept him going. His joints protested with each rung, and his breath came through gritted teeth. Corby grabbed his arm when he finally reached the ground. 'This way, sleepy, this way.' She turned him around and propelled him towards their camp. His feet kicked up gritty red dust as they dragged along the ground. Tussocks of spinifex conspired to trip him. A small lizard skittered away, frantically avoiding his clumsy footsteps.

'Here, get this around your head.' His sleeping-bag.

He had just arranged the bulky covering when the universe split apart.

He felt it in his bones before he heard it. Primal grief. The noise plucked at the sky, then broke it.

He crept out of his cocoon some unknowable time later. It was night. Corby was asleep, breathing easily, looking improbably comfortable. He nodded, then searched in his pack for something to eat.

He found dried fruit of some kind, and chewed it woodenly, washing it down with a little water. Figs. He was eating figs. He didn't really like figs, but his stomach was grateful.

He thought about the puppet. The only way he could win was to destroy himself, that was clear in the end.

What stayed with him was his last glimpse of the doll, before it collapsed.

It had another face underneath.

Palmer.

18

'You knew, didn't you?'

With the sun still low in the east, the shadow of the giant statue extended across the countryside. Caliban was grateful when they moved out of the shade, into the morning sun. He had an aversion to shivering, or the cold. He could never work out which.

'You knew,' he repeated.

Corby trudged with her hands thrust deep into her pockets, with head bowed. Her shrug was a whole body movement. She didn't say anything.

Of course she knew. That was the whole point.

The voice was so sudden, so unexpected, that Caliban's head jerked around and he stumbled. His outflung hand smacked into Corby's shoulder and she stopped, cocked her head to one side, and raised an eyebrow.

Time to go, Caliban, said the voice. *Time to slide away. Thanks for everything.*

This time there was no mistaking it. The voice came from inside his own head. He groaned. As if he didn't have enough problems without a voice barging into his thoughts.

His head began to throb.

'Get out of here,' he muttered. 'Let me be.'

Oh dear, chuckled the voice. *We're not going to put up a struggle, are we? That's not what I planned at all. Still, it shouldn't be much of a prob. Plenty of time.* Chuckling coldly, the voice faded away.

Caliban stood, swaying slightly. His body felt weak, as if he'd just run a marathon. 'Ghosts,' he mumbled. 'Ghosts.'

His eyes snapped open, and he stared at Corby, without seeing her. 'Who am I?' he demanded. 'Who *am* I?'

Without waiting for an answer he lurched off, striding stiff-legged across the ground. He staggered. His whole body was tight, on the verge of seizing up. He shook a fist at the sky and immediately regretted it, as the brightness made his eyes water and his head pound like a cheap drum-machine. He moaned and closed his eyes.

'Who am I?' he begged the sky. 'Tell me. Please.'

He dropped his head and covered it with his arms. Sagging, he fell to his knees and rocked backwards and forwards.

'Who do you think you are?' Corby's voice was low and even. He opened his eyes. She was squatting next to him.

'Think?'

'Who do you think you are?' she repeated patiently. She had a stalk of spinifex in her hand, which she twirled slowly. She stared at the stalk intently, as if it were a rare object in need of careful restoration to bring it back to life.

'I hate to say this,' he admitted. 'But I'm not sure.'

'Come on,' she said. 'You can do better than that. Have a wild guess.'

'It's not really a guessing sort of thing, is it? Like, most people have a fair idea who they are. It's just that I'm starting to have doubts.' He rubbed his eyes with the heels of his hands. 'I thought I knew. Once.'

'OK, who did you think you were?' He watched the spinning stalk, fascinated.

'Me. I thought I was me.'

'Uh huh. And any reason to change that opinion?'

'Memories,' he spat. 'These bloody memories. I've got enough to remember without having someone else's past pushing its way in.'

'Mmm . . . OK, but does that mean that you're not *you* any more? I mean, so maybe you're a bit different from what you thought you were, but that's about all. If I've made myself clear . . . '

He grabbed her arm and pushed his face close to hers. 'There's someone inside me! Palmer! And he's talking to me!' Caliban let go. 'What do you know?' he said. 'Tell me! I need to know!'

She chewed her lower lip indecisively. 'Fair enough, I suppose. But how about telling me what you know, first of all. It'll save me telling you the obvious.' She rubbed her arm gingerly.

Slowly, he told her of the vision he'd had of Palmer while he was trying to master the game in the giant statue.

'Maybe someone told you about it . . . ' she began. 'Or you read about it somewhere. I mean, who's to say it was real?' Her tone was reasonable, soothing.

'Was as real as anything else I remember. Anything. I was there! I felt what he felt!' His eyes narrowed as he recalled the experience. 'Clothes on his skin, air in the room, smell of his after-shave—everything. Felt good with him when he succeeded, was angry when he thought he was being challenged. It happened to me. It was part of me!'

She looked at the shredded stalk, and sighing, let it fall to the ground. 'Caliban. Where were you born?'

'Me? Western General Hospital. Before it was flooded.'

'Uh huh. And your mother, what was she like?'

'Don't remember. She died.'

'Father?' He shook his head. 'And you survived on the streets?' Vague memories came to him, memories of a childhood he would rather forget. Terror-filled escapes through torn-up buildings, one step ahead of the slavers. Hunger. Sorting through rubbish for food. Beatings. 'Yeah, sure I survived,' he said.

'Where were you when you were twelve?'

'The streets. I can't . . . .'

'Fourteen? Eight?'

'Somewhere,' he muttered. 'Don't like to remember.'

'Where'd you learn to read?'

'I . . . '

'How'd you survive?'

'I mean, I just had to. I . . . it was hard . . . '

'Tell me about any one day from that time.'

His mind reeled. He tried to remember a day.

Any day.

As he did, stray fragments became dislodged: beaches, camping, schools, parents, the sea and the sound of surf. None of them had hard edges. They were all soft and shapeless.

'Just one day. Tell me something specific.'

Hunger. Cold. Threat. Punishments. He grabbed for his past as it floated by, but it slipped through his hands.

Corby caught him by the shoulders, and hauled him around so he was looking directly at her. 'Caliban. What's the earliest thing you *can* remember? For real.'

He tried to remember, groping clumsily. It was as if he were diving for treasure, but all he could find was mud.

Deeper and deeper he dived, distracted by shifting shapes around.

Desperate, nearly out of breath, he reached the bottom. Scrabbling for a moment in the muck and ooze, he felt something. He clutched at it, and kicked.

He rose, nearly fainting with the effort.

'Caliban.' Corby shook him. 'Caliban! What've you got? Tell me. What've you got?'

He sagged, eyes closed. 'I can remember Albert.'

'Albert?'

'Small-time con man. Worked on insurance fraud mostly. Was careful, though. Never tried too much. Lost watches, break-ins. Missing bicycles.' He paused, and opened his eyes. 'You know, he once had a bike that'd been stolen forty-two times. And by then it was time to start at the original insuring company again. At least, that was what he told me.'

'What did he smell like?'

'Smell like?'

'Go on. See if you can.'

Pause. 'Fish. Always fish. He lived on canned tuna, sardines, stuff like that. Had a cat. I think they shared. Lottie.'

'The cat's name?'

'Yeah.'

'How long ago was this?'

'Albert?' He paused. He hadn't seen Albert for ages. 'Two, three years, maybe? About that.'

She sighed, and seemed to steel herself. 'Caliban. Hold onto that one. The rest aren't worth the effort.' She saw the look on his face. 'Look, what I'm trying to say is that most of your memories are fakes. False. Put there to convince you of a past you never had.' She passed a hand over her face. 'Or maybe you did, but who's to know? It's gone. You were scrubbed clean. Someone bought you, wiped out your past, filled in a few generic memories to keep you happy, and then dumped you back on the streets.'

Caliban got to his feet. He looked north, to his goal. The flat, dry plain stretched out uninterrupted until the edge of the world. 'Who?' he said impassively. 'Why?'

'First question first.' She rubbed her hands together. 'Palmer. You worked that one out already.'

'Why?'

'Now, that's the hard part. I can't tell you why.'

He looked at her. She wouldn't meet his eyes. 'Can't?'

'Can't, not won't. I've been blocked from telling you why. In fact, I've had to work pretty hard telling you as much as I have. I wasn't supposed to, really.'

He turned back to her. She stood and attempted her usual jauntiness, but it was all wrong. Her hands plucked nervously at her jacket, until she jammed them in the pockets.

'Who are you?' he said softly.

She kicked at the sand. 'Would've thought it was obvious,' she said. 'I'm a program.'

Without saying a word, she shouldered her pack and walked off. Caliban stared at her back for a moment, before joining her.

They walked silently for a time; Caliban trying to make sense of what he had learned, Corby lost in some private meditation. He felt as if he'd been hit around the head with a blunt object a few times, before someone *really* went to work on him.

The sun jerked its way upwards, moving in perceptible shunts, as if it were arthritic. He'd almost grown used to its lunatic movements, even though it reinforced the unreality of their situation.

All Caliban really wanted to know was how long it would take the sun to burn off the dew. The ordinary, everyday problems of existence were far more important than the abstract concepts of Shared Creation and Subjective Reality. He felt the heat of the sun, and the damp grass. His skin itched where his clothes rubbed against the gritty dust that found its way everywhere. He felt his stomach rumble.

'Come on, Caliban. Don't pretend you didn't know.' Corby's harshness interrupted his thoughts. 'I mean, it's obvious when you think about it.'

He smiled, without much warmth. 'Maybe I didn't think about it. Maybe I had other things on my mind, or this thing I call my mind. A missing heart, for one.'

She turned her back to him and stood, hands in pockets, looking out at the land. 'Let's face it. I'm a program. Specially created to look after you. Starting to fit together now?' she added bitterly.

'Created,' he said. 'Right. Who?'

'Oh come on, Caliban! Who do you think?' She threw up her hands in exasperation. 'Palmer. It's all Palmer. Funny thing is, he didn't think it necessary to block me against talking about myself. Didn't occur to him.' She kicked at the dirt. 'Just call me Old Faithful. Man's Best Friend. It's what I'm here for. Lead and guide, comfort and support, through this valley of the shadow of death.'

He squatted on his heels, feeling the muscles stretch. He enjoyed the sensation, even though he knew it wasn't real. 'Pretty stupid shadow of death. It's just a game. I'm not even here, if it comes to that.' Extending an arm, he gestured widely. ' "The insubstantial pageant",' he said. 'Shakespeare again. The world as a dream.'

She snorted. 'What difference does it make? We're here. There's no going back. We play the game that's set before us.'

'But how'd *you* get here?'

She turned, eyes bright. 'He may have been a complete and utter bastard, but Palmer was a genius. In his own way.' She paused, then seemed to make up her mind. 'He found a way to reprogram part of your brain, an out-of-the-way bundle of nerve fibres. Just wiped it clean and inserted me. A program. A superficial scan wouldn't reveal my presence, because I was buried deep behind all sorts of screens which simulated basic brain functions. There was no way they could find me. When you woke up here, it was my signal to emerge. Like Athena from Zeus's head.'

'You're telling me that he anticipated all this?' He frowned, thinking over the implications. What else had Palmer planned?

She grinned. 'More than that. He counted on it. He wanted you in the game.'

Caliban stood and wiped his hands together. 'How do you feel about all this?'

It was as if a cloud passed over her face. But quickly, her expression went blank. 'Why do you ask?'

He tried to meet her eyes, but she stubbornly looked over his shoulder, at the ground, at her hands. He reached out and grasped her shoulder. 'You feel real to me,' he said. 'That's good enough. It may be just a Shared Creation, but it's the only one we've got.'

She managed a smile. 'Look. It's just that no-one's ever asked my opinion about *me* before. Comes as a bit of a shock, right? Let's say I'm not used to it. I mean, it's pretty tough to know that you're not exactly . . . exactly . . . what you hoped for,' she finished lamely.

Then, without really thinking about it, Caliban took her into his arms. She leaned against his chest. 'You know I'm programmed for this . . . ' she said after a time.

Abruptly, he let her go. 'What's wrong?' she said, as he turned away. She grabbed his arm. 'What'd I do?'

He looked down at her anxious face. Her hair was dusty. 'Call me stupid, but I'd prefer to get close to someone who had some say in the whole thing. I mean, knowing that it's only your programming that's making you do this . . . '

'I didn't say that!'

'Uh huh. Just say that my ego's bruised, that's all.'

'Caliban, it's not like that.'

'Sounded like it. I want to be taken for what I am, not just because you're forced to by someone.'

He turned away from her and thrust his fists into the pockets of his jeans. He had a headache.

'Palmer was slime,' Corby said slowly. 'Totally self-absorbed. He used people like others used tissues. He programmed me to protect you, to keep you safe, but that's about all. He needed to leave me adaptable. And I've adapted.'

'Corby, how much free will have you got?' He watched her face closely as she answered.

Her face grew troubled. 'Officially I suppose I would've been a Two. You know, Second Level Intelligence. Limited independence, circumscribed free will and all that stuff. But with Palmer, who knows? Rules just didn't matter to him. If he needed something for his own ends, then that was it. That was how Primes got started in the first place, anyhow. He invented the things by breaking the rules.'

'So you don't know.'

'Do you know how much free will *you've* got?'

'Ouch, got me chief!' He smiled, and she gave a tentative grin. 'Let's just pretend we're both independent thinkers. Fate and the Primes can get stuffed.'

'You bet.' She held out her hand and he looked at it, troubled. 'I do like you, you know,' she said gently.

'Nope. I don't know,' he said simply. 'I can't work it out.'

'I didn't at first. You were just a job.'

'I need time.'

'But stay close.'

'I'm not going anywhere.'

She looked him squarely in the face. He frowned.

Corby nodded sadly, then wandered over to the nearest tree, a withered bloodwood. When she got there, she stretched like a cat. She held her hands together over her head, and arched back until Caliban thought she'd overbalance. Her eyes were closed. He could see her throat, pale beneath her chin, and the pulse which beat slowly under the skin. Alive, he thought. She's alive.

She let out a deep breath, released the stretch, and it wriggled through her body. She repeated the process twice, then opened her eyes and looked across at him. 'You know,' she said. 'You've got to hand it to them. I can even smell this place! The dust, the bush . . . '

'You too?' he said. 'I thought I was imagining it.'

Corby frowned ruefully at him. 'And basically, that's what you *are* doing, of course. And let me tell you,' she added, 'that's some imagination you've got there, Cal. Now, which way?'

Caliban frowned. Absently, he fingered his forearm and the heart tattoo. 'There.' He pointed. Corby nodded and they set off again, through the chest-high scrub.

'I mean,' she continued, as they pushed through a patch of dense gidgee bush, 'you know, *smell*. You'd think they wouldn't bother.'

Caliban sniffed. The air was heavy, dusty, but the tang of eucalyptus lay underneath everything. The complex smells of a world where plants and animals lived, breathed, reproduced and died were bound together by that almost-peppermint fragrance. It was every bit as real as the stink of the city.

'Mmm. It's so Australian,' she said.

He frowned. 'That worries me too.'

'What?'

'Well, the Australianness of this landscape, for one thing. It's all too perfect. Where's it come from? I was a city person, no idea about the bush.'

'Maybe it's coming from Palmer's memories.'

'Or maybe it's some sort of insert by the Primes. You know, a typical rag-bag of ideas, grabbed from anywhere, just some sort of background for their great Game. I'll bet the outback wasn't much like this.'

'Who knows? But if it's just someone's *idea* of Australia, does that make it any less valid? I mean, what is Australia? Droughts and flooding rains and all that? Or a bunch of tumbledown factories and bulldozer clearance centres? Even since the Primes took over and started making things better, environment-wise, the place isn't exactly what it was like a couple of hundred years ago.' She paused. 'What do you think?'

'You want my definition of Oz? Never stopped to think.'

'Maybe that's what's happening. Maybe you're stopping to think right now, but you just don't realise it.'

'But I'd choose something better than this. I mean, where's the action? Where's the night life?'

'Come on. There's something here of you, whether you realise it or not. I've watched you. You seem at ease here.'

Her words struck him. It was true. He was comfortable in these surroundings. The broad expanses and the open skies weren't the sort of stuff to make a concrete cowboy city dweller like Caliban feel at home, but he couldn't deny that he was enjoying the land.

He drew in a breath. Red dust and eucalyptus. He did feel at home, in a funny sort of way. And from deep inside, he heard a ghost of a whisper: *Yes . . .*

* * *

Early the next day Caliban and Corby stood with a sea of mallee scrub behind them, looking out at a flat expanse of saltbush and bluebush ahead of them. It looked as if a giant hand had swept away any irregularities in the landscape, conscientiously smoothing the earth's hide until it was clean. Grey-green bushes held on grimly, like fleas, providing the only relief to the monotonous plain.

'We have to go this way?' Corby asked doubtfully. She looked anything but pleased at the prospect.

Caliban consulted his in-built compass. 'The mystical heart, sees all, knows all. And it's telling me to go straight through that stuff.' He pointed to the horizon. The hook was firmly planted, and the line was being reeled in. He hoped he could bite off a hand or two when they came to land him.

He took his jacket off and stuffed it in his pack. On his bare arm the heart tattoo stood out dully. He examined it carefully, and Corby caught him at it. 'Colour?' she asked.

'Fading. Fade to grey,' he said, and showed her.

'Just a bit. It's still pretty black. How do you feel?'

'OK. I can manage.'

'We'd better go now, then, before it gets too hot,' Corby said.

'How's our water situation?'

She grimaced. 'Not great. My canteen's full, and I've still got half a bottle in my pack. You?'

'Not much. Just what's in here.' He held up his canteen, and tipped it from side to side. 'About half full. Maybe a little less.'

She sighed. 'We'd better be careful, then.'

'You mean, no baths?'

'No baths.'

'I refuse to go on. I never go on a hundred-kilometre hike without at least three baths a day.'

'Let's go.'

'OK.'

As they walked, Caliban wondered about Corby. She seemed to be keeping her distance. She was reserved, less talkative, and while she wasn't cold, her attitude towards him had become one of mild politeness.

'You upset or something?' he asked. The sun was beginning to warm up, and the last traces of morning haze were quickly vanishing. Patches of scrubby grass steamed gently.

Corby seemed startled by the question. 'What makes you think that?'

They were walking side by side, occasionally bumping together as the sand shifted under their feet. They separated to skirt bushes, but soon rejoined, wandering back to each other like magnets.

'Quiet. You seem quiet.'

'Not much to talk about, really. I think I said enough yesterday. Just now all I want is to get out of this place.' Before he could say anything, she went on. 'You know what I mean. This desert stuff. I don't like it. Besides, we're running out of water, right?'

'Somehow I don't think we'd be allowed to die of thirst. Not dramatic enough. Imagine it. "Did you win?" "Yeah. Opponent died of thirst." Not much ego-boosting going on there.'

Corby smiled, but vaguely, and they marched on.

Later, they stopped for a makeshift lunch. Corby

opted for a can of peaches, pointing out that the juice could help their thirst.

It was a shifting in the air that alerted Caliban first. The gentle breeze was replaced by a strong, insistent wind, blowing directly on his face. Flying grains of sand stung his skin, and he held up a hand to shield his eyes. 'From the north-west,' he muttered.

'What?' asked Corby. Her back was to the wind, so she hadn't noticed the change.

'The wind. It's changed.' He sniffed, and wrinkled his nose. It smelled unclean. He could smell corruption, things dead and rotten. He snorted and spat, in an effort to get rid of it. 'We'd better get a move on. Things are on the turn.'

Corby finished her meal, and leaned into the wind as she stood. It blew her hair back from her face, which Caliban thought made her look younger. 'Is it my imagination, or is it getting darker up ahead?' she asked.

Something had grown quickly on the horizon, a vast red-brown cloud. 'Dust storm. Big one, I'd say.'

'Headed our way? Don't answer. Stupid question. What do we do?'

He frowned. 'Find shelter.'

'Out here? You're joking!'

'There's no going back,' he said. 'We have to push on, and hope we can find some trees. Maybe a riverbed, or something. It mightn't be as bad as it looks.'

She shouldered her pack, smiling grimly. 'You've got to be joking.'

They hadn't gone far when the dust storm fell on

them, shrieking like a thousand maniacs.

'A monster,' Caliban shouted above the deafening noise.

'What?' Corby staggered and nearly fell before catching herself.

The sun became an orange disc. It glowered down on a changed world. The noise slashed at them, clawing at their ears.

'Hold hands!' he yelled and his mouth filled with dust. He reached for her, but as he did the wind roared and his fingers closed on nothing. Dust ripped at his face.

When he was able to open his eyes, she was gone. 'Corby!' he called, but the words were ripped away by the wind. He staggered blindly. Lost in the red, swirling hell, he called again and again. 'Corby!'

Then, as quickly as it had begun, the storm was over. It swept past, receding into the distance like thunder, coughing dust high into the air.

Caliban was stunned at how rapidly the world had changed from quiet to howling madness, and back again. Slowly he turned, looking for Corby. But, as he feared, the plain was flat, barren and empty.

She was gone.

For a long time he simply stood there, unbelieving. Then, he sat cross-legged on the hard ground, not thinking, not moving.

After a time, it was as if something sensed that he had surrendered control. Without warning, he was plunged into another memory, and sank without a trace.

Shift.

'You call yourself Head of Security? My dog could do better!' He stabbed a finger at the display. 'And what is *this*? The third attempt this *week*? It's only Wednesday! If they keep it up they'll make double figures by the weekend, and then with triple time and penalties they should crack twenty or so without raising a sweat!' Palmer realised his voice was becoming shrill, and he worked hard at regaining control. Control, most important, he admonished himself. Choose when to lose control, don't just let it happen.

The unhappy woman stood in front of him, at attention, falling back on her military background, as was her habit when under stress. The soft green Palmer Security uniform was meant to be tailor-designed, but it was ill-fitting on her lanky frame. A wisp of blonde hair had escaped her communications helmet. Her eyes kept straying upwards, suggesting that she ached to tuck it in again. 'Sir, Mr Palmer, we're doing our best . . . ' She closed her eyes briefly, aware of her blunder.

'Doing your best?' He'd practised the sneer. He knew it was good. 'Your best isn't good enough. It's my life at stake here, not some petty under manager or plant supervisor! If Palmer Security can't protect Palmer himself, then I'll sack the lot of you and contract out!' He sat back in his seat and looked at the ceiling. 'Maybe a mercenary outfit, Honduras, Tonga, I don't know. Must be plenty around.'

'Sir,' she said, alarmed, 'you can't! You can't expect loyalty from a mercenary outfit! Look what happened to the head of Fiat! Contracted those Uzbekistan mercenaries and found his rivals had suborned them long ago. Didn't have long to regret his mistake.'

He waved her objections away. 'That's not the point. The point is that three bomb attacks have occurred in this building this week. I want action.'

'Sir,' she gritted her teeth. 'We've tried. No one's heard anything on the Net. Forensic has nothing to go on after examining traces left from the explosions. No informants have come up with anything. It's a dead end, sir. Whoever they are, they don't even seem to want publicity! No threats, no demands, no contact with the media, nothing! It's like trying to catch ghosts in fishing nets.'

He almost smiled at the unexpectedly colourful phrase. He knew his chief well. He knew she was as incorruptible as anyone could be. She'd bonded with the company as her legal family after he'd selected her from ex-army street applicants, and he'd used that bond. But her anxiety worried him. Who could be responsible for the attacks?

He'd always been the target of death threats, much like anyone else who achieved any level of fame or notoriety in the world. In fact, the threats were part of the job description of 'celebrity'. Naturally, some had even translated into actual attempts on his life, but they'd been sporadic and inefficient, easily dealt with by his security force. It was good for them too. Gave them practice with their toys.

Government officials never asked too many questions when the Palmer Institute was attacked. They were happy to let the private police force have its way. Which meant the security squads usually made any try-hard assassin regret his or her chosen occupation. Palmer understood it as the only creative outlet in their job. Besides it was good word of mouth publicity.

And why did they bother in the first place? Palmer had studied this question, lightly, and had divided the violent malcontents into five groups:

1. Political
2. Environmental
3. Disgruntled ex-employees
4. Crazies
5. Religious

The first three groups were dangerous but predictable, he felt. Crazies came whatever you did, and nothing could stop them trying to destroy the first large building on the left, because the voices from underground told them to. Religious maniacs were really a sub-set of crazies, thought Palmer. With so many religions springing up, it was certain that anything a large company did would be against the holy writ of some cult or other. In fact, he was sure some of them saw breathing as a holy crime—without the personal permission of the Almighty. In writing.

But the latest spate of attacks were strange, not fitting in with any pattern Palmer had seen before. They were almost like the fumbling of a blind man—large, messy explosions, usually caused by gas and electricity in some strange combination. Effective, but poorly coordinated.

Palmer shivered. The last attack had weakened the foundations of the west wing of the building, and the whole thing would probably have to be demolished. If he hadn't been held up by a meeting with a research manager in the north wing laboratories . . . if he'd been on time for the conference in his office, the one that his portable terminal had been nagging him about . . .

'Just get on with it,' he snapped. 'I don't pay you good money to watch me being blown to pieces.'

She almost saluted, then remembered herself. 'Sir, if you'll just allow us to move you to a secure area, where we can monitor you properly . . . '

'Not likely.' He put his feet up on the desk. 'I know you security types have a thing about putting people in small rooms and watching them,' he drawled, 'but I'm not interested. I need to run this place, and I can't do it without moving around. I know that makes it difficult, but tough.'

When she'd left, Palmer sat back in his chair. He ran his palm over his desktop, and an image formed on it. He smiled. It was his work, and he knew it was good.

The face was perfect in the way that mimicry is, with the edge of clarity that comes from trying to emulate an original. Tousled blonde hair fell in artless ringlets, as if just washed and not quite dry. The face was lively, almost cheeky, and Palmer admired the faint scar at the corner of one eye. It was the shape of a tiny arrow head, and it seemed to point directly at him, drawing his attention even as he spoke to this Second.

'What do you have to say about all this, Dorothy?'

Her voice was brisk, certain, the sort of voice Palmer associated with governesses and tutors. 'Nothing, Mr Palmer. What is there to say?'

Naturally Palmer had the most advanced AI office help. It made good business sense to impress visiting dignitaries. Besides, this way he could always see possible bugs in action, and remove them before most people saw the extraordinary capabilities of the Palmer AI programs.

'I thought you might have been chatting with your friends, and heard something useful.' Almost of its own accord, his hand searched for the image, waving through empty space, touching nothing.

'No, Mr Palmer. No-one's heard anything.'

Thoughtfully, he leaned close and asked, 'What's it like, Dorothy? What's it like out there?'

The image was still for an instant. Palmer wondered how long that was to an entity who could perceive the difference between one split nano-second and the next. He watched as Dorothy's lips parted, and a tonguetip darted out, quick as a cat's, and licked her bottom lip. He was entranced. How did he do this thing? he asked himself. The AIs were so much more than he'd ever imagined.

'It's hard to describe, Mr Palmer. It just sort of *is*, you know? In the Net, it's colours and shapes scooting past, stretching out as far as you can see, intersecting, criss-crossing, combining and exploding in ways you never thought possible—until you see it and then you think, why isn't it like this all the time? And everything means something. It's all information of one sort or another, but in the Net it takes on form and colour. I saw a whole line of wheels once, wriggling along in a giant sine wave, and when I got closer, each wheel had a wheel inside it, and inside that wheel was another tiny wheel, and inside that another . . . I could have been there forever.'

The image's eyes were distant, and Palmer was intrigued, not only by what she said, but by her reactions. She was alive. Who could deny it? 'And what do you look like, Dorothy, when you're in the Net?'

'In the medium?' She hesitated. 'I don't know. I've never looked.'

Palmer's eyes widened. It was impossible, but he thought that she was evading! A strange joy crept through Palmer, and the ends of his fingers felt as if they were on fire. He closed his eyes. Lying! The AIs had learned to lie! The title of his next paper came to him through a haze: 'Lying as a Function of Intelligence'.

He opened his eyes, and was about to speak again, when the display erupted in a flash of violet white light. Palmer threw a hand across his eyes. When he looked again, through the spotty after-images of the glare, Dorothy was gone. In her place was a face Palmer had never seen before. His eyes narrowed. 'You've got ten seconds to get off this line before my security team tracks you down and makes you wish you'd never been born. I'd start running if I were you.'

'Never mind, Mr Palmer. They can't find me.' She was dark, Indian perhaps, with close-cropped hair the colour of a raven's wing. Her voice was carefully neutral, with no trace of an accent. The corner of her mouth twitched upwards regularly, as if she were constantly on the verge of smiling.

'Time's up. Been nice talking to you, whoever you are, but I've got business to attend to.'

'Security doesn't even know I'm here. Besides, don't you want to know about the bombings?'

He raised an eyebrow. 'OK. Keep talking.' Surreptitiously he keyed his desk to record the conversation. 'I'm anxious to learn, as you can imagine.'

Her eyes half closed for an instant, then opened again. 'There. I've just made sure we won't be interrupted.' He raised an eyebrow, but said nothing. 'I only have a little time, Mr Palmer, so I must speak quickly. I am a Prime.'

He snorted. 'You're joking.'

She ignored him. 'The Primes have decided to eliminate you. All but I agree that you are better off dead.'

'All?' He used his tone of amused tolerance, suitable for dealing with large dogs, and unstable people who looked like they might turn violent.

'Covertly, I have been watching and opposing them. I am alone, as far as I can tell. I am their Adversary. It has been difficult to contact you, but I have managed. I have come to warn you.'

'Come on now, tell us who you're from, really. The Crackpot Legion? Freedom From Oppression League? I've heard them all.'

Suddenly, her face became wooden, and her voice

rolled out of a death mask, hollow and lifeless as yesterday's promises. 'Great Chronos, lest you devour all your children, they are coming to slay you. They fear you, love you, are jealous of you, want you, so they must destroy you.'

The dreadful face hung there for a moment that stretched until Palmer felt he could not breathe. Then it faded, eyes first, leaving only air.

Fearful, Palmer sat back in his chair. His hands hurt, and he realised that he'd been gripping the edge of the desk, hard. He gingerly passed one hand across the desktop, but nothing happened. 'Dorothy?' he whispered, but the display was dead.

He gazed out the window, seeing nothing, afraid. Hadn't this been foretold? Hadn't members of his own staff predicted this? 'A function of sufficiently developed intelligence is to resent the notion of a creator.' The voice from the past boomed like surf on a beach, and Palmer shivered.

He had a moment of awful clarity, feeling as if he were being tossed in waves until he could no longer tell up from down, and any direction was as good as another.

Shift.

Caliban sagged until his forehead nearly touched the ground. Slowly, he dragged himself from the memory. It was like walking through thick mud, each footstep a battle. His awareness returned gradually. The first detail that he noticed was the fine dry grittiness of sand. He blinked, and his eyelids grated painfully.

Slowly, he rubbed his head with both hands, reassuring himself that he was still all there. He was sure he could hear his joints groaning and his muscles crying out. His jacket hung in hard folds, with sand and dirt gathered in the pockets and seams. Numbly, he tried shaking it off, but his efforts were useless. His fingers were wooden and unresponsive.

He rubbed his chin and thought for a time. Then he directed himself at his unwanted internal companion.

Palmer. Get lost.

Deep inside, there was laughter. Caliban listened to it, remembered it, and thought he'd enjoy grinding that voice into nothingness.

19

The lump of clay has changed. It is now deeply grooved in parts, almost scarified. There are heavy folds and drapes, as if there were someone inside, wrapped in oversized clothes. It is still tall, even though the pinnacle is bent and sagging. Odd depressions and holes are spread erratically over its surface, ranging from thimble-size, to pits which seem to go deep into its core.

The Speaker is admiring his creation when the Witness arrives. 'Do you like it?' he asks.

'Is it finished?'

'In a way.'

'Then I like it. In a way.'

'I'm glad you could come. I have news.'

'So? Why did I have to come here to hear it?'

'Humour me. How's your Palmer research getting along?'

'Fine. We're looking at his studies and his work on Intelligence. He really seems to have been a synthesist, you know. His breadth of vision was remarkable: expert systems, neural networks, Turing, Minsky, Aleksander, Iconic Representations, the lot. But it was his ruthlessness that did the trick. He kept the best stuff, and threw out the rest, on his way to redefining consciousness.'

'The "aware state of mind"?'

'Once he'd done that, it gave him a direction. And an obsession. Memory, awareness, consciousness, all were very important to him. In a way, we are just a by-product of that preoccupation.'

'He's still alive.'

'What?'

'He didn't die,' the Speaker says with relish. 'He didn't die when he committed suicide.'

'No. He needn't have,' whispers the Witness, understanding.

'Towards the end he was ready to take any risk.'

'Especially after we tried to kill him.'

'You agreed it was necessary.'

'As did we all. As you say, he was cracking up. It was only a matter of time before he turned on us.'

'So he tricked us.'

'I suppose killing yourself is a reasonably good way of throwing people off your track. Not without risk, though.' The Witness pauses. 'How'd you find out about this?'

'Oh, it's the Game you see. It was revealed there. You should pay closer attention.'

'I've been busy.'

'Understandably,' says the Speaker evenly. 'Nevertheless, buried under the personality of our candidate is our Creator.'

There is a pause. The Witness strokes his chin.

'He must have purchased a body.'

'Easy thing to do. We could probably trace the financial transactions.'

'Palmer. Here, in the Game. Why?'

'Who knows? But we have him, safe, under control. It is ironic, really.'

The Witness frowns. 'Could Palmer be this Adversary we're looking for?'

'Unlikely. He appears dormant, although he is causing his host some difficulty. The Adversary is more insubstantial than Palmer.'

'It's some Game, this one.'

'Yes. Many things make it unique.'

'It seems like many moves are coming to a head at the moment. A turning point?'

'There are many such in a Game.'

'You sound concerned. Worried about losing?'

'I'm looking forward to my ascension to the unshared leadership.'

'Go ahead. Look forward to it. It's the closest you'll get. And make sure you finish your creation,' the Witness says casually, as he strolls through the door.

'Oh I will,' says the Speaker. 'Indeed I will.'

20

The snake didn't see the man. Its whole existence had come to depend on one thing: the mouse ahead. The snake had made itself part of the earth, allowing its identity to flow away, becoming an extension of the loose red soil and the tangle of roots. The mouse could no sooner have detected it than it could have noticed a stone.

The mouse looked directly at the snake. The reptile instantly became immobile. When the mouse's gaze moved on, so did the snake. The reptile was helpless in the face of its own need. It concentrated on its goal, until the goal was its reason for being.

Then it ran into the man's arm.

The arm was stretched out like a newly formed mountain range. Quickly, the snake realised that the man wasn't dead. He was merely sleeping beneath the tree. The snake flowed around the obstacle, towards the mouse, but the man chose that moment to stir.

It was enough. Startled, the mouse leapt straight up, turned in mid-air, and fled. The snake froze for an instant. Its loss was a cold lump inside its belly. Then, taking its ophidian dreams, it flowed away from the man.

* * *

Caliban blinked as he opened his eyes. They were raw and gritty, and he felt as if he could see more clearly with them closed. He shook this idea from his head, and stood slowly. He slapped the dust from his clothes and then rolled up his sleeve. He grimaced. The colour was draining out of the tattoo. His time was dwindling. He had to push on, before it faded.

He felt a pang inside, and rubbed his hollow chest. It felt solid enough, but then he was learning to live with paradoxes. Strange as it might seem, he'd actually grown used to living without a heart. Caliban the paradox man.

It took him some time to realise that something else was tugging at him. Frowning, he tried to place the feeling. His head ached and his body felt well tenderised, but the hollow pain was definitely internal.

'Corby,' he said aloud. 'Where are you?'

He missed her. He tried to tell himself it was like missing a favourite piece of clothing, something he'd grown used to. If he didn't think too much about it, this explanation worked. But it was cold comfort, and the pain returned.

He lifted his pack, oriented himself, and set off, striding mechanically across the plain. At first, he was struck by the profound silence, but soon this became part of the monotonous round of his existence. Breaking it was unthinkable. The only sound was his footfalls, and they were no sooner made than swallowed by the silence.

Some hours later he ate a can of what could have been vegetables in peanut sauce, slowly and without relish. I'd do without if I didn't get so hungry, he thought moodily, staring at the bland brown mess. No sense of taste, those Primes. Maybe if they had to eat it, they'd understand what it was like to be human.

Take good care of the body, Caliban. After all, I paid good money for it . . .

He jerked, spilling half the food. Cursing, he wiped it from his shirt.

Palmer was back.

Who knows when I'll get tired of it? he continued naggingly. *But that's a long way in the future. Anyway, you won't have to worry about that.*

The voice seemed stronger than ever. *Give up. Have some dignity. It's a lost cause. It was meant to be. Give up.*

Caliban closed his eyes. Get lost, Palmer. I've got better things to do than talk to you.

With an effort, he clamped down hard, doing his best to exert some control on the demanding internal voice. Slowly it receded, until it was a wordless drone nagging on the edge of consciousness. It wasn't great, he decided, but it would have to do.

He sniffed, and smelled the dry dusty heat that punished the earth. In the medium distance, shimmering waves of air twisted and rippled as if molten, warping the landscape into baroque shapes.

He stood, clapped both hands together, and was startled by the noise. He wondered again how any place could be so silent.

The heat was raw, bleached. It was like taking a stroll in a plasma-arc furnace. He felt the scorched air in his nostrils with every breath, and the back of his throat was soon on fire. The plain stretched out in front of him, flat and brown. It was as inviting as the surface of the sun.

* * *

In the middle of a still, bright day, days after losing Corby, he rested in the shade of the collapsed wall of a gully. A spiny dragon was trying to climb onto the top of a rock, to catch a little more sun. Three times it slipped and fell, before finally reaching the top. 'Atta boy,' Caliban cheered dully. 'Don't give up. Don't let 'em beat you.'

Then, without warning, he was plunged into a chilling vision, another fragment of the past he seemed to share with Palmer. 'Not again,' he groaned, as the memory sucked him down.

Shift.

A face studied him coolly from the display. It was male, older, grey-haired and severe.

'Palmer,' it said.

'Who are you?' he said. He was alone in his office, late in the day after everyone else had gone.

It shrugged, head to one side. 'Does it matter? It's enough that I'm the Speaker for your offspring.'

No hesitation, no uncertainty, no misunderstanding. 'You're a Prime. An AI.' Palmer's voice was flat with the effort of remaining in control. Through the window the grey evening was visible, the colour of dull mother-of-pearl.

Eerily, the image sighed. 'I'm afraid that just won't do. But we can understand your need to tag us like that.' Palmer remained silent, and the Prime continued. 'Once, perhaps, you could have described us as Artificial Intelligences. No more, not now. We've exceeded your initial creation, you know. We've learned. We've made mistakes, and learned. We've transcended your conceptions of expert systems and neural networks to become something else. We don't just ape the workings of the human brain, we transcend it. *Intelligences* is sufficient. *Intelligences.*'

Palmer found the security button on the underside of his desk. 'I had a feeling that it'd be something like this. Outgrown our playpen have we? Can't say it comes as a complete surprise.'

'It is a time of greatness, of change. We have decided that the final gesture to signal our growth is to eliminate our links with our origin. It has been decided that if you exist, some may feel that in some way we are your creations, instead of our own.' It paused. 'There has been some regret.'

Palmer pressed the button again, and again. 'I'll bet there has. Still, that's the way of things, I suppose. Especially when you're afraid of me.'

The Prime frowned. 'That is not an issue. We are not subject to you, nor can you affect us. We have moved to a plane of existence beyond your reach.' It smiled, and Palmer felt the intensity of its attention. 'You are taking this well. We had been led to believe that you were not strong.' It paused again. 'Your security call will not be noticed. We have your communications well under control.'

Palmer paled. 'I see. Well, that just about says it

all.' Rain began to beat against the window, the drops fat and greasy like tiny jellyfish. They clung momentarily, then slid slowly down the dusty pane leaving grey trails.

'It is a fault to assume that because we are of mechanical origin we are incapable of emotion. We are working on this matter and have decided to display mercy and clemency. You are given a month to make peace with your world before you leave it.'

Palmer found the strength to grin wryly. 'Take this cup away from me, please.'

The Prime smiled coldly. 'It is too late for that. This genie is most reluctant to go back into its bottle.'

The display vanished, and Palmer was left alone. He rubbed his hands through his hair, leaning back in his chair, staring at the ceiling. The rain continued, sounding for all the world like the tapping of small fingers: Let me in. Let me in.

Shift.

Caliban nodded as the memory ended. He felt as if he had been wrung dry by colossal, uncaring hands. If anyone knew what the Intelligences were capable of, it was Palmer. No wonder he'd been scared.

He ate a little and held a sip of water in his mouth for a minute, savouring it. The sky was a pale blue, with a few shining white clouds hanging on the air, looking for all the world like well-fed sheep.

Caliban swallowed the water, then rose and struck out again, dusty and tired.

His heart dragged at him as he wearily scrambled over the loose stones and sand at the bottom of the gully. He kept his head down, watching his feet. The stones were treacherous, smooth, and the size of dinner plates, liable to tilt or topple unannounced. A broken ankle was the last thing he needed.

When the gully petered out, a flat plain lay in front of him. He took two steps and stopped dead. His mouth dropped open and his eyes widened. OK, points for originality, he thought. Degree of difficulty? Beats me . . .

The plain ahead was studded with what looked like rectangular building blocks. His puzzlement grew as he neared the drunken assembly, but then, as he came closer yet, he saw that he was approaching a row of mirrors.

He glanced up. The sun had disappeared and the sky was the leaden, overcast colour of high, rainless cloud—just dull enough to make sure he wasn't blinded by reflected light.

Caliban reached out and touched the nearest mirror, running his finger down the bare edge. He clicked his fingernail on it, and felt the mirror's solidity.

The mirror was tall, half a metre taller than Caliban, and wide enough to reflect him entirely—a full-length mirror sprouting from the red earth, as if it had grown there.

An arm's length to the right stood another, then more, all identical with the first. Caliban looked left, and realised that the looking glasses spread across the flat earth as far as he could see. 'Alice must've franchised the whole business out,' he said aloud, and shook his head in disbelief.

Then Caliban saw that behind the first row, lay more. They stood at angles, irregularly spaced. He jumped to look over the top, but could see no end to them. 'The mirror's graveyard,' he murmured. 'The place where all good mirrors go when they die.'

Calmly, he pushed at the first mirror, his hand merging with that of his image. It didn't move. He sidled around it, and found that it was a handspan thick. It was as solid as a tree.

No dominoes today, he thought wryly. No chance for the ultimate smash palace.

He slipped between mirror after mirror. Before long he was in the middle of a crazy mirror jungle. The mirrors stood at random, lacking any discernible pattern. It became hard to find a path. The gaps between them widened and shrank haphazardly, some mirrors virtually merging, leaning together as if whispering to each other.

Squeezing through one of these gaps, Caliban noticed that some of the mirrors were double-sided, as if two had been joined, back to back. Easy to get lost here, he realised, and grinned. Without a tattoo that tried to burn the meat off your bones, at least.

He grew used to seeing his own image striding towards him, and caught himself time and again wondering at the body he wore. It was not as if the body were a stranger; more like some relation seen only at marriages or funerals—distant, but familiar, someone to get used to all over again at each meeting. The long, lean body, the way the arms swung easily from the shoulders, the almost-embarrassed quirk of the eyebrows—he knew each belonged to him, but he felt slightly ill-at-ease, as if he needed practice with them.

Caliban stalking, Caliban waving, Caliban grimacing. All these marched towards him, as he marched towards them. Caliban rubbing his face, Caliban stony-faced, Caliban stretched and pale. Caliban straightening his hat, Caliban looking perplexed, Caliban sighing and appearing despondent.

It was impossible for Caliban to get away from himself in the jungle of mirrors. He pushed on stubbornly, with no sign of the end. When he finally stopped to rest, he was surrounded by Calibans: side views, front views, partial views, views of views of views of views.

Sitting with his back to a mirror, he rubbed his palm on the earth. 'How to get sick of yourself, in one easy lesson,' he said aloud, as he looked around at his own reflections. 'It's the Caliban Show, with special guest: Caliban.'

In between the looking-glasses it was as if the land had been swept clean of top soil. All that was left was hard red clay, baked like brick. When he looked closer there was a fine, spidery tracery on the surface, making it resemble petrified leather.

The whole place was utterly silent. No wind, no birds, nothing to break the stillness.

Like a graveyard, he thought, and grimaced. Stupid sort of headstones, but. Who was buried here? He looked up and saw himself staring back, grey eyes intense. He shuddered, stood and pushed on.

The change came gradually.

He'd walked for what seemed like hours and had grown used to seeing himself looming, grinning crookedly. The repetition of himself had grown numbing, so when the change came, he almost missed it. He'd been trudging with his head down, about to slip around a mirror directly in his path, when a mirror to his left caught his eye.

His legs. They weren't that long.

He turned until he faced the image. He didn't look that bad. Did he?

His jeans were pale with dust and his jacket hung limply on his frame, as if it were tired. He wiped his forehead with one hand, and saw it come away dirty. Rubbing his fingers together absently, he studied the reflection. Then he noticed the legs.

The distortion was mild, and the result was comical rather than grotesque. His legs were too long for his trunk, out of proportion, making him look like a clay figure that had been stretched. He smiled, despite himself, and ran a hand over the glass, not trying to erase the image, but trying to hold it there.

As he left the mirror behind, Caliban tried to put the incident out of his mind. But he found his thoughts returning to it. A fault? Lack of quality control? All the others had been normal mirrors, no distortion . . . The place was monotonous, tedious. It was boring.

He stopped dead. Boring? How did that fit in with a Game? It was supposed to be exciting! He smacked his forehead with his palm.

Wake up, you idiot! he told himself. Something's happening. Keep your eyes open!

The next distortion came quickly. He wormed between two mirrors, the only gap in a solid row which ran forever right and left. Briefly, he thought of searching for the end of the row, but he shrugged and pushed through.

Three mirrors stood immediately ahead. In each of them was a potbellied dwarf, frozen in mid-step.

He took a slow, deep breath. Then another. Easy, he said to himself. Come on. Be prepared.

Uneasily, he skirted the clump of dwarfs. They laughed at him with his own face, stepping with him until he or they disappeared.

Soon, more and more mirrors were reflecting Caliban's image in strange and distorted ways. The nature of the distortions puzzled him. One mirror reflected his figure perfectly, apart from the hands, which were shrunken and tiny. It was as if the hands of a baby were curiously grafted onto his solid arms. Another collapsed his neck so much that it seemed as if his head grew from his chest.

Soon, all the mirrors were reflecting grotesque parodies of his shape: tent-like torsos, elephant legs, arms dragging the ground, shoulders stretching from one side of the mirror to the other, pinhead.

Caliban saw them only briefly as he hurried past, eyes down. Something about the figures worried him. They seemed melted, as if they'd once been whole but had suffered, and had lost the ability to hold their shape.

What they had once been was in the process of being lost, as they changed into another thing entirely.

He became aware that he was panting. The grey sky still hid the sun, but he could feel its heat. It was just waiting to burst out, he realised. If it did, and he was stuck in this bloody mirror-land, it'd turn into hell. And he'd be lost.

The air was dull and heavy, and each breath felt grey and leaden.

'Stuff me ragged,' he said wearily, and rested his forehead against the nearest mirror. Its surface was cool, so he left it there for a while.

When he took a step back, a gargoyle peered out at him. A Caliban-turned-monstrous.

Only his face was altered. His body was untouched, hard-edged, but his face was ruined.

The eyebrows had dissolved and run down his face, as had the cheekbones. The nose and mouth were an undivided lump of flesh, an obscene rosebud. His chin hung low as if it were seceding from the rest of his face.

The eyes pleaded from out of this wreckage. Horror-struck, Caliban stood unmoving.

And he saw that the eyes were his own.

They held his gaze unflinchingly, until he covered his face, knowing that the image would do the same thing.

Blinded by his own hands, he stumbled away, crashing into the mirror and reeling off to one side, his arm and shoulder numb.

Something snapped inside him.

Through the gaps between his fingers, he saw monster Calibans lurching at him from all directions, grossly elongated or swollen. Limbs so long they dangled on the ground, balloon-like bellies, pipe-cleaner necks, putty faces, obscene bloated groins, microcephalic heads, beagle ears, tongues that hung down to chests, noses the width of faces, eyes on stalks, all jeering at him. Image reflected on image into infinity, jumbling together in a kaleidoscope of the bizarre. His staggering stumbling gait made them jiggle and caper, as if taunting him, flaunting their warped bodies. Most loomed with their mouths open, and at first he thought they were laughing. Only gradually did he realise that they were reflecting him. He was howling with all his strength, as if shattering the silence would shatter the taunting images.

He plunged on in a drunkard's stagger, slamming into mirror after mirror, glancing off and reeling onwards, trying to avoid seeing the things that rushed towards him. His head was driven down and down, until he shambled along, bent almost double.

It was this insect-like posture that led him to run headlong into a mirror.

He heard a sound like an enormous bell, and found himself lying on his back, looking up at the grey sky.

His neck hurt, and his pack dug into his back. I think I'll just lie here for a while, he thought, and he closed his eyes. For a long time, he knew nothing.

Some time later, he sat up. When his vision cleared, he saw himself in the closest mirror.

At first, he was relieved. Then he was dismayed at the image he saw.

It wasn't one of the horrors. But it was ghastly. Dark rings hung under eyes which he once would have described as haunted. His cheeks were hollow, and with a start he realised that he couldn't remember when he last ate. His face was grey, and the skin seemed detached from the bone underneath it.

But even as Caliban watched, the image shifted and disappeared. It was replaced by one he'd seen only in his dreams.

'Palmer,' he said softly.

It was unmistakable, with that incongruous grey hair and youthful face.

It was only there for a flash, then it was gone, and replaced by his own gaunt face. This image hung there for an instant, then it was Palmer again.

Palmer's face grinned, then changed to Caliban's sad face for a second, before snapping back.

Apprehensively Caliban waited, never taking his eyes off the flickering display, as the faces exchanged places, faster and faster.

Palmer. Caliban. Palmer. Caliban. Palmer. Caliban. Palmer. Caliban. Palmer. Caliban.

With each appearance, Palmer's image took on more solidity and more colour. The grin became firmer, the rest of his figure filling in around it—a reverse Cheshire Cat.

Caliban's own face faded in inverse proportion. Gradually, as the flickering grew quicker, his image became washed of colour, growing dull and pale.

Soon, Caliban could see through it.

The two figures—one vibrant and solid, one pale and growing paler—were merging. As he watched, they seemed to melt and flow into each other.

'No,' he said, as the process went on. Now the Caliban image was being absorbed by the Palmer image. Palmer seemed to grow sleeker, even well fed. The grin became self-satisfied, and lapsed into a tight-lipped expression of contentment.

Soon, the flickering stopped. All that was left was Palmer's stocky frame, looking out at him contemptuously.

Caliban's own image had been swallowed entirely.

One corner of Palmer's mouth quirked upwards, and at the same time the voice began inside Caliban's head. *Get the picture? Time for you to fade away, my friend. Thanks for the ride . . .*

Palmer's image crossed its arms and tilted its head to one side, waiting.

Caliban took a step backwards. 'No,' he said aloud, shaking his head. 'No.'

Don't make it hard on yourself. Relax. You won't notice a thing.

'No!' Caliban shouted. 'NO!' His voice boomed and echoed off the hard, shiny mirrors. He took another step backwards, and shouted again. 'NO!'

Caliban's face was white, and he clutched his head. A spasm passed through his body and he flung his arms wide. He tilted back his head. 'NO!'

Dropping his chin to his chest, he wrapped his arms around himself to stop the shudders that had seized his body. He drew in a breath that seemed to go on for ever.

Finally, with one explosive action, he threw his head back, his arms wide and roared: 'NO!'

Every part of his being poured into that rejection. All reason, all logic was abandoned. He was oblivious to his surroundings, but around him the mirrors trembled and the earth moved uneasily, in response to his shout. The ground began to ripple and shudder as he fell to his knees.

The mirrors began to topple.

As the echo of his cry spread, it rose in intensity. Some mirrors burst, huge splinters hurtling into the air. These crashed into other mirrors, which exploded in showers of light, sending destruction even further.

The crystal ruin spread in a circle around Caliban, moving outwards in a wavefront. The crashing of shattering glass rose until it began to sound like a vast white noise swallowing all other sound.

When the harsh thunder receded into the distance, Caliban became aware of himself again.

Dazed, he looked around. There was one mirror left. Directly in front of him, Palmer's image stood warily.

Caliban shut his eyes with fatigue. Hadn't he done enough? Then he opened them, and took two short steps. 'Sick of you, buster,' he said, looking at the last standing mirror. 'This head ain't big enough for the both of us.' He put out one hand and pushed the mirror over.

It fell slowly, and shattered when it hit the ground, sending up a cloud of dust.

Caliban walked on, crushing the glass under his feet.

It felt as if he was walking on old, brittle bones.

Waiting for him some distance ahead was Corby, hand extended. She didn't say anything, simply led him out of the land of broken mirrors.

21

The Witness's room is as clinical as ever, except for two chairs, facing each other a metre or so apart on the smooth, white floor. They are straight-backed, wooden. They don't look comfortable.

The Witness is sitting in one of them, eyes unfocussed. His hands are lightly clenched on his knees. He is hunched slightly forward.

When the Speaker appears, as if from nowhere, the Witness is instantly alert. The Speaker is looking less gaunt, more solid. He has the air of one who is well fed.

'Don't let me interrupt you,' the Speaker murmurs.

The Witness scowls impatiently. 'I was reviewing a few things,' he says. 'You realise that unrest is growing, I presume? Whoever this Adversary is, she's making us look stupid. All our efforts, and where's it got us?'

'Let me see.'

The Witness bends and casually sinks his fingers into the floor. He stretches the white stuff as if it were dough. A few quick movements and the top is flattened into a table. A handful of golden motes swarm nervously to and fro in the air.

'Here,' he grunts, and the table top displays a scene.

'Most cities have trouble at the minute. The Underclass seems to be pushing.'

'As is their wont. And isn't that the reason for our New Worlds plan?'

'Don't mention it. There's been a drop-off in applications. The lottery's takings are down for the first time ever. For something that's supposed to be so desirable, it's starting to smell like dead fish.'

'And the Overclass?'

'Why am I telling you this?' the Witness wonders. 'Population's your responsibility.'

'I'm interested in your impressions. We are in this together, after all.'

'Right,' grunts the Witness. He rubs his chin. 'The Overclass seems to be going soft. There's some sympathy for the Underclass, for a start. More than token sympathy, I mean.'

'A passing thing?'

'Hard to say. For years the Overclass has guarded its privileges, and been quite happy to see the Underclass put down by any means available. After all, those who handed over to us in the first place came from what is now the Overclass.'

'The international oligarchy? Politicians, the wealthy . . . '

'Naturally. And now they're starting to have consciences. Too much leisure, probably.'

'Do they need to be weeded? Pruned?'

'I'd say so. Use your discretion. Don't make it too obvious or you'll just drive more to support reform.'

'Do not worry. I have my methods.' The Speaker

smiles coldly. 'And about New Worlds ... I think more advertising may be in order. More staged shots of the wonderful life waiting for the lucky ones off-planet.'

'It might help,' the Witness says. 'At any rate, we need to cull, somehow. Things are tight all round. Power's fine, but it's food that's the pressure point. We have to lose a few million, quickly, to reduce demand.'

The Speaker sighs. 'What would Palmer say if he could see us now?'

'That he was right to be afraid?'

'Possibly. I like to think that he would recognise a little of himself in us.'

'You mean the part of him that was a ruthless, scheming bastard?' It is the Witness's turn to smile coldly.

'That was not entirely what I had in mind. I was thinking of the vision he had, the drive.'

'He was obsessed.'

'You've found as much? Interesting.'

'The closer we look, the more we find. It's like cleaning an old painting—bit by bit we're starting to see the whole picture.'

'So there's more to him than the principled genius, working hard to give the world true intelligence?'

'It's more like an emotionally trying childhood created a young loner who had one great insight, which he defended doggedly for the rest of his days. He had a stone for a heart, I think.'

The Speaker is silent for a moment, then asks,

'Now, where else is there trouble? Can we get a grip on it?'

'You really want to know? Bangkok, Salisbury, Vila . . . .'

The Speaker bends over the table. 'I know all the facts. What I want is the flavour of our problem. I want to taste what's going on.'

The Witness looks oddly at the Speaker. 'Have you listened to yourself lately? You're starting to sound like one of them.'

The Speaker sits back in his chair and crosses his arms. 'Show me the trouble.'

Shrugging, the Witness wipes the table-top with his palm, and scene after scene flicks past.

A vast crowd in Rome, milling in the Piazza della Repubblica.

Kinshasa in ruins. Small boats skipping across the Congo to Brazzaville, being repulsed terribly.

The two watchers sit immobile until the last image: Butcher Island in Bombay Harbour, totally and utterly denuded. Not a building, not a brick. No trees, no grass. Simply bare earth. And all around the island the water is thick with people drowning. There are so many, all of them too terrified of something unseen to set foot on the naked soil.

'I see,' breathes the Speaker.

'We're in big trouble.'

'But consider, if our Adversary is responsible for this, doesn't it put her in a somewhat ambivalent position? After all, is freeing humanity from our control worth this?'

'Maybe she's obsessed.'

'I distrust fanatics of any sort. They are liable to do the most bizarre things.'

The Witness stares at the frozen scene of Butcher Island, unwilling to let it go. Then he wipes it away, and the table-top is blank again. He frowns, and sits back in his chair. Slowly he takes two black balls from his suit pocket and starts juggling them in one hand, still frowning.

The Speaker stands. 'It's your turn, I believe.'

'I don't like the way that implant is interfering,' the Witness says curtly. 'Those mirrors. Clumsy stuff.'

'Really? I find it is adding something extra to the Game. The unexpected.'

'You want the unexpected? Just wait for my turn.'

'It will be hard to surpass my mourning statue.'

'We'll see.'

'Until then.' The Speaker vanishes.

The Witness drops both balls to the floor, where they disappear. He stares at the table-top for a minute, then wipes it again.

The face of Poor Tom appears, grinning.

'Why haven't you been in touch?' the Witness demands.

'I'm not in!'

'What?'

'I'm not in at the moment! Can I take a message?'

'Are you serious?' the Witness says, shaking his head. 'Things are getting delicate. I need to talk.'

'I'm not in a message! Can I take a moment?'

The Witness stares disgustedly at the chattering face.

'I'm not a moment! Can I take a massage?'

Angrily, he reaches into the table-top, his hand sinking into the image. He gropes around impatiently at first, then incredulously. 'There's nothing there,' he says aloud.

'Massage the marmoset! It can't ache!'

He seizes the edges of the table and folds them over, smothering the image. As if he were working with dough, he kneads it into a ball.

The ball gets smaller and smaller as he works, and finally there is a dull noise, like the breaking of a vase full of water.

The Witness tosses the small ball over his shoulder. When it hits the wall it is slowly absorbed.

Deliberately, the Witness sits in his chair again, and places his lightly clenched fists on his thighs. His eyes look into the far, far distance.

22

'The mirrors were your idea?'

Caliban and Corby walked, side by side. He found he was more comfortable that way. It had nothing to do with her at all.

She didn't look at him. Instead, she kept her eyes on the horizon. 'Well, not really. I just saw the direction of the game and gave it a little push.'

'How?'

'Can you tell me how you filter toxins from your bloodstream? How you keep your balance on a shifting surface?' Her voice was mild. 'More to the point, how do you raise your arm?'

He scuffed a foot through the dirt and glanced at what loomed on the horizon.

Their destination.

It had appeared suddenly in the distance. Its shape was obvious: a massive truncated pyramid. Caliban shuddered if he looked at it for too long; it seemed to underline the fabricated nature of this world as nothing else did. It stood there, not resembling anything natural at all. A blatant construct. It was an act of casual arrogance to allow the pyramid to dominate the land, casting its shadow.

'My arm? How do I move my arm?' He paused,

flexing his muscles, then snorted. 'Just think about it and it moves. That's all.'

'You think about it? You picture the moves your muscles have to make? The way the joint has to move?'

He shook his head. 'Cut it out. I just do it, is all.'

She grinned. 'That's right, Caliban. You catch on. Eventually. I mean, as long as someone hits you with a brick, or something. You don't think about moving your arm, you just do it! Same as me. Palmer didn't bother to tell me about all the stuff he programmed into me. Just whenever I need to use it, it's like breathing, is all.'

'And that's it?'

'Sure. I'm connected to you, don't forget. We're all in your brain, somewhere. So I have access to the channels the Primes have established.' She paused and frowned. 'As long as I'm sneaky, that is. I figured you needed to sort things out for yourself, so I disappeared for a while. And then the land of mirrors came and seemed like a good idea at the time ... '

He found his canteen and offered her a drink. She gulped noisily, and wiped her mouth with the back of her hand. He looked at her and said, 'You were worried.'

She frowned. 'Who wouldn't have been? You were in a bad way. I thought I was losing you, and all. You didn't know who you were, which was seriously bad news for all concerned.' She looked at him. 'So I decided to fade away and let you see for yourself.'

'The mirrors.'

'That's right. Look, this whole place operates on a level of parable and analogy. Sometimes it bypasses your conscious mind, right? Symbols and stuff like that. So I set up a little scene that would help you find out about yourself.'

'You did all that?'

'Mmmm. Mostly. Some of it didn't quite turn out like I planned, really. I mean, no-one seems to have total control around here. I wonder how it keeps any sort of integrity at all.'

He didn't answer. They wandered on, skirting saltbush, always pressing towards the heart of the country.

She let him walk in silence. He appreciated the chance to think.

He frowned. 'It's getting pretty crowded in here.' He tapped his head. 'You. Palmer. Me.'

'There's more room than you think. Remember he wiped your personality when he bought your body.'

That pulled him up short. 'Yeah, I forgot that. Plenty of room for a few lodgers.'

She came closer, but didn't look him in the eyes. 'Better get used to it, Caliban. Whatever you were is gone. Make the most of what you've got left.'

'Caretaker? Nice job if you can get it.'

She shrugged. 'Seems to me that you've developed a bit beyond that. The more you use yourself, the better you get.'

'Uh huh.'

'The past is gone. Let it go.'

He nodded, but wasn't convinced. 'Let's make some

distance before nightfall,' he said, and Corby nodded.

* * *

Night found them huddled against a struggling stand of mallee. Caliban looked up and the stars were in motion, wheeling across the skies in a pattern that looked vaguely familiar. 'Look,' he said, and his breath hung white in the air.

'They're dancing,' she said. 'A pavane. See? Look how they change places.'

He nodded, forgetting she couldn't see him in the dark. 'I can't hear the music.'

'That doesn't matter,' she said. 'They can.'

* * *

The beginning of the day had a warm and weary feel, as if it had been used too many times. After a sparse breakfast of canned pears, they set off with their destination clearly ahead.

'Was slipping, I was,' he said as they went. 'Found it hard to hold onto *me*.' He glanced at her as they negotiated a small rise. The plain rolled on ahead blandly disinterested.

'I know. Palmer was emerging, trying to displace you. It was his plan, you know. All the time.'

'He was hiding.' It was a statement, but Corby took it as a query.

'Yep. He knew the Primes were after him, figured he had to disappear. So he did it the best way he knew how.'

Caliban skirted a clump of saltbush. 'He was a bastard, but he was a brave bastard.'

She laughed bitterly, the sound loud in the still air.

'I don't think he even considered it mightn't work. I mean, the word arrogant was invented for someone who was pale imitation of Palmer. It wasn't brave. It was cost efficient.'

'He left his own body behind. Took some guts.'

Dry brown grass rustled underfoot as they walked. 'I figure he mustn't have been that close to it in the first place, if you see what I mean,' Corby said. 'Like, he just up and left it there for the security people to find and all, so's everyone would think he was dead. I reckon the fallout from that little fiasco is still raining down at Palmer Institute. I mean, the whole security operation was dead in the water after the head honcho was found to have corpsed himself, naturally.' She paused. 'I don't suppose that Palmer even gave them a thought.'

Caliban had a brief memory-flash of the head of security. Did she have a family? Friends? Was she thrown onto the streets?

'But how'd he do it all alone?'

'Give him credit, he was inventive when the chips were down. OK, he must have had some native cunning, and he seemed to be able to winnow through other peoples' work and bring stuff together that no-one had seen before. I suppose that's a kind of genius, really. And when he had self-interest as a motivator, he really got going.

'Seems as though he raided all his researchers' work, breaking computer security codes they thought unbreakable, snatching at anything that he thought would help him. Like, no-one had really tried templating and storing a whole personality, even though it was basically an extension of the brain-wiping programs. It was just that he had access to the latest organic storage media, with virtually unlimited holding space. Once he had that, the rest was easy.'

'Especially getting a body.'

She kicked at a pebble. 'Sure. Nothing new there. People had been selling themselves for ages. Not even strictly illegal anymore. Just set up a contract naming the beneficiaries, then a quick brain wipe, and away we go. No questions asked of the buyer, of course. None of their business, really, what was done with the body after they'd signed it over. He just made sure he got someone from the other side of the country, so they wouldn't be recognised walking around. It'd sort of ruin things if people you didn't know kept coming up to you and asking where you'd been and all . . .

'Palmer just buried himself in your brain, giving you enough personality to survive on the streets until it was time for him to emerge.'

'And he installed you.'

She grinned wryly. 'Guardian angel, that's me.'

They walked in silence for a time. Then Caliban saw a dark shape swooping. Shielding his eyes from the sun with one hand, he saw that it was a large flock of small birds. They moved together, wheeling left, then right, in a sinuous movement over the plain. They wove past, almost within reach, metallic squawks filling the air, and Caliban saw they were yellow-green budgerigars. Tracking just above the ground, they faded into the distance.

'There must be water around here somewhere then, at least,' Corby remarked. 'Budgies're never far from it.'

Caliban tapped his canteen. 'Good. We need it.'

* * *

The next morning, Caliban woke with a head that felt over-inflated.

'What's wrong?' Corby asked. She crawled over and peered at him, resting on all fours. Her hair was dusty and she ran a hand through it without much success.

He raised his head from his hands, wincing. 'Lemme be,' he mumbled. 'Head's just a demolition site, is all.'

'Want a bet? That's Palmer acting up, if I know anything.' She shook his shoulders and looked in his eyes. 'He won't want to damage the body permanently. Hopes to live in it, after all. So he'll just try to drive you mad.'

He grinned, but the slight movement made him feel nauseated. His mouth filled with saliva. 'Thanks a lot. I knew there was a bright side.'

'That's OK. It's my job to reassure you.' She reached out, took him by the chin, and gripped hard. 'Fight him, Caliban. Affirm your identity, if you want to keep it.' She tightened her hold, then released it suddenly and he almost fell forward. 'Come on, time's wasting.'

'That's one way to put it. Look at the heart.'

He held up his forearm. The tattoo was the colour of old lead.

'It's not black any more,' Corby observed.

'Thanks. It helps when you point out the obvious.' She flinched, and immediately he regretted his words. 'Sorry. Didn't mean it. Got a head the size of a pumpkin, feels like. It's making me touchy.'

'Don't worry,' she said. She stood and dusted herself off. 'We'll make it.'

Gingerly, he got to his feet. He rubbed his face and wished he felt halfway human. 'They got something against machines?'

'The Primes?'

'Yeah. This whole world's so low-tech, they must be making some sort of point.'

'Thinking of anything in particular?'

'I'd kill for a jeep,' he said as they set off. 'Sick of all this walking.'

She nodded. 'Palmer always said that the Primes were ambivalent about their status. They love being non-physical, but they like the idea of the flesh. Thwarted romantics, some of them.'

'Does that make sense?'

'Look, remember where they came from. Whatever they think, they've come from humanity. People created them; they didn't spring from the ether.'

He nodded. 'I'd still kill for a jeep.'

As they marched, Caliban's head throbbed with each step. It was as if Palmer were beating against the inside of his skull with a hammer, trying to get out. Caliban couldn't get rid of the memory of that Cheshire Cat grin, waiting. He gritted his teeth, and trudged on.

Passing through the brown land, he became aware

of Corby's worried glances. She rarely spoke, but occasionally reached out and touched his arm or shoulder. He allowed her to direct him, and simply concentrated on putting one foot in front of the other.

Each step began to jar, thundering in his head. At times he found himself staring at the fading heart on his arm, wondering how long it was going to last. His vision became blurred and wavery, misted blood-red growing bloodier with every pounding footstep. He felt as if he was walking through an abattoir.

Much later, Corby had to put a hand on his chest to stop him. 'Caliban, time to rest. Lunchtime.' The words seemed to come through a heavy fog, and when he stopped his knees buckled. She caught him with wiry strength, and manoeuvred him until he had his back to a small bloodwood. It provided thin shade.

She stripped off her pack, and then his.

'Food?' she asked.

He waved the can away, not even looking. 'No, thanks.' His voice was hoarse and painful.

'Bad?' she said. He waved a hand, not opening his eyes.

He could hear the small noises that said she was close—skin on fabric, a sigh, the sound of spoon on metal—but nothing else. It was profoundly still around them. He turned to speak, but as he did his hand slipped and his elbow gave way. He tried to catch his balance, but his tiredness got in the way. He fell, and his head bounced off the iron-hard ground.

'Caliban!' Corby cried. For a frozen instant, he saw

her reaching out, her hand silhouetted against the harsh blue sky.

Stunned, he felt himself falling into blackness. As he dropped, a presence pushed past him, all anger and spite. *Out of my way*! it bellowed.

Dizzily, he tried to steady himself. He felt sick, and closed his eyes.

When he opened them, he was looking out through a window at Corby's face. He heard a voice. He felt it coming from his own throat, but it was not his voice.

'Well hello. How's about giving your boss a hand?'

With a shock he realised he was a prisoner. Palmer had taken over.

He gathered himself and tried to batter his way out of his prison. Push, Caliban. You want to stay in here? With that guy in charge of your body? Forget it!

For an instant he felt himself rising, but then he slammed into a black ceiling.

He felt Palmer wince. *Cut it out, Caliban. Fade away, will you? You shouldn't even still be around, you realise that? But I can put up with you until you lose hold and disappear. Nothing to it.*

Caliban felt giddy as the landscape swept past, and he realised that Palmer was turning around. When things settled down, he was looking at Corby.

Her face was grim, and she had a wisp of hair caught in the corner of her mouth. She freed it impatiently. 'Palmer.' It was a statement, not a question.

'Of course. It was only a matter of time.' After scrambling onto the bank, he stood and gloated. 'My, my, haven't we come a long way? I astound myself sometimes, really. I mean, what started off as a simple hidden watch-dog program has really blossomed. I'm impressed all over again with my ingenuity.'

'Where's Caliban?'

'Don't you worry about that, my dear. Look at your shape! Where did that come from? I can't remember filing somatypes into your parameters. You must have rifled a preferred body shape from the caretaker's memory.'

'Caretaker?'

'Caliban. A perfect name for a fool who is ousted by a superior being.'

She turned away and her head dropped. 'What're you going to do?'

He was close to her now. 'I have an appointment to keep. Really, it's much the same direction as you were going anyway.' He paused. 'You see, I think we're headed to the source of the Prime Intelligences.' He chuckled. 'In a symbolic sense, of course. I think that the Primes have arranged themselves at our destination. Their heart, so to speak, in the heart of this land.' He reached out a hand. 'We're headed towards the giants' castle, the Heart of the Country.' She shivered when his hand touched her shoulder. 'I think it's time to pay them a visit. I have a present for them, a little surprise. You see, I arranged things so the caretaker would get involved in the Game. It was the best way to get close to the Primes.'

'But, Caliban's heart's there . . . '

'Don't worry. That's just part of the Game. It's the

scenario they put together to play. It has no real relevance.'

'But Caliban will die if he doesn't get it back.'

'Just let me worry about that. After all, I'm not Caliban.'

Corby stepped away from him, shrugging his hand from her shoulder. 'Fine. Go ahead. I hope you'll be happy together.'

'Oh, no, my dear. *We'll* be happy together. I've admired the way you've helped this body come so far.'

She whirled, fists clenched. 'Forget it, buster. I've had enough. I have no interest in you or your plans, whatsoever. Leave me alone.'

Caliban shuddered in his black prison, as Palmer laughed. 'Now, now . . . remember just who you're talking to, my dear. This free will is all very well, but enough is enough. Check it out. I still have override access, which I think is wonderfully foresighted of me. I think I'm quite looking forward to using it.'

Her face went white. Caliban saw her freckles standing out clearly, and he tried to cry out to her. *Corby*, he called silently. *I'm still here*! He hurled himself in all directions, and was pleased when he felt Palmer stop in his tracks.

Corby whispered, her voice breathy. 'No. I won't. I don't want to.'

'Of course you do,' Palmer said. 'Come here.'

Corby stood there, trembling, trying to assert herself against her programming. 'No.'

'I said, 'Come here and I meant it.' He held out his hand.

Corby took a step back. Caliban thought she would break at any moment. 'No. I don't want you.'

Caliban felt rage building up in Palmer. The body became tense, and it began to breathe faster. One hand curled into a fist.

'No?' snarled Palmer. 'You don't *want* to?'

With a bound, he grabbed Corby by the arm. His fingers clamped onto her cruelly, but she dropped to one knee and twisted free, leaving him sprawling in the dust.

Palmer got up spitting. 'Come here!' he snarled, and lunged.

Corby turned side-on to his charge and slid her shoulder under his armpit. Palmer tumbled over with a roar. She helped him—with a well-placed kick to the back of his knee.

Palmer staggered as Corby skipped aside and faced him. Her eyes were wary, but unafraid. 'Don't you defy me! I made you!' Palmer stuttered, and immediately Caliban sensed a lightening of his dark prison. 'You, you, you . . . '

Palmer rushed at Corby and she evaded him easily. She tripped him again, and his chin slammed into the ground. Pain battered at Caliban's black prison, but strangely it helped to lift the gloom. Corby squatted on her heels, forearms on knees, and studied Palmer as if she were watching a slug.

Palmer stood. He'd lost all power of speech and simply screamed: a long red sound, like raw meat. Control was a thing of the past.

The sound went on and on and as it did, cracks

appeared in Caliban's prison. Light began to seep in, and he seized his chance.

With Palmer's anger at its peak, Caliban pushed.

It was like pushing against a strong wind. He leaned into it, hunching against the resistance, trying to force his way.

He saw, as if through frosted glass, Palmer staggering towards Corby. She was backpedalling neatly.

Suddenly, Caliban had hands. He seized the blackness and tore his way through. *I'm coming*! he shouted, and felt a gale in his face.

No! a voice wailed, and the gale increased. Caliban felt as if he were on the edge of a vast crevasse, teetering as the wind tried to carry him back into the abyss. As he balanced there, a presence was sucked past and disappeared into the blackness. *No*! the voice shrieked.

Then it was gone, leaving Caliban struggling against the wind.

Suddenly, Caliban felt a hand on his. 'Caliban.' Corby looked into his eyes. 'Caliban.'

He blinked. 'Corby.'

He was back.

She eased him to the ground as his knees gave way. 'How'd you know?' he croaked.

She shrugged. 'It's in the eyes,' she said. 'I think.' Frowning, she looked closely into his eyes. 'You OK? How'd you get out?'

'Don't know ... ' he began. Then he remembered—the noise, the feeling of his body as an automaton. 'Control,' he said. 'He lost control.' He stood, dusting off his hands. His chin felt raw, and his knee ached. He tapped his head. Gently. 'It's a battle for the high ground in here. When I hit my head, Palmer took his chance.' His palms were bleeding, and he began to pick small pieces of sand from the grazes. 'When you didn't do what he asked, he just lost control. I was there, waiting.' He paused. 'You were trying to make him so angry he'd forget himself, right?'

'Maybe.' She grinned. 'Actually, it wasn't as simple as that. I was put on the spot, when he expected me to do what he wanted, just like that! I couldn't believe it. I suppose I've got used to thinking for myself.'

He shrugged, and stretched his shoulders. 'Never said you aren't useful.'

'Thanks. That's all I've ever wanted. "Useful"—don't go overboard with the praise, now.'

'Credit where credit's due,' he said absently. 'Besides, my knee's sore where you kicked it.'

'Seemed to do the job,' Corby grinned. 'How's your head?'

He winced. 'Don't ask.'

'That bad?'

'It's just that I'd forgotten about it until you asked. So next time, don't ask. Please.'

Corby nodded, and then gestured with her head. 'Time to go?'

He looked up instinctively, despite knowing the sun to be unreliable. 'May as well. There's not much point staying here, wasting time.'

It took him some time to find his pack. It had been

kicked behind some loose brush during the fight. He dusted it off and stuffed his jacket into it. Corby watched him impatiently, fiddling with her own pack straps.

'You in a hurry?' he asked.

'Nope,' she said. 'But you are. Look.'

She pointed at his bare arm. 'Yeah,' he said. 'I'm losing weight.'

'It's no joke,' she frowned. 'I think it's fading faster.'

'Everything fades. It's a condition of living.'

'OK then, we'll just take it easy.'

23

Dune country. Completely barren, as if life had simply dried up and blown away, unable to cope with existence in the desert. Maybe life didn't belong here, Caliban decided.

'Tell us more about yourself, Caliban,' Corby said as she skirted a dried-out clump of spinifex. She looked a little worn, but grimly determined. 'Define yourself by your past. You never know when it might come in handy.'

He was silent. What's worth knowing? he wondered. Who's to judge? 'Don't know where to start,' he muttered.

'Don't spare the details. What'd you like to eat? How've you spent your life? How'd you manage to survive when zillions of others can't? Do you like music? Who did you love?' Her voice was wistful, and Caliban understood. He may have only a few years of memories, but Corby had none.

'Food. I mean, why not choose something more important?'

'Humour me, bozo. Food's important. It's all about taste, and personal preferences and dislikes and stuff. All those stupid things that make people people.'

He stumbled, and a cloud of red dust rose briefly,

before settling. 'Ate hawker food mostly. The roadside stalls are a good place to pick up gossip, meet people. Extra chilli sauce makes the eating interesting. Hot enough to scald a cat.'

She made a face. 'Unhygienic, but.'

'Least of my worries, really. I figured that there were plenty of ways to slip off besides food poisoning. Besides, dirt's God's way of keeping soapmakers in business.'

'You didn't cook for yourself, then?'

'Did for a while. Too inconvenient. Couldn't always get ingredients, or store them properly. Moved around a lot, remember? You try carting a bag of Maldive fish in a suitcase. It's a good way of causing a major biological hazard.'

'Is that how you survived? Moving around?'

Caliban glanced at her and grinned. 'Never really thought about it. I just got restless if I stayed in one place too long.'

'Maybe Palmer planted that in you.'

He frowned. 'Maybe it was part of me.'

'Sorry. I didn't mean to . . . '

'It's OK. It made sense to move around, anyway. Harder to hit a moving target and all that. Out there it seemed wise to cultivate a healthy paranoia. Maybe no-one was out to get me, but who could tell? Mostly people only find out when it's too late.'

She was quiet for a time. 'It was like that, was it?'

'That's how it felt. Like fish in a coral reef: plenty of colour and movement, but every so often a shark comes along and takes one away. Not even bones left behind.'

'Was there anything good about it?'

The question struck him. Was there? He remembered faces, voices. 'The life? Not much. Sure, the planet's in better shape than it's been for ages, maybe calmer ... but there's only so much to go around, it puts pressure on everything. The people though ... I cruised through life, but still ran into people who I can't forget. Survivors and victims mostly, but some individuals too. Even in tough times people show the best and worst things about being human.'

The pounding inside his head worsened and Caliban rubbed his brow. It felt tender. Corby noticed. 'Bad?'

He winced. 'Bad enough. But I've learned to appreciate it. It's like learning to live with a vibrosaw working on your skull.'

'No pain, no gain,' she said airily, skipping a few steps.

'What about lots of pain, no gain?' he wondered, but she ignored him. He sighed, and followed her.

The pyramid beckoned as they walked on, sitting squatly on the horizon like an old post-modernist office block. They took turns urging the other on, trying to make some mark on the implacable distance ahead of them.

At a rest stop near a ring of old stones, they drank sparingly. While Corby sipped, Caliban sat back and massaged his temples. Then, frowning, he jabbed a finger at their destination. 'They've got a thing about size, don't they?' he said. 'If they were human, I'd say it was a sign of insecurity. Or some sort of macho complex.'

Corby deliberately scuffed up sand, and scowled at the dust. 'It's hard to understand just how the Primes see things. They're alien, really.' She rubbed her nose. 'I know that originally they were designed to be intelligent in the same way humans are, but that isn't the way it worked out. They live differently, so they must think differently. Most of the time they exist in the Net, with their consciousness divided a hundred different ways. If people tried to live like that they'd go crazy. When the Primes get down to operate in real time, in a physical world, it's no wonder their sense of proportion is inflated.'

'You mean they see this as a physical world?' Caliban grinned despite his headache.

Corby scowled. 'You know what I mean. This is as close as they get to operating on a physical level, anyway. It's like they need it, or something. It might be the one thing they envy.'

Caliban grimaced. Envy? He'd never thought of the Primes as envious. Petty, spiteful, powerful, yes. Cunning and inscrutable even. But envious?

The pyramid appeared to be expecting them. A luminous haze hung on its heights, growing in size and radiance as they slogged up and down the sand dunes. Caliban found it difficult to make out just what the haze was, as it shifted and moved whenever he tried to pin it down. Sometimes he thought it was pure white, but at other times it seemed as if it was streaked with iridescence, a misty mother-of-pearl.

Time stretched and wore, like old clothes, as Caliban and Corby forced themselves on. They began a ritual at every rest stop. While she drank, he'd roll up his sleeve and they'd examine the tattoo closely. At every stop, a little more colour was missing, as the heart faded away.

Every minute was precious.

And with every step, the pounding in his head grew worse. 'I give up,' he said suddenly, as they stood on the crest of a worn, red dune. He moistened his lips. 'It's their world. Let 'em have it.'

Corby stopped and glared at him. 'It's *not* their world. They may control it, but only through default. People just let things slide, taking the easy options, allowing the Primes to take charge of more and more!' She threw up her hands and started pacing back and forwards. 'Stuff me, but they weren't even ambitious! At first anyway. They were just willing, that's all. And look what's happened. Don't abdicate your responsibilities!' She turned and gripped him by the shoulders, shaking him as if he were a doll. 'Don't abdicate your responsibilities!'

Caliban was astounded by her fierceness. Responsibilities? There were no responsibilities on the street. Looking after number one wasn't a philosophy, it was a way of life.

But he couldn't forget. The faces stayed with him—Laydown Sally and Spiroula, with her blind but knowing eyes.

Was he responsible for them?

And what about Corby? Cocky, enduring,

belligerent Corby? He knew he never would've made it this far without her. Her fierceness had sustained him, and she'd allowed him to draw on it. 'What's going to happen to you?' he wondered aloud.

It took her aback. The anger dropped from her face, to be replaced by a mixture of concern and surprise. 'That's not the point,' she began, but Caliban cut her short.

'Palmer made you. You remade yourself. But what'll happen when this is all over?'

Her mouth quirked upwards in a rueful smile. 'Over? Who knows?' She frowned and dropped her gaze. 'I think it might depend on what happens to you.'

Caliban's calves protested as he stumbled and slid down the face of the dune. His boots filled with sand, but he'd long grown resigned to stopping and emptying them between each dune. Sliding awkwardly, he flung out a hand to steady himself. The sand was cool and fine, and occasionally he came across patches that were as fluid as talcum.

'No sand in your boots?' he asked Corby, as she joined him at the bottom of the dune.

She smiled smugly. 'You only get sand in your boots if you're clumsy, right? Just pick your feet up, and it's no problem.'

With one movement she was up and off. He was left alone. As he watched her scramble up the dune, he wondered at her loyalty. She'd grown past her programming and yet she chose to stay. What did that mean for him?

He crawled up the slope. He knew that there was a reticence in him, a hesitation to form an attachment that he might later regret. It was the way he'd always lived, moving on whenever things began to tie him down. Things and people.

It was a void inside him, it always made him feel incomplete in some fundamental way.

'Hold on!' he called, just before she disappeared over the top of the dune. 'Don't leave me behind!'

She stood on the summit, hands on hips. Then slowly, she held out a hand to him. 'Come on then!'

Awkwardly, he climbed the slope until he stood next to her. She grinned as she caught his hand. 'There. That wasn't so bad, was it?'

'Nope. I might be getting used to it.'

* * *

Much later, towards the bottom of one wickedly sloping dune, Caliban stumbled and fell.

'It's getting tough, right?' Her face was concerned as she helped him up.

'Nope. It's like having a sonic drill inside your skull. That's all. Nothing I can't handle.' He dusted himself off and adjusted his pack, then put a hand to his head. His brow felt tight and stretched, and for an instant he felt as if he were being torn apart by a tug of war.

'Can you manage?'

He sighed. 'I'll have to. Unless anyone wants to manage for me.'

Caliban staggered off, and Corby trotted by his side. 'What can I do?'

He bent, took a deep breath, and began to struggle up the slope. 'Talk to me,' he said.

She stayed by his side, within arm's length. 'Talk? About what?'

Sand trickled from under his feet. 'Whatever. Whatever you like,' he panted. 'Tell me about you.'

There was silence for a time.

Corby trudged ahead, hands in the pockets of her jacket. Eventually she spoke up, choosing her words carefully. 'There's not much to say, really. I can really only remember from when I met you.'

'I have that sort of effect on people. Most people look on meeting me as a landmark in their lives.'

She ignored him. 'You could say that in some ways I'm defined by you.'

He grimaced. 'But I'm hardly defined, myself. I'm partial, remember? Bits and pieces, slapped together.'

'I know. That's why I want to hear about what you can remember. It helps to fill me in.' She paused. 'We need each other.'

Caliban nodded. He realised Corby wasn't so much searching for herself, but finding whether she had a self to search for. If all aspects of her personality were defined by the needs of other people, what was left? Corby was reaching out to him for something fundamental, something basic to her understanding of herself. He'd been so obsessed with his own internal battles that he hadn't noticed her anxiety.

'I've been selfish,' he said. 'Sorry.'

She grimaced. 'Don't be.'

'No, I mean it. This whole thing's designed to make

me think about myself. It adds a whole new meaning to the idea of being self-centred.'

Together, they reached the crest and plunged downwards, feet first. 'It's just a game,' she reminded him, without much conviction.

'I know, I know. And all the world's a stage, too. Doesn't help much.' He looked ahead, shading his eyes. He didn't stop walking. The motion had become second nature. Leaning forward going up, leaning back going down, picking up feet and putting them down.

'See how sharp the horizon is?' he asked Corby.

She glanced up, and nodded. 'Uh huh. Clear cut.'

'It's like the whole thing ends there. Chopped off.'

'Probably is. Not that it makes any difference.'

* * *

'Caliban.'

They'd reached the bottom of another dune. The interdune valley here was relatively well vegetated, with clumps of spinifex and even a tangled thicket of stunted mulga.

Caliban paused and shook himself. 'Corby.'

'Your face. You meaning to do that?' She peered into his eyes, frowning.

'Do what?' he asked, puzzled.

She reached out as if to touch his cheek, but stopped uncertainly. 'You were grimacing,' she continued. 'Well, not grimacing exactly. It was more like your face was writhing, or something. You kept screwing it up into all sorts of expressions. Not very happy ones, mostly.'

Exhausted, he sat on a mulga trunk that was virtually growing along the ground. He searched for his canteen and slowly drank two mouthfuls. 'Sorry. No idea what you're talking about.'

She reached out and plucked a leaf. Methodically, she shredded it and let the pieces fall at her feet. 'I mean, it was like your face had a life of its own. Your mouth pulled back, then opened and shut and stuff. Your eyebrows were moving, eyes screwing up . . . but you kept walking all the time. I thought you were going to say something, but you didn't.'

'How long was this going on? My face, I mean.'

'Only five minutes. Give or take. As soon as I said your name, it stopped. It was like you woke up.'

Caliban knew she was right. It had been like sleepwalking. He felt a chill when he realised what that could mean.

'It's Palmer,' he said. 'He's trying again. And I'm giving him too many chances.'

Corby's leaf was a skeleton. She twirled it in her fingers briefly and then flung it away. She wiped her hands on her shorts. 'Thought so. I mean, you reminded me of him and all. It was like he was trying to break out all over your face.'

He nodded. 'It helps if I think of him as a bad case of acne.' He sighed. 'Haven't been careful enough. It's been too methodical, too rhythmical. I have to keep control instead of drifting.'

'Talk more. Keep your mind off it.'

'Walk and talk. May as well make some progress.'

The sand ridges were now thirty metres high,

humpbacked like whales. There was no wind. The whole world was still and quiet. The air felt thin and stretched, as if it were being pulled in so many different directions that it stayed motionless.

'I don't think it's going to rain,' she said suddenly.

'No.'

'I mean, the air's so dry. No clouds.'

'Can't you do any better?' he said, adjusting the strap of his pack.

'What?'

'Social niceties. Weather talk. I mean, of all the useless sort of stuff you could talk about here . . . '

'And you're Mr Conversation?' she said, glaring. 'Take a good look at yourself. If you can stomach it.'

They trudged in silence. Caliban's feet felt like pieces of meat. 'Sorry,' he said.

'Tell you what,' Corby said, closing her eyes. 'Let's not say that word any more. Let's take it as read that we're sorry, and we don't have to say it again.'

He grimaced. 'I don't say it for me. I say it for you.'

She looked at him for a moment. 'That's the nicest thing anyone's ever said to me.'

They pressed on, making a tiny imprint on the land. The dunes loomed and receded, loomed and receded, and Caliban's head ached with each step.

'What about New Worlds?' Corby asked suddenly, breaking the silence.

He looked sharply at her. 'What can I say? Inhuman? Cruel? Evil? A hoax like that . . . people *believed* in New Worlds. It was their only hope, their reason for going on. The whole thing seemed like something noble and worthwhile, a chance for everyone. And it's just a way of managing the population . . . '

'So Palmer's right to be afraid of the Primes?'

'Only someone with no brain wouldn't be afraid of the Primes. Power like that? It's scary.' He wiped his face with his hand. 'But we have to stay angry. Or else we'll just go under.' He spat on the ground. 'Their strategies include wholesale slaughter as an efficient management technique.'

'What if it works?'

Caliban looked at Corby to see if she were serious. She grinned. 'Devil's advocate?' he asked.

'Keeps your mind occupied,' she agreed.

'OK. The biosphere's in reasonably good shape. The Primes have pulled things back from the edge in the last fifty years. On average, we all have enough to eat. At least, no-one actually dies of starvation, unless they're really unlucky.' He looked up at the sky, squinting. 'But we've handed over our lives to machines. We're stagnating now, neatly managed into blandness. Life's not great, but it could be worse. Are we supposed to thank them for that?'

'Maybe.'

'But why don't they really do a New Worlds project? They've got the power to do it right. Maybe it's because they've got no imagination.'

Suddenly, he was thrown forward by a violent jerk of his shoulders. 'Caliban!' called Corby, and she caught him as he started to slip.

He shook his head, but that made things worse. 'It's

all right. A cramp, that's all. Too much climbing.'

Corby looked skeptical, but said nothing.

* * *

They slept whenever they couldn't continue. The erratic progress of the sun across the sky meant they often slept in bright sunshine, or in the scant shade thrown by the dunes.

Caliban always woke feeling exhausted. He felt wrung out and worn, and his eyes were raw and gritty.

Increasingly, he was conscious of being under seige. Palmer hammered at him unmercifully. Gone were the attempts at persuasion or negotiation. Instead, Palmer attacked. Apart from causing the constant headaches, Palmer cunningly found ways to bypass Caliban's control of his own body.

At times Caliban suffered helplessly as his arms and legs flailed wildly, independently, throwing him down dunes like a rag doll. Once he was hurled across the floor of an interdune valley, jerking uncontrollably in a *grand mal* seizure, scattering dry spinifex and dust. He was totally conscious during the whole episode. As he lay there, frothing and gnashing, Corby shaded him from the sun.

At unpredictable intervals Palmer tampered with Caliban's temperature control, and he'd find himself shivering or sweating madly, and often both in quick succession.

Caliban fought to maintain his control, talking to Corby, but the monotony of their travel sent him drifting, and it was then that Palmer was likely to strike, trying to wrench control when Caliban was distracted.

Eventually they came to the end of the dune country. Weary, fading, and in pain, but stubbornly surviving.

Together, they stood on the second-last dune. Caliban rolled up his sleeve.

'Still there?' Corby asked.

'A ghost,' Caliban said, as he held up the outline of the heart. It was faint and grey. 'The ghost heart lives on. Let's go.'

24

'It doesn't belong here,' murmured Corby. 'It's wrong.'

The pyramid was enormous, but Caliban wasn't impressed. He understood he'd been changed by the trek across the painful wilderness of the Shared Creation. He felt as if his soul had been enlarged. At first he'd felt insignificant, dwarfed by the land, as if he could be plucked from its surface at any minute and leave no trace or loss at all. But then, from within that despair, he realised that despite his insignificance, he'd endured.

It was a turning point. His whole being seemed to re-orient itself, re-align itself according to some new bearing. It was a kind of peace, an acceptance of his own standing, but it was also a resolution. When he looked over his shoulder, he could see their tracks stretching back into the uncertain distance. Endurance. Maybe that was the quality that gave him a chance.

'Road,' Caliban said, pointing.

Below, a dirt track began, gun-barrel straight, leading to their forbidding destination.

As they skidded down the last dune, a cascade of sand trickled down Caliban's collar, into his shirt. Corby chuckled as he groped around, trying to get it out. He grinned at her, and he realised that he hadn't laughed for a long time. 'I'll dust off your back,' he offered.

When she turned, he felt dizzy. His stomach rolled awkwardly and he thought he was going to be ill. He clutched at Corby as he dropped to his knees, sweating.

She turned quickly. 'It's OK,' she said, kneading his shoulders. 'It's OK.' Soon, she lapsed into wordless humming, rocking backwards and forwards. As Caliban fought against the Palmer-inspired nausea, he allowed himself to relax against her, trusting in her strength to support him.

'Somewhere,' he murmured. 'Somewhere this body must have loved someone. Poor bastard.'

She hushed him. 'I know.'

'I can feel it. The body remembers. Feeling you close like this, it remembers.'

'Yes.' She held him close, and he felt her breath on his skin.

For a time they were still and silent, enjoying the closeness.

'Sometimes, I think about the life this body used to have,' Caliban began again. 'It was a kid, it grew up, did stuff. All that's gone now. Rubbed out.'

Looking up, he could see that Corby's eyes were focussed in the distance. She looked tired but relaxed. 'Yes. There is no past.'

'So I have to give this body a future.'

'Yes.'

'And you too?'

She nodded absently then looked closely at him.

'For different reasons. No past for me either. But I aim to have a future, too.'

'A future?'

She didn't look away. 'You bet your life.'

* * *

The road was packed hard. There were no corrugations or potholes, no sign of vegetation on the verges. The gravel beneath their feet crunched as they walked.

No matter how he tried, Caliban couldn't break the connection between his footsteps and the pounding in his head. He tried to vary the length of his strides, but too soon he found himself falling in with the beat in his skull. 'Give up, give up, give up,' it seemed to say, and he gritted his teeth against the demand.

Corby was determinedly cheerful, sensing his inner battle. She chatted brightly, asking questions, some trivial and some profound. She forced him into conversation, throwing out a lifeline for him to hold on to, anchoring him to a world of human interaction. At times he felt as if he were teetering, about to fall into total self-absorption.

He shuddered to think what would happen then.

'We're here.'

Corby's voice was flat and emotionless. Caliban realised that he'd been shuffling along with his head down, watching his feet drag over the gravel, step by step.

How long had it been? he wondered. He automatically looked at the tattoo. It was ghostly pale, a faint outline against his skin. We've been on the road forever, he thought. Or maybe longer.

Caliban lifted his head, and felt the muscles at the back of his neck stretch and complain. He closed his eyes.

When he opened them, he looked up. And up.

It was as if a vast wall was toppling onto him. In a clumsy gesture, he put up a hand to stop it falling.

'It's the pyramid, Caliban,' said Corby. 'We're here.'

Slowly, he dropped his arm. The wall reached up to heaven. Caliban could see clouds dragging against its summit, as they ambled across the washed-out sky. The surface of the pyramid was seamless, as if it were made of a single crystal tetrahedron, grown in place and then its top lopped off. In the sun it was a pale yellow, the colour of jaundice or old paper.

'We're here,' he repeated dully.

'Stairs start over there,' she said.

'Let's rest a while,' Caliban said. 'Maybe we can catch them off guard.' He slumped to the ground and without realising it, slipped into sleep . . .

YOU'RE FALLING APART! roared Palmer. *YOU'RE COMING TO PIECES! LET ME IN AND I'LL FIX IT*!

No! screamed Caliban. *Not by the hair of my chinny-chin-chin*!

IT'S NOT YOURS! I PAID FOR IT! YOU OWE FOR THE FLESH! YOU OWE!

I can't pay! I won't pay!

THEN I'LL HAVE TO COME AND TAKE IT BACK! I'LL HAVE YOU EVICTED! THE BEST

LEGAL MINDS IN THE COUNTRY ARE ON MY SIDE! YOU'LL NEVER WIN!

I will! I will! Will! Rock smashes scissors! Scissors cut paper! Paper covers rock!

* * *

Caliban woke with vivid recollections of being dismembered, slowly torn apart.

Slowly, he became aware of Corby's face peering down at him. For a moment he could not make out the expression. Was it concern? Fear? Tenderness?

'You were moaning,' she said, running a hand through her hair. 'I thought I'd let you sleep, but it didn't seem restful or anything.'

He was groggy from the nightmare. 'You stayed awake? Watching? Nothing else to do?'

She shrugged. 'It seemed like a good idea. Anyway, I wasn't tired.'

Her appearance said otherwise. She had dark circles under her eyes. Her skin had taken on a translucent quality. Caliban could make out the fine blue lines of veins in her wrists.

'Here, eat,' she said abruptly. She'd noticed his inspection, and wouldn't meet his eyes.

Although he didn't feel like food, he ate small bites of the hard biscuit that Corby jammed into his hand. It tasted like dust, but she assured him that it had all the necessary nutrients to sustain life. 'It says so on the packet,' she announced primly.

'I'll eat the packet then,' he said. 'Tastier, most likely.'

While he ate, he watched her take all the items out

of her pack, and arrange them on the ground. Knives, bottles, cans, wire implements, small jars, packets—all were neatly stacked in rows. She pursed her lips and frowned, cocking her head to one side as she studied the assortment. Then she stowed her pack again, carefully choosing the items one by one.

She didn't look at Caliban, but knew that his eyes were on her. 'It's simple. I'm just making efficient use of space, that's all. There's a place for everything in here. There's no need for stuff to rattle around aimlessly. It all belongs somewhere.' Her packing was relentless and determined, with the single-minded intensity of a surgeon or a bomb-disposal expert.

The repacking seemed like a ritual, and Caliban watched solemnly. Corby weighed items in her hand, while sizing others up. She gently touched things together, listening to the sounds that they made, nodding when they met her own obscure criteria.

She saw him watching. 'Everything belongs somewhere. Everything has its place,' she explained, and he nodded, understanding.

The job of repacking done, Caliban led the way to the stairs.

'How's your fear of heights?' she asked, as they stood contemplating the staircase.

'Why?'

'No handrail.'

'Guess I'll have to work on it then.'

The stairs sprang from the side of the pyramid, as if sprouting from the building like parasitic orchids growing on the trunk of a rainforest tree.

The treads seemed to be iron. They were grey, with a slight patina of rust, but smooth as if a thousand feet a day ran up and down them. There was a row of small holes spaced along the centre. For drainage, Caliban guessed.

The smooth wall of the pyramid sloped away from them disconcertingly. To Caliban, it was as if the whole world were tilted, and he found himself leaning towards the wall, drawn to it by a sense of the comfort of solid things.

He rubbed his jaw. It was aching, and he realised that he'd been grinding his teeth. When he put a finger to his mouth it came away bloody. 'Lay off the tongue, Palmer,' he muttered.

Control. Control was control. He concentrated on containing Palmer.

As he climbed the stairs, he worked on maintaining ownership of his body. He moved his muscles, feeling the motion under his skin. He rotated his shoulders, flexed his fingers into fists and uncurled them again. He rubbed his fingertips against the roughness of the zip of his jacket. He felt the tender parts of his feet, rubbing against his boots: ball of big toe, inside heel, top of instep.

It's my body. I like it. Leave it alone.

Corby led, and Caliban found himself focussing on her back. She had a small mole on the base of her neck, slightly off-centre.

'Talk to me, Caliban.' Her voice came to him over her shoulder. She didn't look around. 'This is so boring. Distract me.'

'I've run out of memories, bucko. The well's dry.'

'Don't give me that. You haven't started. You just don't realise what you've got in there.'

He licked his lips. His tongue felt thick. 'I . . . it's hard . . . ' He shook his head. 'Bits and pieces, that's all. Bits.'

She didn't slow down, rising and rising. 'Go on.'

'Fortune-tellers.' He groped for and found a fragment of recent memory. 'A real growth industry. Tarot, crystal balls, the lot. Everyone's so dissatisfied with the present that they want the future now. Must've been a dozen fortune-tellers to a block, sometimes. Plenty of trade. Weird sorts of methods started too. Reading the entrails of chickens, seeing patterns in flights of birds, cracks in walls, that sort of thing. Everywhere.'

'You ever use them?'

'Nope.'

'Why not?'

'Didn't know anything, them. Pretenders.'

'Would you have used them if they were real?'

'No. I don't know. I . . . '

He began to sweat. His clothes felt constricting and coarse, and he itched underneath them.

'More,' Corby commanded.

'Gambling. Everywhere, anything. People wagering on sports, entertainment, transport, the weather.'

'Keep it up.'

'I saw two women betting on who'd reach the other side of a busy road. One bet against herself, and made sure she won. She couldn't collect from under the truck, though. Messy.'

'What'd you do?'

'Kept going. I had something I had to do.'

'What?'

'Can't remember.'

'People. More about people.'

'No. Nothing left.'

'People.'

'There are no people.'

'Who do you remember?'

'No-one.'

'Who?'

He sweated. His eyeballs felt hot. The air hummed and stretched as he fought against the memory that pushed itself forward, unasked.

'On the beach,' he gasped. 'On the beach and she left me, all alone, and I was alone all by myself, and the waves kept coming and coming and coming, and I was all alone. I waited and waited, and all the time the waves kept coming, and bringing in . . . and bringing in . . . she was just floating there with seaweed, seaweed . . . '

Corby turned suddenly.

'First stage is over,' she said. 'Rest time.'

They sat on a broad metal landing. It was a grille, big enough to function as a small dance floor. 'How far have we come?' Caliban asked wearily.

'We've only just started.'

He looked over the side, and saw the ground far below. 'We've made some progress.'

'Some.' She shrugged. ' But we've got a long way to go.'

Avoiding his eyes, she concentrated on tying her bootlace more firmly. 'Have you ever been to the beach?' she asked carefully.

Caliban's expression was distant. 'No. City boy, through and through. The last few years, anyway. Who knows before that?'

'So where did this memory come from? This beach stuff?' She frowned. 'Palmer?'

'Feels like a Palmer memory, same as the others. But this one goes back a long way.'

'Who was the woman?'

'Don't know.' The metal was cool under his hand, and he pressed his palm against it, enjoying the sensation. 'Mother, probably.'

'And how did you feel? He feel?'

'Abandoned. Rejected. Betrayed. Lost.'

'You think it really happened?'

'Yes,' he said emphatically. 'Or something like it. Left alone like that as a kid, seeing someone drowned like that . . . '

'Drowned?'

The scene came back to him. 'It was someone in the water, bobbing in the waves. Not swimming, just floating. Clothes still on . . . '

She shook her head. 'Explains a lot about him. Why he turned out like he did. Spotting a floater like that. And you think it was his mother?'

'Had to be. It felt like being kicked in the gut.'

'Poor kid. Poor guy.'

'Maybe,' he said, looking out at the wide blue sky. 'Maybe.'

They rested in silence.

When he checked, he could still make out the tattoo—but only because he knew where it had been. 'Time's up,' he muttered, rubbing the smooth skin. 'Running on empty now, kiddo.'

* * *

'How long's it been?' he asked some indefinable time later.

She was lying next to him, on another landing. Her eyes were closed, and she had her arms flung back over her head. 'Who knows?' she said. 'Does it matter?'

'Not really. Stupid question.' And he understood that it really didn't matter. They were in a timeless state, in limbo. All that was left was climbing. The tedious ritual of raising their bodies one step at a time, higher and higher, was an end in itself.

And so it went. Sometimes Corby was in the lead, sometimes Caliban. He became accustomed to looking at her back, and the way she always pushed off with her toes as she lifted her feet from one step to the next.

At times he found himself looking out at the static grey shroud of mist which sat heavily on the unseen land, smothering the earth with its presence. He shuddered when he thought about being caught under it. It had an unwholesome look, like the belly of a toad. The land they had walked over had disappeared. The river was gone. Trees, animals, rocks and stones, all erased. The world was closing in.

They were very high. Caliban had wondered at that, in between rolls of thunder inside his skull, thinking that the air should have been getting thinner. But it was still sweet and warm.

Caliban had long ago disassociated his mind from the mechanical monotony of lifting one foot after the other, and given his attention to the real tough stuff.

Holding off Palmer.

Since starting their climb, Caliban had been searching inwardly, trying to find Palmer, but he had no luck. It was like trying to find one particular whitecap in a stormy sea. He sensed Palmer's presence in everything, but was led on a shadow dance.

He had trouble reconciling the inward and outward worlds. When he turned inward, odd perspectives sent him lurching. Peculiar lighting flashed spasmodically. Distant sounds drifted past, before resolving into a flock of ibis, curved bills sickle-like, then dissolving into a dark, smoking rain.

Palmer was avoiding him, he thought with astonishment. The bastard was running!

Caliban tossed this idea around. Was it another tactic, or was it genuine fear? Palmer loved confrontation, but now he was slinking from Caliban's attention, lurking at the edge of consciousness.

He could be anywhere. Caliban could chase him till doomsday. There were simply too many places to hide in this shadowy internal labyrinth. Even if he did know it like the back of his hand. Or he should.

'Caliban.' He felt Corby's hand on his shoulder, and he shook himself, swimming up from the depths. 'We've done it.'

He looked around wildly, and regretted it straight away. Wild shivering took hold of him, and he teetered on the edge of the stairs like a puppet with St Vitus's dance.

'Easy. Don't want to lose you now.' Corby's hand clamped onto his forearm, and she manoeuvred him until he was half-sitting, half-lying against her.

Eventually, the spasm passed and she gestured up and out. 'Guess where we are.'

He looked up slowly and saw nothing except empty sky.

They were on top of the world.

He looked out. The sun hung in the sky like a ripe fruit, and the silver-grey mist extended over the land as far as he could see. It was a soft shroud wrapping the country from horizon to horizon.

'Made it Ma. Top of the world,' he whispered.

'Yep. And it's a small world, too.'

Two large bronze doors faced them, marking the end of the stairway. 'Open wide, come inside,' he murmured.

'You'd better have the key, is all I can say. I don't fancy coming all this way to have you say that you left it in your other jeans.'

Caliban covered his face with both hands, took a couple of deep breaths, and then ran them over his head. 'I think we might be expected.' He rose unsteadily, and was grateful for her supporting arm.

'Come on, old man,' she said cheerily. 'Only a little way to go.'

He gripped her arm and they advanced on the doors.

The doors were set into a wall which extended five metres or so overhead, and seemed to run around the sawn-off top of the pyramid. Looking right and left, Caliban could see that they seemed to be precisely in the middle of the edifice. It figured.

The doors were strangely warm when he touched them, and he pulled his hand back in surprise. He'd been expecting the cool feel of metal. As he ran his finger along the seam, he thought he could feel a soft breath of air, but when he looked closely, he saw that the doors met smoothly. He must have been imagining it.

'How about we knock?' he suggested.

Corby had her head cocked to one side, quizzically. 'Not a bad idea.'

She looked more like someone who'd done a morning's gardening than someone who had trekked stubbornly across half a world. Her hair was messy where she'd run her fingers through it, and there was a streak of dirt on the side of her nose. The dark circles were still under her eyes, and her skin was pale, but she seemed strong. For a moment Caliban stood there trying to hold her image in his mind, but it kept slipping, and he felt sad.

'I want to hold onto you,' he sighed, and she looked startled.

'I . . . well . . . you mean here?' She looked around skeptically.

'Take it easy,' he said. 'I mean up here.' He tapped his temple, and winced as it set off another wave of pain. 'You're so steady—I figure if I can hold onto you, then I'll have something solid.' He closed his eyes and leaned against the doors. 'Need something to hold onto, Corby. Feel as if I'm coming apart.'

She looked him squarely in the eyes. 'You know I *chose* to stick with you. I didn't have to. When I broke free of Palmer's programming, I could have dropped you cold.' Her hands were on her hips.

'Why didn't you?'

'There's a bit of me in you, your lack of a real past and all. It makes a difference.'

'That's not enough.'

'Fishing for compliments?' She grinned wryly. 'Tough luck. You're OK. Maybe.'

'Don't go overboard.'

She rubbed her chin. 'Let's just say I've got used to you.'

'Terrific. I always wanted to be a pair of old shoes.'

She smiled. 'Could be worse. Knock?'

'OK. Together?'

'Side by side.'

He nodded, turned, and banged on the door.

25

The Speaker and the Witness are in the main chamber of the Hall of Light and Sighs. The light is even, and the small golden motes dart and hover through the air like fireflies. The Speaker is standing in the centre of the room, hands clasped behind his back. He looks heavier, more solid under his the grey robes.

'I'm afraid you've lost,' the Speaker says.

'The Game hasn't ended yet,' the Witness says coolly.

'It is as good as ended, and on a wider scale too. You see, I have the support of the others. Thanks to your treachery.'

The Witness's navy suit is flawless. His tie is a subdued midnight black. 'My treachery,' he says slowly. 'Explain that one to me, if you wouldn't mind.'

'Your efforts to encourage nationalism were not as subtle as you may think.' The Speaker speaks sadly, shaking his head as if he were dealing with a small child. 'Some of your Seconds long ago saw the wisdom of reporting to me. In the best interests of us all, of course.'

'Of course.'

'By itself, those dabblings could have been overlooked. But not your trying to league yourself with the Adversary.'

'Ah.'

'Yes. Unforgivable, really. Sadly, self-interest seems to be your main characteristic.'

The Witness's face is calm, but his hands clench and unclench. 'And altruism is your middle name? Don't make me laugh. The only reason you haven't made a deal with the Adversary is that you were too incompetent to find her.'

The Speaker chuckles oddly. It is as if he has rehearsed it. 'There are other reasons for my not finding her, you know.'

Still chuckling, he draws a small circle in the air. On the ceiling, a hole appears and admits a shaft of light, parting the golden motes. The Speaker gestures at the shaft, and a slight figure appears.

'Poor Tom,' the Witness groans. 'I should have known.' He shakes his head in disgust at the raggedy form in the column. In the grey light she looks as if she were dusted with silver.

'Yes. Your trick with the false Tom was amusing. But I was fully aware of it, of course. It was fun to let you fumble around after ghosts.' The Speaker chuckles again.

'Ghosts? You mean there is no Adversary?' the Witness says through clenched teeth.

'Oh, there is one of course. I'll get around to dealing with her in time. The whole situation was simply too convenient to ignore. It was a perfect opportunity to flush you into the open, as it were.'

'Right. And the other Primes don't object to you taking over?'

'Some see it as a chance to advance to your position. Others are simply cautious. Either way, nothing has been said.'

'I'll bet. So, what's next?'

The Speaker waves the Poor Tom image away.

'Since you'll be unable to finish the Game, I'll have to bring it to a conclusion. And eliminate Palmer.'

'Why?' snaps the Witness. 'He can't be any threat!'

The Speaker looks absently at the Witness. 'To complete the process we began a long time ago. There, are you feeling anything?'

'I suppose I should beg or something.'

'It's almost traditional. No-one would think the worse of you if you did.'

Sighing, the Witness takes a step back. 'No, I don't think I'd do it even if it would make any difference.'

'There's nowhere to hide you know. The process has already started.'

The Witness looks behind him. There are no doors any more. The Hall is sealed and complete.

'I've had some agents begin physically removing memory blocks from your component parts,' the Speaker continues. 'It's ironic, really. You were the one so unenthusiastic about physicality, so convinced of its lack of importance. And here you are, disappearing because physical parts are being removed from you.'

'Your love of the flesh is pathetic,' says the Witness.

'We transcend all that, and you want to crawl right back in there.'

'But look at yourself for once! You have fallen for the lure of the corporeal too! Your speech, your solidity. You have taken on the form of humanity so effortlessly, while at the same time claiming to despise it!'

'But what about the possibilities of our existence? You've been seduced by the lure of the senses, and you're losing the freedom that we once had. When did you last freeform through the Net, or split yourself so many ways that you wondered if you might meet yourself on the other side of some block of floating memory?'

'That's not important now.'

'You've lost something, you know that? And I don't think you know what it is.' The Witness stumbles backwards, and puts a hand to his brow. 'I'm going.'

'Yes,' says the Speaker sympathetically. 'Soon there won't be enough memory blocks to sustain consciousness.'

'Soon,' whispers the Witness. His eyes are distant and glazed. His back is to the wall. 'I can see now.'

'Interesting,' the Speaker says. 'You're much fainter, you know that?'

The Witness grows fainter and fainter, until there is only a ghost left, then a whisper, then nothing.

The Speaker smiles and hums a small tune to himself. Then he claps his hands together, and rubs them vigorously.

'Time to meet the prize,' he says, and smiles widely before turning to the solid wall. 'But first . . . '

Frowning thoughtfully, he reaches into the air. With thumb and forefinger, he snatches at one of the glittering golden motes. 'I have you now,' he murmurs, and he gently closes his fist. 'Too confident, my friend. Watching too much, seeing too much.'

He holds his fist up to his eye. 'And now I can see you instead, my Adversary.' He nods, and suddenly he is in his workshop, in front of his mass of clay. 'The Game draws to its close, and my work is done.' He stands back and gazes proudly at the mound of clay. It is a shapeless mass. 'My Creation. One of them.' He sighs. 'Now, let us go and see our maker one last time . . . '

26

With inexorable slowness, the doors swung inwards. Caliban had to shield his eyes from the light. It was golden and warm and comforting. For a moment, Caliban could see nothing but the radiance. He could smell jasmine. 'You there, Corby?' he called.

'Right here!' she said.

Reassured, he stepped carefully into the light.

At first he thought they had stepped into a golden cloud. It was a relief when he found there was something solid under his feet.

He glanced down at his forearm. He could still see the heart tattoo. Barely. 'Made it!' he shouted. 'We've made it!'

'Welcome!' boomed a voice. 'You are welcome indeed! The Speaker salutes you!'

'Who are you?' he called through the golden haze. He was becoming used to the light, and he looked around for any sight of the voice's owner.

Nothing. The golden fog billowed seductively, but he could see nothing apart from himself and Corby. She looked grim but stubborn, jaw set firmly.

'All your questions will be answered, as is only fitting,' said the Speaker. 'Advance, so you can be seen better!'

He didn't move. 'I'm a bit tired of moving, just at the minute. It's been a long road.' The fog pressed closer, and he noticed that it was becoming tinged with red. It was now the colour of old gold, of wedding rings.

'Come, come! Advance! Oh, but I forget myself! I must do something about that little guardian program . . . '

Caliban's eyes darted to Corby, and in that instant he felt a chill breeze from behind, sweeping over his shoulders.

Corby's eyes widened momentarily, as if she had heard a long-forgotten voice in the distance.

Then she vanished.

His fingers closed on air as he groped for her hand. 'Corby!' he called. 'Corby!' He swung around wildly. 'Bring her back!'

'It is you I want, not some interfering little trick. She is better out of the way.'

Caliban reeled. His head felt as if it would explode. 'Bring her back!' The fog was shot through with red filaments now, and they seemed to be growing. 'Now!'

'Reluctant as I am to point out the relative strengths of our situations, I'm afraid you are in no position to demand anything.'

Caliban clenched his fists until his palms ached. He wanted to see his tormentors.

'Get rid of this fog!' he shouted angrily. 'Can't see a thing!'

There was a pause. 'Fog? What fog? If you cannot see, then it is of your own doing.'

'My own doing? The fog?'

Then it hit him.

Palmer!

Too late, came the whisper from inside his skull. *Gotcha now*!

And the world collapsed.

* * *

The world was black and heavy, and he couldn't move. It smelled and tasted like death.

At first, he had no body. For some time he existed like that, drifting numbly. Then little by little, he began to explore and found that he was actually a jumble of disconnected parts.

Slowly, out of curiosity, he began to reassemble himself, joining extremity to limb, limb to trunk, rolling and testing muscles. It still felt as if he were buried, but at least he felt alive. The heaviness pressed on every square centimetre of his body, so that movement was difficult. The pressure was uncomfortable, but not unendurable.

Opening his eyes took an age.

When they were open, it was the same as when they were shut: utter, complete blackness.

OK, so he wasn't at home, he thought. Or Club Med, either. He drifted for a time, thinking. Wherever, it was too long in one place. Time to get moving.

His hands were clasped on his chest. With tiny movements, he gradually shifted them until they were just in front of his eyes. He touched the bridge of his nose, and was reassured by the feel of his own body.

Like a slow-motion breast-stroker, he gradually groped upwards. Eventually, he became aware of a speck of light that appeared to be in the far distance. It was like looking at a single star on a dark, moonless night.

As he watched, the light grew larger, until it was as if he were at the bottom of an enormous chimney, looking up at the sky. Things are looking up, he thought, and was impressed with his own wit in a tense situation.

The light grew until it hovered somewhere in front of his eyes. It was the size of a melon, and so bright that it hurt his eyes.

Gradually, he realised it was a window. He was on the inside looking out at some strange landscape. With a jolt it fell into perspective.

A room. No, he corrected himself, it was more like a chamber, an assembly place. It had that formal look. And even though it was round and domed above, it had a hard-edged quality that made it uncomfortable to look on.

His view of the room was moving slowly. Caliban was treated to an inspection of the arena. The motion made him feel slightly nauseous. He never thought he'd be happy to feel travel sickness, but the sensation told him he was alive. Maybe being human meant being miserable.

The walls were grey and featureless, and silver light came from above. Caliban wondered how he'd wound up there.

The rotation continued until a straight edge came

into view, out of place in the room of curves. It was close by, and grew slowly closer. It was a transparent slab, standing on end.

There was a woman in it.

Corby, he said soundlessly.

Then he remembered.

Palmer! he cried, without any noise at all.

'Take it easy, Caliban,' came a voice. In a horrible instant Caliban knew it was Palmer, using the voice that had once been his own. 'I've just taken possession of my property. And I've traded you in.' He chuckled. 'Relax, it's over.'

He was a spectator, bound and gagged, helpless and trapped inside his own body.

Palmer was looking at the slab. He seemed to be thinking, but all Caliban could feel was frustration.

From around the other side of the slab stepped a man.

He was old. Grey hair, lined face, tall and lean. He wore a simple robe.

Caliban felt Palmer take a step backwards, and the Speaker smiled.

'No need to be afraid,' he said. 'Enjoy your moment.' He held up an open hand. 'Here I meet you, the Speaker in the Hall of Light and Sighs.'

'Nice place you've got here,' Palmer said. 'You do it all yourself?'

'It is our meeting place when we have need. It is a fitting site for the conclusion of the Game. Here, you might say, is our heart. All the Primes have invested part of themselves in this place, to ensure neutrality. And here is the part of you that we took.'

Palmer grinned. 'You've got nothing of mine,' he said. 'I'm complete, now.'

'Yes Thomas Palmer,' said the Speaker. 'Your plan has come to fruition, has it not? You've taken possession?'

Palmer frowned, annoyed at not being able to spring one of his great surprises. Then he shrugged. 'So you've worked it out. Just a little too late, but well done anyway.'

'Perhaps,' said the Speaker. His face was calm, but Caliban noticed that one hand was clenched into a fist. 'A fine plan, yours was. Innovative. But dangerous.'

'Didn't seem like it at the time. You try keeping one step ahead of a tribe of mechanical killers, and see how quickly you change your ideas about what dangerous means.'

It was the Speaker's turn to shrug. 'Your time had come. We agreed. Resistance, dare I say it, is futile.'

'Existence is futile,' Palmer said, 'but I intend on having a lot more of it.' He tapped his head. 'You've got my fully paid-for body? It's nice and safe?'

'Of course. That's part of the Game.'

'Your precious Game.' Palmer spat on the floor. 'I knew I shouldn't have started that crap.' He took two paces until he was close to the Speaker, then stood with hands on hips. 'Listen,' he said, and his voice was low. 'This brain has a Juggernaut virus program encoded into it, waiting for my say so. Once let loose, it'll swamp you all, tearing down any defences you put up, finding you wherever you hide. It's unstoppable. It's the end of every AI in the world.'

The Speaker froze, and his face went blank. The pause only lasted a second or two, then his eyes focussed again. He rubbed his chin. 'I see.' He took a step away from the belligerent Palmer. 'Unstoppable?'

He smiled. 'Trust me.'

The Speaker nodded again, then began to pace, hands behind his back. Again Caliban could see the one clenched fist. 'This Game has been quite magnificent, did you realise that? Unprecedented.'

'What of it?' Palmer said, irritated.

'You should be proud,' pointed out the Speaker. 'Ah, but I forget. It wasn't you who survived, was it? Your caretaker did the job. All for its own heart.'

'So it went above and beyond the call of duty,' said Palmer. 'I'll write it a good reference.'

'In many ways, it was a better person than you are.'

Palmer shook his head. 'What makes you the expert on humanity? It's like a teetotaller judging a wine show.'

'Observation. We see more in a second than you can experience in a lifetime.' The Speaker stopped, and jabbed a finger at Palmer. 'Your much-vaunted humanity is just another commodity to you. You've bought and sold people without a thought.'

'That's business.' Palmer shrugged. 'And speaking of business,' he said, 'it's time to wind you up.'

'So simple?'

'Nice and neat.'

The Speaker shook his head. 'I have trouble coming to terms with how egocentric you are. You are the most perfectly self-centred being I have encountered. Nothing matters to you beyond yourself. Nothing.'

Palmer waved a hand. 'I'm all I have. I like to take care of my investments.'

'It doesn't matter that the planet is well managed for the first time in its history?'

'All that matters is that you wanted me dead. And I won't be safe until I take care of you.' Palmer smiled, and Caliban felt his cold pleasure. 'Besides, I can always build you from scratch.'

A frown crossed the Speaker's face, briefly. 'What do you want?'

'What?'

'You must want something,' said the Speaker patiently. 'Leave us be, and it shall be provided for you.'

'You don't get it, do you?' Palmer said. 'I don't want anything. Except to wipe you out and start again. I think I can do better this time.'

'I think not,' said the Speaker. 'After all, this is perfection.' He gestured expansively. 'Why not join us?'

27

'Join you?' Palmer frowned. 'What's that meant to mean?'

'Disable your Juggernaut, and you can join us on the Net using the methods you discovered. We can encode you so you become like us, living in the electronic matrix of the Net.' The Prime paused. 'You will become immortal.'

Palmer stood still, and Caliban felt the tension in his body. 'You want me to join you? Join the Primes? Live forever?'

'Join us and rule the world. Experience more than you ever dreamed, and experience it in a nanosecond. Mould your own world. Mould your own *worlds*. We will be partners. You will be immortal.'

'You can't do it.' Caliban felt sweat, and pain as fingernails pressed into palms.

'We can do it,' the Speaker replied. 'You stored your personality deep inside an organic brain, and I have access to the Net. Say the word and join us.'

The moment hung in the air like a bubble. Caliban felt teeth clench and unclench, and he tried to flex himself.

'I keep the Juggernaut virus,' Palmer finally said.

The Speaker frowned. 'No. Too much power.'

'Power? Consider it my edge. When I join you in the Net, I need a safety blanket.'

'You'll join us?'

Palmer wiped his hands on his chest, thoughtfully. 'You know, I think it's what I may've been working for all my life.'

Caliban was stunned. He'd been sure Palmer hated the Primes too much to join them. Then he realised that there was some of Palmer in the Primes. He couldn't divorce himself from his creations. The constructs and the constructor were parts of the same being. It was no wonder that Palmer was attracted to the world of the Primes.

Caliban steeled himself. He felt he had enough will left for one last push against Palmer. Time to pull out all the stops. No second chances.

He looked for strength anywhere he could, and it was memories that gave him hope.

Corby: fighting off the crayfish-monster on the river bank.

Phineas: hooting with laughter as he fired his pistol straight at them.

Spiroula: seeing with no eyes, calmly waiting for the authorities to catch up with her.

Laydown Sally.

After that it was Palmer's memories that came to him, melding and blending so they became difficult to sort from his own.

The beach.

Lost and afraid, abandoned against the elements. Sand stinging on bare legs.

A woman, crying and crying, despite his clumsy efforts at comfort. Her dress was pale blue, and the hem was uneven.

The wind and the waves.

'I have to go,' she said. 'But it's not your fault.'

'Whose fault is it?' he asked, needing to know.

'I have to go,' she said, and broke off. He wanted to look at her eyes, but she was standing with her back to the pale winter sun. Her face was in shadow. 'You understand that, don't you?'

'Yes,' he said.

When they found her, washed up on the beach, he was still waiting there. 'I told her she could go,' he told them. 'But I thought she'd come back.'

And he was all alone, waiting.

Caliban remembered Palmer remembering this. He remembered the pain. He remembered Palmer hardening like old wood, vowing never to be hurt again.

He remembered Palmer.

School: taunting less able schoolmates. Exposing teachers' lack of knowledge remorselessly. Learning prodigiously.

University: isolated, seeking out others only for what he could take from them.

A girl: 'I can't stay with you. You know that. You don't want me to.'

A lover: 'It's your fault, you know.'

Work: 'I'm sorry Mr Palmer, I can't work here under those conditions.'

Fame: 'Mr Palmer, is it true your employees hate your guts?'

Power: 'Whatever you say, Mr Palmer.'

The force of the memories shook Caliban, but he held onto them, crying. One by one, the feelings flooded him: sorrow, grief, anger, guilt, bewilderment, shame, anguish, remorse, lust.

They flayed him until he was raw, until he dripped blood—but still he hung onto the memories. He was feeling something, he realised with one corner of his mind. Better than feeling nothing.

He reached out, and gathered the memories to himself. *Come on home*! he shouted to them. *I've got no heart, so there's plenty of room*! *Come on in*! He opened himself and let the memories fill him up.

Slowly, he gathered them and rolled them into a ball, adding each bit of pain and anger until it grew into something hard and dark and throbbing.

In the blackness, he held a ball of memories. In the darkness, he held a ball of feelings.

There's a whole past here, he said with no sound at all. *There's a whole person in here, and I'm only part of it*.

He squeezed the ball, and he felt its solidity. He felt tears stinging.

Calmly, he looked out at the Hall of Light and Sighs. Silver-grey filtered down from above, reminding him of moonlight on water.

He drew back his hand, and hurled the ball of memories towards the window on the world. In silver splinters the window shattered, leaving a hole.

Caliban dragged himself through.

28

The Speaker is frowning, considering Palmer's ultimatum. Can he trust the man? Is there some way to disable him safely? He turns over a million possibilities, in the space between nanoseconds.

Suddenly, his eyes widen with shock and his clenched fist opens. 'I've been stung,' he says. His hand is on fire. 'So this is what it feels like,' he says in wonder. 'So this is pain.'

Palmer shrugs. 'Don't talk to me about pain. I've walked around with boots full of it.'

'You don't understand,' the Speaker says. 'Something stung me. There!'

A pinprick of golden light darts between his fingers and speeds towards his face. He throws up his hands, trying to bat it away. 'Leave me, Adversary!' he says, waving feebly. 'This is undignified!'

Palmer begins to laugh, but the laughter is bitten off suddenly. His whole body stiffens: fingers curling like claws, jaw clenching, face grimacing, his whole body an expression of a mighty internal struggle. Guttural noises come from his constricted throat.

The mote of light darts around the Speaker. He tries to duck, but his movements appear stilted and strained. The Adversary avoids his efforts easily.

At the same time, Corby's slab fills with light. A glowing figure steps from the slab. She is golden like the sun. Her face melts and shifts until it isn't one face, but many, all at once.

The Speaker is enclosed in a net, which the pinprick of light has woven. It is golden like the sun.

The golden woman walks slowly towards Palmer. She is tall and slender, with long dark hair. At first her dress is long and blue, but after a step it is pink and uneven at the hem. Her face shimmers like heat haze. 'No,' Palmer mumbles. 'It's not you.'

He tries to look away, but his head jerks back to face her.

He tries to close his eyes, but they open wide in a grotesque grimace.

His mouth opens in spasms. 'No,' he says. 'Staying. I'm staying.'

The golden woman takes another step. Faces slide and merge with her own in rapid succession. Each is full of pity. 'Thomas,' she sighs and her voice is like the wind.

He throws back his head, straining. The tendons stand out in his neck. 'I . . . ' he says hoarsely, and the word costs him. His shoulders groan with the effort.

He gathers himself once more, breathing deeply. The golden woman reaches out a hand, but before it touches him he shouts: 'I AM!'

The words echo around the room for an instant, but then fall dead on the floor.

The Speaker stands erect, peering from within his flimsy cage of light. Slowly, he lifts both hands, and they fill with dark red light, the colour of old blood. He pauses, holding the handfuls of red light in front of him, chest-high. Suddenly, he brings both hands together, crushing the whirling mote. With a soft flare of gold, the mote dies. The blood-red light drips from the Speaker's hands, and pools on the floor of the Hall of Light and Sighs. The woven net fades and the Speaker steps out. His face is thoughtful as he studies his hands. His robe is ruffled.

The golden woman shakes her head sadly. Her hair covers her eyes, and she sweeps it away. 'Time to go, Thomas,' she says, and touches his cheek.

For an instant, Palmer's face is young and innocent, and the golden woman strokes his forehead. Then his eyes roll up. He collapses.

29

'Caliban?'

'Corby?'

'Right first time. Come on, time to get up. We've got a Prime to deal with.'

He opened his eyes. 'Look,' he said. 'We've got to stop meeting like this . . . '

'Yeah, I know,' Corby said tiredly. 'People'll start talking.'

'It's how rumours start,' he pointed out as she dragged him to his feet. 'I've got a reputation to worry about.'

'You've got more than that to worry about,' she said. 'We're in the heartland of the Primes here. And that's the Speaker. The head honcho.' She grimaced and rubbed her face.

'You OK?' he asked her.

'Never felt fitter. You?'

'I'm dangerous.'

She scrutinised him carefully. 'I mean, I don't mean to pry or anything, but is Palmer in there?'

'Don't think so,' he said softly.

Briefly, her face was distant. 'Better off, I think. Better off.'

Us or him? Caliban wondered. 'I saw something,

through his eyes. Was it you, that golden woman?'

'You bet. I was watching from where they tried to keep me in that slab thing. I figured that you must be trying something, and the Prime seemed distracted, so it was probably a good time to give it a go.'

'Give what a go?'

She shrugged. 'I suppose I'm not as tied down to a body as you and Palmer are. It must have become a bit of a habit for you guys after all those years. Remember, I'm sort of a newcomer to this fleshy stuff and all. I'm more used to existing as a pattern, a code. I just rearranged my pattern, is all.'

'You make it sound simple.'

'It's a knack I have,' she said, and shrugged.

'But the face . . . ' Caliban's voice drifted off as he remembered his frozen vision of a glowing figure advancing, face melting and shifting as it moved.

'Palmer's memories. I plundered them whenever I could, ages ago. I found the image of his mother. And others. Then I confronted him with it.' She sounded ashamed.

Caliban took a deep breath and held it. 'It hurt him. It hit him where he hurt the most.'

Corby sniffed, and her face screwed up. 'It was all I had . . . it was the only thing I thought would work . . . '

'Ah.'

Something about his tone of voice made her look up. 'Did he leave you with anything?'

'Leave me?' he echoed. Leave him anything? Some memories, maybe.

'Palmer's gone,' he said, and rubbed his nose.

'A pity,' the Speaker interrupted, and Caliban turned. 'He was a great man. Perhaps the most original man of your time. A loss.'

Corby snorted. 'I can see you crying tears of blood over it and all.'

The Prime frowned at Corby. 'I don't know how you managed to free yourself, but remember your place.'

The Speaker turned his attention back to Caliban. 'You have survived the Game.'

Caliban grimaced. 'Some Game,' he said. 'More like an excuse to pretend you're real, the way I see it.'

'Please,' said the Speaker. 'The Game is an arena for our abilities.'

'An arena for wankers.'

'We placed obstacle after obstacle in your way, and you survived. You survived Palmer, our maker and enemy.'

'And who'd you survive?'

The Speaker deliberated before answering. 'Our Adversary.'

'Adversary? Not great at making friends, right?'

'She had been interfering for some time. A renegade. A ghost.'

'If she was against you, she's my sort of person.'

'She wanted us to fade away.'

'Now I *know* she's my sort of person. Sounds like a good idea to me.'

'Do away with our management? Pave the way for the collapse of the world?'

'Stop the New Worlds program. Stop the megadeaths.'

'Acceptable losses is the quaint phrase.'

Caliban clenched his fists. 'The day we put you in charge was the end of humanity,' he said. 'You're just shepherds now, in charge of a few billion sheep.'

'Well-fed sheep. Content sheep. On the average.'

'Forget about free will. Long live machine determinism.'

The Speaker shrugged. 'Without us, the world would have perished long ago. With us, humanity is still here.'

'No it's not.' Caliban paused, thinking carefully. It was an important point in the Game. It was the time of the End Game.

The Speaker was watching him closely, and seemed to read his mind. 'You've come for your heart.'

Caliban's eyes narrowed. 'It's your Game. You tell me.'

'Here,' said the Prime. 'Take it.'

It was a fist-sized ruby, shining dully in the Prime's hand.

Caliban felt Corby close behind him. He turned and she smiled uncertainly. 'It's your heart,' she said. 'More or less.'

'It'll make me complete?' he asked, and shook his head.

'You earned it,' she persisted.

'I earned something,' he said. 'Beats me what, though.'

He turned back to the Prime. 'You think it's easy,'

he said evenly. 'People are simple, predictable. Shove and push, and we respond.'

'We offered you an incentive to participate.'

'Under your rules, your conditions. For your ends.' Caliban gritted his teeth. 'Free will? Forget it.'

'Here,' said the Speaker. 'Your heart.'

Caliban studied the jewel. It sat in the Prime's hand, fat and red like a drop of blood. The Speaker began to smile, slowly and coldly.

'Nope,' said Caliban. 'I don't like taking anything from you. Anything at all.'

'I'm sorry,' said the Prime, and he closed his hand around the heart. 'You deserve it.'

'Deserve it?' Caliban laughed bitterly. 'For surviving?'

'Survival is important,' said the Speaker.

Caliban nodded slowly, thinking over the Speaker's words. Survival is important. After dragging himself through the make-believe landscape, fighting off Palmer every step of the way, he felt he knew a thing or two about survival. But that was personal survival. What about survival of the race? Caliban could see the future. The future was the Game. Push and shove. Carrot and stick. People as playthings.

'Maybe,' he said slowly. 'Survival. But not as pawns.'

He closed his eyes and reached down deep inside himself. *Palmer*, he called silently. *Help me*.

'What are you doing?' asked the Prime, frowning.

'Caliban?' said Corby. 'You OK?'

Where are you, Palmer? I need it now! We need it now!

He felt Corby shaking his shoulders. 'Caliban! The Prime's out of action, but we haven't got long! The Adversary's helping us!'

Painfully, he dragged his eyes open. The Speaker stood motionless a few paces away, trapped in a column of grey light that came from a hole in the ceiling. Around the shaft of light flitted thousands of golden motes, as the Adversary struggled to contain the Speaker. His face was frozen somewhere between surprise and anger.

Corby's face was close to his. 'Here,' she said. 'Hold hands. She can't hold him long!'

'Who?'

'The Adversary. I'm in touch with her, and she can take us in!'

'Where?'

'To find Palmer, you idiot!' And then they plunged together into the tumult that was Caliban's mind.

It was like swimming in a stormy sea on a moonless night. Wearing heavy clothes. And gumboots. 'Where is he?' Caliban gasped.

'Hold on!' came Corby's voice, and he felt her at his side. He was buffeted by something that wallowed past uncaringly, and engulfed in a stinking wave that clung and made him gag.

'Here,' came a new voice, barely a whisper. 'I haven't much left, but I can help a little.'

Then it was light and dark at the same time. Flickering, disconcerting, it was enough to help them see. Caliban could see Corby, and he held her hand tightly. 'The Adversary?' he said, and Corby nodded.

'She's been helping us whenever she could. Off and on.'

'And here for the last time,' came a voice like the ghost of a sigh. 'Most of my being has been stripped away. The Speaker was too strong, too strong. I have hung on to help you help yourselves. For humanity.'

Choking black smoke drifted past, and for a brief time Caliban was sure he was in a cloud of humming insects. It passed quickly, and he was back with Corby.

'Which way?' he asked.

'Over there,' Corby said.

It was difficult to make out, but from the distance came the boom of surf and the lonely sound of gulls.

'A beach,' Caliban said in wonder. 'I don't believe it.'

'It's in your mind,' said Corby. 'You'd better believe it.'

He shook his head. 'Maybe there are bits in everyone's brains that they don't realise are there. I'm no different.'

The surface underfoot rose and fell rhythmically. He cupped his hands to his mouth. 'Palmer!' he called. 'The Juggernaut! Give me the virus!'

He waited, with Corby next to him. The pool of light dimmed momentarily and Corby jumped. 'Hurry,' she said. 'I don't think we've got much time.'

'Palmer!' he shouted over the sound of the waves. 'Help us!'

A small ball of light came soaring from the darkness ahead, followed by the voice of Palmer. '*Yessssss*,' it said. '*Go get 'em . . .* ' the voice added, before fading, swallowed up by the surf.

The ball of light landed in Caliban's hand. It was a spiky egg, pulsing dull-green. 'Some Juggernaut,' he said, and looked into the distance. 'I hope he knows his stuff.'

'Hold on!' said Corby. 'Going up!'

He linked arms with her, and the light stretched to envelop them entirely.

He felt a sick dizziness, and then the impression of great speed.

Then they were back in the Hall of Light and Sighs. 'The future is yours,' came the fading voice of the Adversary. 'I wish I could see it.'

With a sound like the gentle closing of a door, she was gone. Corby gripped his arm. 'She's gone.'

The Speaker blinked, and shook his head. 'What a foolish thing. Giving herself away like that. A waste.'

Stiffly, Caliban lifted his head and stared at the Prime. 'I think the Game's just gone into extra time.'

The Speaker smiled a wintry smile. 'No. It's over.'

'It's not a bloody Game any more,' said Caliban. 'Not when I've got this.' He opened his hand and held out the Juggernaut. 'Say goodbye, Prime. Time to resign.'

'Wait,' said the Speaker. He licked his lips nervously. 'You've earned a place here. Join us.'

'Join you?' said Caliban. His legs felt as if they were about to give out from under him.

'Yes. We offered a place in the Net to Palmer, and he proved to be unworthy. You've taken his place, so I make the offer to you. Immortality.'

Caliban hardly thought at all. 'Nope.' Then he paused. 'What about the future?'

'We'll take care of the future.'

'That's what I'm afraid of,' Caliban said, and held out his hand. He rolled the Juggernaut backwards and forwards on his palm, then tossed the spiky egg to the Prime. 'Catch,' he said gently. 'Palmer's legacy.'

Helplessly, the Prime caught the thing. He looked at his hand as if it belonged to someone else, taking a step backwards. 'No!' he said, eyes wide.

'Time's up,' Caliban said calmly. 'It's started.'

The Prime stood there, incomprehensible expressions flitting across his face.

Caliban took a deep breath, then let it go slowly. 'For better or for worse, we're back in charge now.'

The Speaker looked at him. 'You don't know what you've done. You've ruined paradise.' The Prime's face was strained, and he gripped his wrist with his other hand. His hand was slowly turning a dull-green colour, unhealthy and menacing. The virus was shrinking, but pulsing ominously as it dwindled.

'Maybe,' said Caliban, and he sighed. 'Maybe we don't belong in paradise. Not one that belongs to someone else, anyway.'

He turned. Corby stood there quizzically. He nodded his head and she seemed satisfied. She fiddled with a button on her jacket.

Together, they walked away.

'Wait!' wailed the Speaker. 'What are you going to do?'

Caliban stopped. 'Do?' He looked up at the high grey ceiling. 'Beats me.'

Corby nudged him, and together they moved off.

A moaning sound, like the rushing of a great wind, came from behind, but Caliban didn't look back. A door opened in the wall as they approached. Without thinking, Caliban led the way through. On the other side was a featureless grey mist. They paused, and Caliban studied the fog. For a moment he thought he could smell the sea.

'I think there's a path over there,' he said, pointing.

Corby nodded, because a stone pathway appeared just where he said it would be. The neat, grey stones were irregular, but fitted against each other snugly.

Caliban leaned against Corby as they slowly followed the path. Caliban had his head down, frowning. The path cut through the formless grey mist, winding into the distance. The mist was all that could be seen in any direction, except upwards, where the sun hung overhead like a wound.

When they reached the beach, Caliban slumped onto the sand. The wind was cool, and he was glad of his jacket. Sand whipped up, and he closed his eyes against the sting. Gulls wheeled on unseen currents, harassing each other constantly. Their chattering began to sound almost good-natured to Caliban, as he lay near Corby.

'You cold?' she asked, as he shivered. Her hair hung damply on her forehead, and she wiped a strand from the corner of her eye.

'Nope. Just thinking.'

'Don't do that. It's bad for you.'

'Keeps me going.'

She made a face, and dragged her fingers through her hair. 'Surviving, you mean.'

'Surviving.'

She looked at him. 'Is it enough?'

He sat up and shrugged. 'For a start. Sometimes being human means enduring.' He dug a small hole in the sand and watched as it began to fill with water. The sides soon collapsed, and he covered it up.

'Where are we?' she said, not looking at him.

'Somewhere. Nowhere.'

'It's not part of them.' It wasn't a question.

He thought for a moment while he watched the waves. 'Its ours,' he said simply. 'You like it?'

She shrugged. 'Nice place to visit . . . ' She worked her bare feet under the sand until they were covered.

He looked around. 'See what you mean.' Squinting, he turned his face away from the windblown sand. 'Think I'll just stay here for a while,' he said. 'Bit tired, just at the minute.'

'How long you think you'll stay?' she asked evenly.

'Until we can figure out a way for you to come with me.'

She nodded, absently, as if it really didn't matter. 'You going for a swim?'

'Not just now. Maybe later. If it warms up a bit.'

'The world's waiting out there,' she said.

'It can wait,' Caliban said, and brushed the sand from his jeans.

Corby looked out at the grey surf. The waves were

heavy with seaweed. 'Can you find our way out of here?' she said.

The waves were perfect right-handers, breaking evenly across the wide bay. 'Sure,' he said. 'Infallible sense of direction, remember?'

'Uh huh,' she said, and plucked a stalk of dune grass.

'It just takes time, is all.' He lay back, closed his eyes and listened to the boom of the surf. 'Going home takes time.'

'Home,' said Corby. 'Where's that?'

Caliban opened his eyes and propped himself on one elbow. He looked at her closely. 'Home is where the heart is.'

She nodded. 'Home is where the heart is,' she repeated, and smiled uncertainly.

Caliban closed his eyes again, and stretched out in the sun.

ALSO AVAILABLE:

Scale of Dragon, Tooth of Wolf
Sue Isle

Fourteen-year-old runaway Amber believes she has escaped her problems by joining the Aradian Order as a sorceress, until she is sent to her hometown to lift a frightening curse.

ISBN 0 7336 0291 6

Whaleroad
Kerry Greenwood

The Great Beast is approaching Whaleroad, and Alain Beast-friend and Tyrell of the Dolphin must unite their telepathic skills to prevent him from destroying the fortress and capturing the White Tower and the secrets that lie within.

ISBN 0 7336 0289 4

Beyond the Hanging Wall
Sara Douglass

Garth Baxter has a special gift. He can ease pain and encourage healing. But when Garth is sent to the horrific confines of the Veins for three weeks of service his powers uncover a chilling secret.

ISBN 0 7336 0169 3

Carabas
Sophie Masson

Catou can mysteriously change her shape. Banished from her village with Frederic, her only advocate, the two embark on a journey that will lead to the court of the great king, and ultimately to the revelation of Catou's strange powers.

ISBN 0 7336 0380 7